Through the Fire

ERIC LUPPOLD

RESOURCE *Publications* · Eugene, Oregon

THROUGH THE FIRE

Resource Publications
An Imprint of Wipf and Stock Publishers
199 W. 8th Ave., Suite 3
Eugene, OR 97401

www.wipfandstock.com

PAPERBACK ISBN: 979-8-3852-2283-4
HARDCOVER ISBN: 979-8-3852-2284-1
EBOOK ISBN: 979-8-3852-2285-8

VERSION NUMBER 06/27/24

Map of Canaan by Niday Picture Library

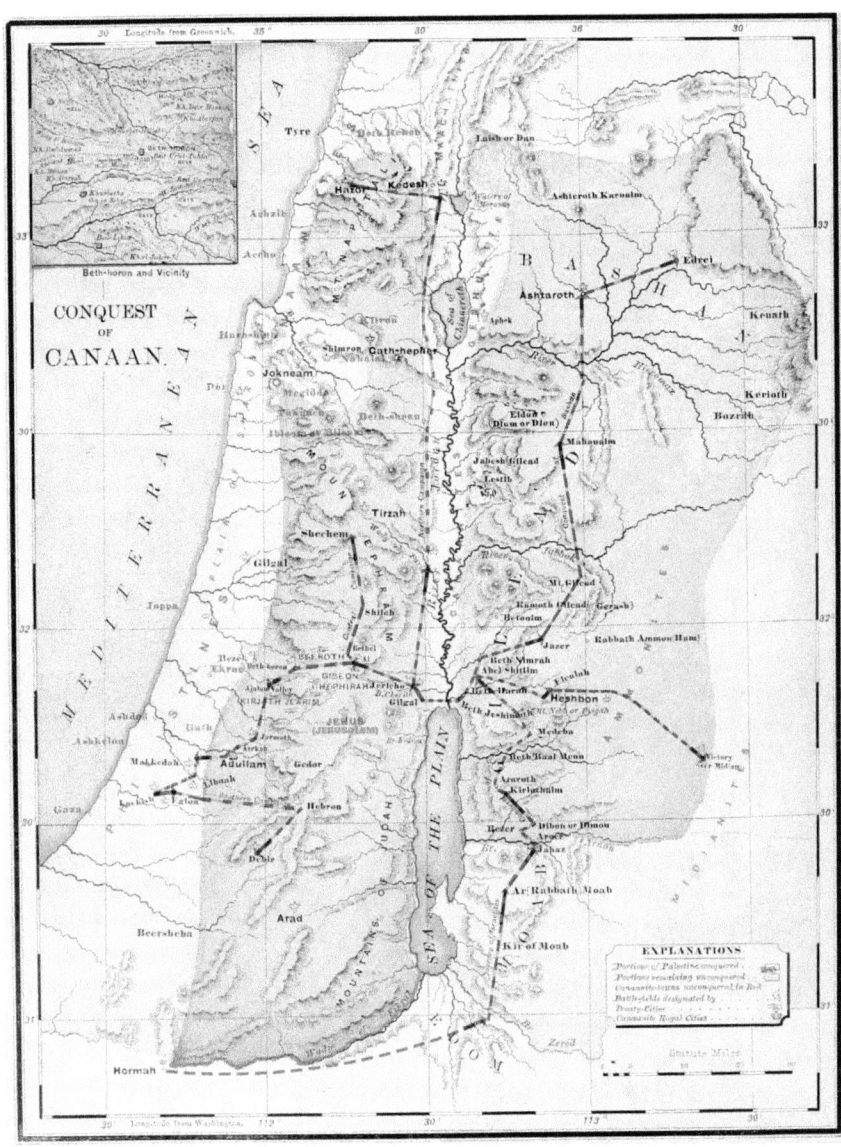

Israel's Conquest of Canaan

Timeline of Israel's Invasion
(1407–1406 BC)

1407 BC

1 Av (~July 14)—Aaron dies on Mount Hor

Av (July/Aug)—Israel defeats the Canaanites at the Battle of Hormah

1 Elul (~August 13)—Israel proceeds after mourning for Aaron

Elul (Aug/Sep)—Fig harvest takes place before the autumn rains arrive

Tishri (Sep/Oct)—Israel defeats Sihon at Jahaz and destroys Heshbon

Cheshvan (Oct/Nov)—Israel occupies King Sihon's territory

Cheshvan (Oct/Nov)—Time of olive harvest andthe autumn rains

Kislev (Nov/Dec)—Israel defeats Og at Edrei and occupies Bashan

1406 BC

1 Shevat (~January 7)—Moses reminds the Israelites of God's law

Shevat (Jan/Feb)—Israel kills Balaam and five chiefs of Midian

7 Adar (~February 12)—Moses dies on Mount Nebo

Nisan (Mar/Apr)—The Jordan River rises to its highest level

7 Nisan (~March 13)—Joshua sends two spies into the city of Jericho

10 Nisan (~March 16)—The Israelites cross the Jordan River

28 Nisan (~April 3)—The Battle of Jericho takes place

Iyyar (Apr/May)—Barley harvest takes place prior to the wheat harvest

6 Sivan (~10 May)—Israel celebrates the Feast of Weeks

PROLOGUE

Rabbah,[1] Winter 1407 BC

NIKKAL GROANED IN PAIN. Sweat ran from her brow as the contractions became fierce. She quit trying to stifle her cries hours ago, no longer concerned about what others might think. With each wave of pain, she sent prayers to all the gods of the Ammonites.

Thankfully, Nikkal was not alone. Her midwife and sister-in-law, Arsay, was with her as coach and comforter. It was Nikkal's first pregnancy and so, as she was often told, she should expect it to be the hardest. Those words had certainly not made things any easier.

"Nik, you need to keep pushing!" Arsay commanded.

Nikkal strained, her knuckles white as she gripped the edges of her mat. Her long black hair stuck to her sweat-covered skin.

She could not tell how much time had gone by, only that it seemed to be a never-ending cycle of pain, breathing, and pushing. *I can't do this.*

"Just one final push! Hard!" Arsay commanded.

Nikkal exerted all her strength and felt the pressure inside her subside. A few moments later, the cries of her firstborn child filled her ears.

"Well done, Nik!" Arsay exclaimed. "It's a boy!" She held him up for Nikkal to see.

Nikkal's heart fluttered with joy as she lifted her head and gazed at her son. His bluish hands quivered with every cry.

Arsay took the boy to a nearby basin and began to wash him.

---

1. Also known as Rabbath-Ammon.

Breathing a sigh of relief, Nikkal let her head fall back on the rush mat. The stink of oxen hit her nostrils, and she realized that she could breathe through her nose again. She was glad to have the function back, although she had not missed the odors that constantly arose from the room below.

The thought of oxen caused her to glance over at the terra-cotta statue on the wooden stool next to her.

The goblet-sized idol had the body of a man and the head of a bull, with its arms outstretched. It was a depiction of Moloch, the chief god of the Ammonites.

Nikkal focused on Moloch's arms extending toward her. She could not tell if he wanted something from her or wanted to offer her something. Perhaps he desired both.

She looked away and watched as Arsay rubbed her trembling son with salt before swaddling him. Arsay then walked over and handed him to her. "Here he is."

"Thank you." Nikkal sat up to receive her son.

Arsay demonstrated how to hold him. "You need to support his head, like this."

Nikkal nodded, careful to mimic her movements.

Once she had a secure hold on him, she brought him in close. His cries ceased and he became calm as he nursed. Her connection with him filled her heart with joy and affection. "I love you," she whispered.

Arsay started to clean up the room and, after some time, came back to check on them. "How is he?"

"I think he's asleep." Nikkal looked down at the boy's closed eyes. Her fingers brushed the small amount of hair on his head. Brown, just like his father's.

"Should I get Tobi?" Arsay asked.

Nikkal nodded.

Arsay turned and climbed down the ladder to the main floor of the pillared house.

Nikkal listened as Arsay spoke with Tobimelech, Nikkal's husband. Though she could not make out the words, she sensed the excitement in her husband's voice.

In an instant, Tobi's head appeared through the opening, his face full of anticipation. Nikkal could tell that he had been stressed, probably about whether his wife and newborn baby would survive.

He was dressed as if he were about to go water the flock, which is what he had been doing hours ago when Nikkal's labor began. He apparently had not taken the time to either wash or change.

Tobi stooped slightly as he stepped onto the floor. The habit always reminded Nikkal of how tall he was, above average for an Ammonite but not as tall as the giants of the land, or Zamzummim, as the Ammonites called them.

She smiled at him. "Come say hello to your son."

Tobi strode over to her and knelt. The boy appeared to be blissfully asleep. Tobi studied him for a few moments, then looked at Nikkal and smiled. "He has your face."

Nikkal nodded. "But your hair."

Tobi chuckled.

She caressed her son's head. "What is his name?"

Tobi's face turned thoughtful. "Well, I was thinking we should name him after my father, Aliyan. Perhaps call him Ali for short."

Nikkal nodded. *Aliyan is a lovely name.*

"May I hold him?" Tobi asked.

"Of course." Nikkal supported Ali's head, as Arsay had instructed her, and demonstrated the same posture to Tobi. "Just be careful not to wake him."

Ali squirmed as Tobi took him, but the boy's eyes remained closed.

Once Tobi appeared comfortable holding Ali, he stood. "Father will want to meet him." He turned and walked back to the ladder.

Although Tobi descended to the first floor with great care, Nikkal's stomach churned with anxiety. She yearned to hold Ali again, to keep him safe. She would not let any harm come to him.

She shook her head. Tobi loved him and would be a good father. Her son would be fine. She laughed when Tobi reached the bottom and exclaimed to the rest of the family, "His name is Aliyan!"

Amidst the cheers and congratulations, she heard shouts of, "Praise Moloch!" and "Moloch be blessed!"

She glanced back over at the idol of Moloch next to her. Her thoughts turned worrisome as she considered what the god required. No, she should not think like that. Moloch had blessed her. He was not against her. He would not take what he had just given.

Just then, a wave of fatigue washed over her. She did not want to think about anything right now. Laying back down on the mat, she closed her eyes. The last thing she heard were the joyful cheers of her family.

PART ONE

The Child

CHAPTER ONE

Rabbah, Summer 1407 BC

THE SMELL OF LENTIL stew filled Nikkal's nostrils as she set the bowl of figs onto the table. She shot a glance over at Ali. The six-month old rolled around on the earthen floor in a fit of giggles. Nikkal shook her head and turned back to her duties.

"Nikkal," said Naamah, her mother-in-law. "Can you go tell the men to come in for dinner?"

"Yes, mother." She checked Ali's last known position and then hurried out the front entrance of the house.

Once outside, she shielded her eyes from the setting sun and walked straight ahead. From the edge of her vision she noticed the walls that surrounded the rectangular courtyard and led to the lone gate on the western side. The walls stood high enough to obscure the family fig tree orchard to the south, but Nikkal knew it was still there. It was her favorite place to go when she found time. She sighed. *Probably not today.*

The sound of male voices forced her to look up. Squinting, she caught a glimpse of Tobi, along with his father, Old Aliyan, and older brother, Zakar. The three men stood just inside the courtyard walls, deep in conversation. Each man gestured forcefully as he spoke, although Nikkal could not make out the words.

She signaled to them. "Tobi! Dinner's ready!"

Tobi looked over at her and nodded. He then rejoined the conversation with his father and brother.

3

Nikkal turned to head back but noticed Zakar's two sons, Hanun and Peduel, wrestling each other in the dirt. "Boys!" she shouted.

They stopped immediately and stared at her.

"Go inside for dinner!"

They both made a face, typical for boys aged four and five, but then obeyed. She watched as they raced toward the house, sprinting past the donkey's stable and around the clay oven. Nikkal shook her head as she followed.

When they reached the front door, she cupped her hands around her mouth. "Don't forget to wash your feet!"

They looked as if they did not hear her. But, after a moment, they complied.

As she watched them remove their sandals and use the nearby water basin, she thought of their mother Arsay. When Nikkal had arrived at the farm as a new member of Tobi's family a few years earlier, Arsay and Zakar had already been married. Adjustment for Nikkal had been difficult, but Arsay—who was a Canaanite like her—helped her feel welcome.

Nikkal reached the boys' position by the time they finished and gestured for them to go in. After following them inside, she looked for Ali on the floor but found him in Arsay's arms.

"I caught him trying to roll out the door after you." Arsay smiled and carried him over to Nikkal.

"Thank you, sis," she replied.

"Are the men coming?" Naamah asked from across the room.

"They're on their way." Nikkal kissed Ali on the forehead. "They were busy talking about something serious."

"Men and their talk," Naamah muttered.

Old Aliyan was the first to come in. At around sixty, he was not particularly old. Everyone just called him that because he had children so late in life. His oldest, Zakar, was in his mid-twenties. Old Aliyan's daughter, Tallai, lived in Jericho with her husband. Tobi, having just turned twenty, was the youngest of the siblings.

Nikkal avoided Old Aliyan's gaze as he moved his overweight frame past her and stood at the head of the table. While Ali squirmed in her arms, she found her own chair near the opposite end and sat down.

She still had not gotten quite used to sitting in a chair at a high table to eat. Old Aliyan had purchased the set from Jericho several months earlier. It was the new style these days, and probably cost more than they could really afford. She knew that he, like many other Ammonites, had an obsession for all things Canaan. That is why he had wanted her as Tobi's wife. She had come from a successful Canaanite family.

Nikkal glanced up as Tobi and Zakar entered the room. Their conversation appeared unfinished as they moved to their assigned spots.

Tobi sat down next to her, gave her a nervous smile, and kissed Ali on the head.

As soon as Old Aliyan sat, everyone quieted down. He then reached for the wine and poured a generous amount into his cup.

He handed the wine jug to his wife, Naamah, who then filled her own cup before passing it to the next person.

Once everyone had received their wine, Old Aliyan raised his cup in salutation. "Thank you again, ladies, for this wonderful meal."

He then gestured with his cup toward an idol of Moloch, similar in size and color to the one in Nikkal's room, that sat in the center of the table. "Moloch has truly blessed us," he continued. "Let us never forget his great mercies—" He glanced over at Nikkal and Ali. "Nor his judgment . . ."

The rest of them raised their cups and drank with Old Aliyan.

Nikkal pretended not to notice his glance and instead focused her attention on her squirmy son. She moved her cup away from him so that he would not knock it over.

As everyone took food and began to eat, Tobi broke the awkward silence. "It's good to finally get out of the heat."

Zakar nodded in agreement as he reached for the figs. "Yeah, it's been a bit hotter than usual." He popped one in his mouth. "When I went to the market, I heard some folks say that it's a sign of coming judgment."

Tobi shook his head. "Come on, Zak, let's not start this again. It's just temporary. Nothing to panic about."

"Sure." Zakar grinned. "Just like the recent insect swarms." He pointed a finger at Tobi. "Did you know that Yarikh's brother died from one of those rare wasp stings that are going around? I guess they aren't just rumors after all."

"You trust Yarikh?" Tobi laughed. "He's a drunk!"

Zakar shrugged. "Well, that doesn't mean he's wrong."

Tobi turned toward Old Aliyan. "Father, please tell me you don't believe that killer wasps and strange weather is a sign of judgment."

Old Aliyan grunted. "All I know is that things are changing, and not for the better." He took a long drink from his cup. "Your generation is losing respect for the gods, which is going to lead to punishment."

Naamah spoke up. "Oh, don't be so hard on them. They're faithful, even if not in the way you'd like."

Old Aliyan shook his head. "Faithfulness is seen in actions, not mere words." He looked at Nikkal again. And again, she looked away. A sense of shame and guilt grew inside her. She already wished that dinner would end.

Zakar gestured to Tobi. "Well, what about the Israelites? How is that not a judgment from the gods?"

The room fell silent. Even Hanun and Peduel stopped eating.

Old Aliyan's face turned red as he pointed at Zakar. "I told you not to mention them at the table!"

Zakar looked down in shame. "I'm sorry, father, But I believe that the gods are warning us. The heat, the droughts, the deadly insects, and now the Israelites on the move? How could it not be judgment?"

Out of genuine interest, Nikkal spoke up. "Is that what you three were talking about outside?"

Tobi nodded. "Yeah, and I was hoping it would have stayed out there." He shot an angry look at Zakar.

Nikkal continued, her curiosity unquenched. "What do you mean, on the move? I thought that the Israelites were gone."

Zakar answered before anyone could stop him. "Well, they were never really gone. After they escaped from Egypt, they just wandered around the wilderness for decades."

"But why so long?" she asked. "Why have they reappeared now?"

Zakar shrugged. "Who knows? Maybe they finally figured out where they wanted to go." He grabbed some more figs and popped one into his mouth.

It was now Arsay who asked a question. "And why is that a big deal?"

Zakar responded to his wife between chews. "Because this time they beat the king of Arad."

Nikkal sensed everyone's eyes shift to her at the mention of the Canaanite city. Her grandfather, Shalim, had grown up in Arad and had fought against Israel almost forty years earlier. Back then, Israel had been defeated and Shalim had come away as the brand-new owner of an Israelite slave that he had captured in battle. Not long after that, he moved east of the Jordan River and settled down in Betharan.[1]

---

1. Also known as Beth-haram.

Old Aliyan waved his hands dismissively. "It doesn't matter if they defeated the king of Arad. These days, anyone could beat that fool. He had it coming."

He reached for the wine jug and refilled his cup. A scornful laugh erupted from him. "Apparently, he attacked the Israelites first. And then he got himself conquered. Pathetic!"

Zakar turned to Old Aliyan. "But father, don't you think this defeat is a warning from the gods? Don't you think we should do something?"

Old Aliyan slammed his cup down, splashing wine onto the table. "Of course!" he shouted.

He then lifted his cup into the air. "We need to honor the gods now more than ever. The Canaanites in Arad failed to do that, and so they got what they deserved. But if we're faithful to Moloch, he'll protect us from this upstart pack of sheep herders."

Old Aliyan took another drink and then pointed an unsteady finger at Tobi. "That's why, son, you must not hesitate to do the right thing."

He jerked his cup toward Nikkal's direction. More wine spilled out. "You've waited long enough. If you care about this family and our people, you'll honor Moloch!"

Tobi lowered his gaze. Nikkal could sense him searching for the right words. "Father," he replied, "we haven't really discussed it yet."

Nikkal glanced down at Ali, who had already fallen asleep. Fear and anxiety began to surface in her heart.

"What's there to discuss!" barked Old Aliyan. "Consider your brother. He's been faithful. Look at how Moloch has blessed him and Arsay!"

The words stung Nikkal. Her eyes shifted to the idol of Moloch on the table. She felt as if it were glaring at her, judging her. Afraid, she then glanced up at Arsay, who gave Nikkal a nervous smile but remained silent.

Tobi held up his hands. "I promise we'll do it, father. We just haven't had time."

"Well, then make time!" Old Aliyan replied. He took another long drink and then threw the empty cup onto the floor. "Don't be faithless like her grandfather!" He pointed at Nikkal.

She felt as if a lightning bolt had erupted from his finger and struck her in the chest. *Faithless . . .*

The outburst startled Ali, who began to cry. Nikkal felt tears fill her eyes, but for much different reasons. She knew she had to get out of there.

She took hold of Ali, got up, and fled through the doorway that led to the attached oxen stable. She then climbed the ladder to her and Tobi's room. Once she believed herself to be out of earshot, she began to sob.

Attempts to calm Ali and control herself failed. She felt both fear and shame. Shame at what her grandfather had done and fear at what she was supposed to do.

She took several deep breaths and forced the sobs to cease. She then rocked Ali and began to shush him. After several moments, her efforts paid off and he calmed down.

The ladder creaked and Nikkal looked over to see Tobi's head emerge from the opening. She said nothing as he came over and sat down.

He placed a hand on her shoulder. "I'm sorry Nik. When my father drinks he can be—harsh."

"But maybe he's right!" Nikkal replied. Anger now replaced her fear and shame. "Maybe I am faithless like my grandfather!"

Ali stirred but did not cry.

Tobi's words were gentle. "Nik, I know that you've always served the gods. I don't know why your grandfather abandoned them, but that was his decision. He rejected his people and his family. That's not your fault."

"But what if I can't do what your father wants me to do?" she sobbed.

"You can," Tobi replied. "We can do it together."

"I don't think I can, Tobi."

For a moment, neither of them said anything. Nikkal sensed that Tobi wanted to speak. He always wanted to fix the problem and correct her when he thought she was wrong. But this time, he said nothing. She thanked him for that in her heart.

Nikkal let out a deep sigh and wiped her eyes. "I'm tired, Tobi." She waited to see how he would respond.

Again, she sensed that he wanted to argue but instead he just gave her a thin smile. "Okay." He leaned over and kissed Ali, and then Nikkal, before he got up to leave.

Nikkal smiled at him. *Thank you.* Once he went back down the ladder, she laid on the mat and placed Ali next to her. She watched her son as he fell back asleep. "I love you." She then felt her eyes begin to close.

After what could only have been a few moments, Nikkal opened her eyes and found herself still on the mat. Only this time, the space where Ali had been sleeping was now empty.

Nikkal jumped up. "Ali!" She turned to the right and left. There was no sign of him.

Just then she heard what sounded like his cry. It came from below.

"Ali!" She ran to the ladder and climbed down. When she reached the bottom, she saw that the room was empty. No people. No animals. *That's strange.*

She then ran to the main room of the house. Still no one. There was no evidence of life at all. "Where is everyone?" she asked out loud.

As if in response, Ali's cry reached her ears. This time it came from outside.

She ran to the front door and burst out into the night air. But it was not night. It was near sunrise. She scanned the courtyard and, not seeing Ali, sprinted west toward the location of her son's cries.

As she reached the gate of the family compound, an immense storm cloud formed right before her eyes.

Darkness spread across the sky as peals of thunder reached Nikkal's ears. But even as the storm grew loud, she could still hear Ali's cries. This time they came from where the storm began. She ran toward it.

"Ali!" she screamed. She froze in terror. A black funnel cloud, immense in width, came down from the sky and impacted the ground in front of her.

The whirlwind moved in her direction. She turned to run away but then heard Ali's cry again. It came from inside the storm, behind the swirling clouds and howling wind. She stared into the tempest. *How is that possible?*

As the whirlwind drew close, she felt the dust and debris sting her skin. She shielded her face and tried to locate Ali but only saw darkness interrupted with periodic flashes of lightning. Despair and fear filled her soul as the storm enveloped her. Feeling the air ripped from her lungs, her vision swam, and she fell to the ground.

Nikkal sat up, drenched in sweat. Her whole body shook. She looked over and saw that the spot next to her was empty.

"Ali!" She sprang to her feet.

"Shh," Tobi whispered.

She turned and saw Tobi on the other side of the room. He stood near the open window rocking Ali. The early morning light illuminated his face just enough that she could detect a look of concern.

"Are you all right, Nik?" he asked.

She regained her composure and let out a sigh of relief. "Yes. I'm sorry. I just had a nightmare."

Tobi nodded, though his worried look did not disappear. "He woke up fussing so I figured I would try to quiet him to give you some more time to sleep."

Nikkal flashed him a quick smile. "Thank you." She held out her arms. "Here, I'll take him, so that you can get started with the animals."

Tobi walked over to her. Nikkal felt a slight twinge of guilt. She knew that he wanted to make up for what happened at dinner last night. The topic of Ali's dedication could not be avoided, and she figured that Tobi wanted to ease her worries before that conversation came up again.

He held Ali out. The boy reached eagerly for her as she received him.

Tobi then kissed Ali on the forehead and Nikkal on the cheek. "Can we talk later?" he asked.

She nodded.

"Okay," he replied. He gave her a faint smile and then turned and descended the ladder.

Nikkal knew he would not be back until the evening meal, yet she already dreaded the conversation that would inevitably come.

As the day went on, Nikkal and the other women of the house performed their regular duties, although Nikkal spent much of her time tending to Ali. While she tried to remain focused on her work, every time she looked at Ali she was reminded of the impending talk with Tobi. It tied her stomach into knots.

After putting Ali down for his afternoon nap, Nikkal went to help Naamah hang the laundry. She walked out into the courtyard and glanced up at the cloudless sky. It felt hotter than usual, even for summer. At least the clothing would not take long to dry.

Nikkal found Naamah and walked up next to her. Without a word, she grabbed a wet cloak from the basket on the ground between them and hung it onto the clothesline. For a while, they worked in silence, broken only by the occasional breeze.

Then, Naamah spoke. "I know what troubles you, daughter."

The unexpected statement caused Nikkal to drop the blanket she held. She did not reply as she bent to pick it up.

Naamah continued. "But you don't need to worry."

This time, Nikkal could not stay silent. "How can I not worry?" Anger crept into her voice. "I'm going to lose my son!" Her outburst surprised even herself, and she looked away in shame.

Naamah did not seem bothered at all by it. She continued her work without hesitation, as if she had expected Nikkal's reaction. "But he is not your son." Her voice came out cold and calm.

Nikkal did not know how to respond. *What is she talking about?* She waited for her mother-in-law to explain herself. When she did not, Nikkal decided to press the issue. "What do you mean?"

Naamah picked up a tunic from the basket as she spoke. "He belongs to Moloch. Ali was set aside for him before he was even born. And it is Moloch who has granted fertility to your womb. That's why the boy belongs to Moloch, not you."

She paused and looked straight at Nikkal. Her voice turned solemn. "To give Ali to Moloch is to give Moloch what is rightfully his."

Nikkal shook her head in disbelief. "But I can't stand the thought of losing him—" She paused to stifle her tears. "And to see him suffer."

Naamah gave Nikkal a sympathetic look. "And you're right to feel that way. But if you refuse to give the boy to Moloch, he will suffer far worse."

"How is that?"

Naamah let out a deep sigh. "Many years ago, my sister refused to give her firstborn child, a daughter, to Moloch, despite my family's pleas. One morning, when my sister went to nurse her, the child did not move. She had died in the night."

Naamah held up a finger. "And that is only one example. There are some children who are cursed by Moloch for life, unable to say or do things that normal children can do. They end up on the streets, or worse."

She walked over and took hold of Nikkal's hand. "I say this not to upset you, but to help you understand the bigger picture."

Nikkal tried to process her mother-in-law's words. *Bigger picture?*

Naamah gave Nikkal's hand a gentle squeeze. "You say you don't want Ali to suffer. Well, if you refuse to dedicate him to Moloch, the boy will be cursed forever and shall have a life full of pain and suffering. But if you give him to Moloch, both you and the boy will be at peace."

With her free hand, Nikkal wiped several tears from her eyes. "But I want a family. And now that I have a son, I should just give him up?"

Naamah smiled as if she had foreseen Nikkal's question. "Moloch is testing you, my dear, to see if you'll do the right thing. But think about the family you'll be given in the future if you serve Moloch now. You'll have more children, healthy children, and good harvests to feed them with."

"How so?"

"Well," Naamah began, "have you noticed how much work you've been unable to do lately?"

Nikkal became defensive. "It's not my fault. I've been taking care of Ali. He's a handful!"

Naamah nodded. "No doubt. And before that, your pregnancy was so difficult that you could barely do anything the last few months of it."

"What are you saying?" asked Nikkal.

"I'm saying that if you honor Moloch, you'll be able to work and earn more for yourself and for the family. And with that wealth, you'll be able to properly take care of your future children. But to dishonor Moloch will incur his wrath, upon yourself and upon others."

Nikkal sighed. "I—I hadn't really thought about it that way."

Naamah leaned over and hugged Nikkal. "I know that you're just trying to do what's best for Ali and for the family. We all want that. But being faithful to Moloch is what's best. Without his blessing, the people of Ammon, your people, will suffer."

She pulled back and smiled at Nikkal. "And remember, being a mother takes planning. You don't become one just because a man goes into you. Moloch offers you a choice and wants you to choose wisely. Delaying motherhood allows you to grow in wealth so that, when you do decide to become a mother, it will go better for you and your family."

Nikkal nodded in understanding.

Naamah gestured to the half-empty basket next to her. "Can you finish up here while I start to prepare the evening meal?"

"Sure," replied Nikkal.

As Naamah turned to go, she spoke over her shoulder. "When a seed goes into the ground, it dies. And in that moment there is sadness. But when the harvest comes later, all sorrow for the seed disappears. Think on that." She then walked off.

Nikkal paused in thought for a moment before continuing her work. She considered her mother-in-law's words. If they were true, then Nikkal's perspective had been all wrong. And she had no reason to doubt

Naamah's wisdom. In fact, Arsay had dedicated her first child to Moloch, earned more wealth for the household, and now had two healthy and capable boys.

Nikkal then recalled her recent nightmare. Maybe it served as a warning from Moloch that wrath would come if she disobeyed. But if she demonstrated her faithfulness, both her and her family would be protected from further pain and difficulty.

Upon finishing the laundry, she picked up the empty basket and turned toward the house. With each step she took, she began to feel better about the decision she would make. *I will honor Moloch.*

CHAPTER TWO

Rabbah, Summer 1407 BC

As Nikkal placed the waterskin with the other supplies, she heard Ali giggle and glanced over at him. He sat on the floor playing with a small hand-carved wooden horse, oblivious to the world around him.

It had been several days since Nikkal's conversation with Naamah and her subsequent talk with Tobi. Tobi had been ecstatic to hear that Nikkal felt ready to dedicate Ali to Moloch. They had spent the days since then in preparation for their journey.

Nikkal turned to Tobi, who had just concealed a dagger in his tunic. His sword, an Egyptian-made khopesh, lay on the table in front of him with its sickle-shaped blade wrapped in leather.

"Is the journey really that dangerous?" she asked.

He remained focused on the task at hand as he spoke. "Yes. It's one day south to get to Heshbon and then another two days west to cross the Jordan River and get to Jericho. From there it's about a half-day west to Jebus.[1] If we can't find a larger caravan to travel with, it'll be just us, and we'll need to protect ourselves."

Anxiety crept into Nikkal's heart at the thought of camping at night on the road to Jericho, unprotected and vulnerable. Folks from Rabbah were used to going to Heshbon, but traveling all the way to Jericho was a different story.

---

1. Jebus would later be known as Jerusalem.

Suddenly, she thought about Betharan, where her grandfather still lived. What if they stopped there? It would help break up the trip from Heshbon to Jericho, and her grandfather could meet Ali.

She bit her lip nervously. She knew it would be risky to even mention it, but she decided to try anyway. "There's a place we could stop on the way to Jericho—."

Tobi's head snapped up and he gave her a stern look.

She already knew what his response would be.

"Absolutely not," he replied. "I'm not going to your grandfather's, no matter how convenient. I'd rather take my chances with highway robbers than be associated with that traitor." He placed extra emphasis on the last word.

Nikkal opened her lips to reply but decided against it. She felt torn. She knew that her grandfather had betrayed the family. But why, after nearly two decades of no contact, did she still feel a strong desire to see him? Was it just to have a safe space to stop at on the road to Jericho? No. For whatever reason, she yearned to talk to her grandfather again.

Her thoughts shifted to the last leg of the journey, the most dangerous one. "But do we really have to go all the way to Jebus? Can't we just stay in Jericho and perform the ceremony there?"

Tobi shook his head. "No, because Tophet is where the high priest of Moloch holds his services. And Tophet is at Jebus."

This time, Nikkal decided to push the issue. "Does Moloch really care where we dedicate Ali? I mean, I just don't think it's worth the risk."

"Shouldn't we trust Moloch to protect us?" Tobi shot back.

Nikkal remained silent and turned away from him. His words hurt. Tobi must have realized this, because Nikkal heard him walk up to her. She felt his hand on her shoulder.

He sighed. "Nik, I know you're scared. I am too. But my father wants us to dedicate Ali at Tophet."

She turned and faced him. "I know what your father wants, but what do you want?"

Tobi gave a weak smile. "Well, I might not be as traditional as my father, but I think we need to serve Moloch as best as possible. Going to Tophet will show our commitment."

Nikkal nodded. She knew that Tobi was right. They were fully capable of going to Tophet. To take the easy road by finding a local priest either in Rabbah or Jericho could incur Moloch's wrath. She had already tested the god's patience by delaying Ali's dedication this long. To give a half-hearted effort now might make things worse.

Tobi turned his attention back to packing the supplies.

Nikkal considered asking if they could at least visit her cousin in Jericho, but then decided against it. Nikkal's family was already suspect, so she felt it best not to even bring it up.

An hour later, Nikkal stood outside holding Ali, with Arsay next to her. The three of them watched as Kenaz, a slave that Tobi had purchased in Heshbon several years earlier, helped Tobi secure the supplies to the family's donkey.

Kenaz nodded in satisfaction with his work and then turned to Nikkal. "Are you ready to go, my lady?" His accent revealed his Edomite origins.

"Yes," she replied. She handed Ali to Arsay and then stepped forward. She lifted herself onto the beast of burden and, with some help from Kenaz, eased herself down. She nodded to Kenaz. "Thank you."

Arsay handed Ali back to Nikkal, who seemed eager to return to his mother.

Tobi and Nikkal said their farewells before Tobi led the donkey on foot through the compound's gate and in the direction of Rabbah. From Rabbah, they intended to take the King's Highway to Heshbon and then the road to Jericho.

Outside their walled compound, Nikkal felt the hot blast of the summer wind. While not as bad as the dreaded east wind that came out of the Arabian Desert, it made her quite uncomfortable.

Tobi seemed to feel the same way. "This heat is something else, isn't it?"

"I know," Nikkal replied. "It's good we packed extra waterskins."

Tobi nodded in agreement. He then looked up at the clear blue sky. "Let's hope that the autumn rains will be good. If not, next year's harvest will be worse than this one . . ."

Nikkal sensed the concern in his voice.

After a moment, Tobi let out a sigh and began leading the donkey down the dirt path.

Given that the family farm lay just east of Rabbah along the Jabbok River, it did not take long before they reached the city gates. Though the city's mud-brick walls were not nearly as impressive as Jericho's, its strategic location and access to water made it easy to defend. Thankfully, the gates were open and the guards, who knew Tobi well, let them through without hesitation.

When they reached the King's Highway, which ran through the city, they turned and followed it south. As they went along, Nikkal spotted the usual merchants peddling their wares. She fought to avoid eye contact with them, having no desire to enter a conversation about spices, perfumes, or jewelry.

Nikkal had not been to Rabbah since before getting pregnant. Looking around, she noticed how different it seemed. Her eyes caught sight of several packs of wild dogs in search of food scraps, as well as numerous orphans looking for a handout, or a pocket to pick.

"If anyone comes up to us, just ignore them," said Tobi. He placed his free hand on the hilt of his sword.

Nikkal shifted Ali in her arms. "Has it really become that dangerous?"

Tobi's voice grew grim. "The past few months have gotten bad, that's for sure. More beggars and orphans than ever."

Nikkal nodded. As she looked from beggar to beggar, she felt both sadness and sympathy wash over her. *Why did no one help them?* There were many wealthy families in and near Rabbah. Or at least they appeared to be wealthy. It seemed as if they all spent their money on the latest and greatest thing from Jericho while ignoring everyone around them. Old Aliyan fit that description perfectly. He complained about the homeless and the terrible economy, but kept spending money on unnecessary luxuries.

Nikkal chose not to say this to Tobi. Instead, she just looked down at Ali, who had dozed off.

Due to Rabbah's small size, it did not take long before they reached the southern edge. While the number of travelers on the streets diminished, the number of beggars did not.

The moans of a man in deep pain reached Nikkal's ears. "Help me . . ."

She looked to her right. There, a few steps away on the side of the road, lay a middle-aged man covered in sores and welts.

Tobi gestured toward him. "Plague." He then led the donkey several steps away in order to keep distance.

Nikkal turned her head to watch the man as they passed him. He did not move but just continued to moan.

Memories of her parents flooded her mind. They had died of plague in Heshbon just months after her and Tobi's wedding. A terrible death, and one that she tried not to think about.

They then approached a group of four orphans, who appeared to be around ten years old. As they drew closer, the boys turned and addressed them. "Money, please, or food. We're starving!"

Tobi did not respond but just kept leading the donkey forward. As a result, the boys began to curse and jeer at them.

As they passed the group, Nikkal saw one pick up a rock and move as if he was about to throw it. "Tobi!" she shouted.

Tobi drew his blade and turned to face the boy. "Get out of here or I will gut you!"

The boy dropped his rock and ran off as the others shouted after him.

After a moment, Tobi sheathed his sword, grabbed the reins, and continued.

Soon afterward, they approached the bridge that crossed the Jabbok River, which served as the boundary between Ammonite territory and that of the Amorite king, Sihon.

Nikkal noticed the shallowness of the river. It seemed much lower than usual. *I didn't realize how bad the drought was.*

They then moved to cross the bridge when a voice called out from a nearby clump of cypress trees. "You'll get stung! Bees, hornets, wasps, all of them! Or eaten—eaten by lions and jackals!"

Nikkal turned her head as an old man stumbled out from behind one of the trees. The elements had turned his skin leathery, and his long hair and beard were wild and unkempt. The man coughed and sputtered before taking a drink from the wineskin in his hand.

"Hello, Yarikh," said Tobi. "I'm glad to see that you're still able to afford drink."

"Ah, Tobi son of Aliyan!" Yarikh wiped his mouth. "Leaving Rabbah for good? Going to visit the Israelites? Ha!" He let out a drunken laugh. "Don't have to wait too long! They're coming here. Coming for you! Coming for us!"

Yarikh's eyes grew wide when he spotted Ali in Nikkal's arms. He dropped his wineskin and stumbled over toward the donkey.

Tobi drew his sword and moved to intercept. He leveled it at Yarikh's neck. "Don't," he said sternly.

Yarikh stopped but fixed his eyes on Nikkal. He then raised a finger and pointed. "You going to honor the gods? The baby too? Moloch's baby. Blessed baby. Burnt baby!"

Tobi grabbed Yarikh by his tunic and shoved him backwards. "Shut up you old drunk!"

Yarikh fell to the ground with a cry.

Tobi grabbed the reins and led them away at a quick pace.

Nikkal watched as Yarikh got to his knees. "Good for baby!" he shouted. "Better to burn now than later! We'll all burn! Israel is the fire! Ha!" He found his wineskin, took a drink, and then waved at them. "Farewell burnt people!"

Nikkal looked away and focused her attention on Ali. She gave her son a protective squeeze and kissed his head.

"Don't let him bother you, Nik," said Tobi. "He's just crazy. I probably should've just put him out of his misery." He gave her a look of concern. "Are you all right?"

She lied. "Yeah." Glancing down, she noticed her hands were trembling and forced them to stop. *He's just a drunk, Nik, that's all. Ignore him.* She took a deep breath and hoped that the rest of the journey would be easier.

It took only two days to get to Jericho.

Nikkal gazed up at the city's massive double walls. Though she had visited Jericho years ago, she had forgotten just how impressive they were.

She looked down and noticed that Ali too was fixated on them. "Can you say 'Jericho'?" she asked.

Ali made an indiscernible sound and pointed.

Tobi led the donkey through the double gates and then turned to the man next to him. "Thank you for allowing us to travel with you." He held out his hand.

The man, a merchant whose name Nikkal did not remember, grasped Tobi's hand. "You're quite welcome, Tobi. When you get back home, please tell your father that I expect a significant discount."

"Of course." Tobi bowed his head in respect.

The merchant signaled to the bodyguards with him and continued forward while Tobi led the donkey down one of the side streets.

"Greedy bastard," Tobi muttered.

"Your father always makes the nicest friends," said Nikkal.

Tobi chuckled. "Well, my father screwed him over often enough in their dealings. So, I suppose it was only a matter of time before it came back around."

She nodded. "Your father might not be happy about it, but I'm glad we had that man's protection."

"Me too," he replied. "Traveling alone on a road swarming with bandits would not have been fun."

Nikkal held Ali tight as she glanced around at the large crowds. "Is Jericho any safer?"

Tobi did not answer.

Nikkal's feeling of awe wore off as they made their way through the city. Disgust and anxiety soon took its place. The smell of animal and human waste was profound, worse than anything she had experienced in Rabbah. That, coupled with the shouts of merchants and the throng of people, threatened to overwhelm her senses. Had she been alone on foot, she probably would have panicked.

After what seemed like an eternity, they finally stopped in front of a small home near the inner wall on the northern side of the city.

"Here we are," said Tobi. He stopped the donkey and held out his hands for Ali. Nikkal passed the boy to him and then dismounted.

When Tobi transferred Ali back to Nikkal, he turned and knocked on the wooden door.

A few moments later, the door opened, and a brown-haired woman appeared. She stood taller than Nikkal, with a complexion like Tobi's. It was his sister, Tallai.

"Tobi!" Tallai exclaimed. She threw her arms around him.

"Hey sis." He hugged her back.

"And Nikkal!" she exclaimed. She released Tobi and moved to hug Nikkal. She stopped when she noticed Ali. "And who is this?"

"It's your nephew," answered Tobi. "His name is Ali."

"Oh, little Ali!" Tallai said. She leaned over and kissed the boy's forehead before giving Nikkal a kiss on the cheek. "It's good to see you both again. Please come in." She gestured for them to follow her. "Baalis is out selling his wares at market, but he should be back soon."

Once inside, Nikkal looked around for a place to set Ali down for his nap.

Tallai noticed, and pointed to the back of the room. "You can put him on our bed if you like."

"Thank you." Nikkal walked straight back to the small sleeping area in the corner. The entire home had been structured as one large room, with a few small nooks for storage.

She set Ali down on the mat and began to soothe him. As she hummed, she noticed various idols of stone and metal piled nearby. She recognized the images of Baal, Asherah, and Moloch, along with some others that were unfamiliar to her.

Convinced that Ali would not fuss if she departed, she stood to leave. When she turned, she felt her arm brush up against one of the idols. Several toppled over as a result.

The sound caused Ali to stir but, to Nikkal's relief, he did not cry.

Embarrassed, she began to pick up the idols but then heard Tallai's voice behind her. "Don't worry about it," she said. "I'm always tripping over my husband's work."

Nikkal noticed that one of the idols she had knocked over had been of Moloch. Fear gripped her, and she panicked at the thought that Moloch would be angry if she left his image face down on the floor. She grabbed the idol and set it upright before heading back to Tallai and Tobi.

Tallai handed Nikkal a cup of wine and gestured toward the bread and grapes on a nearby table. "Please, sit and eat."

"Thank you." Nikkal took the cup and sat down next to Tobi, who had already begun eating.

Tallai sat across from them. "So, what brings you to Jericho? Will you be staying a while?" She appeared eager for them to say yes.

Tobi shook his head as he finished chewing. "Just a day or two. We're only here to dedicate Ali at Tophet. Then we'll head back to Rabbah."

Tallai frowned. "Why don't you stay a bit longer? I mean, Baalis and I don't get many visitors these days."

"There's too much work to be done back home." Tobi took a sip of wine. "Father needs all the help he can get. Things are tough these days."

An angry look appeared on Tallai's face. "You think you have it tough, Tobi?"

Tobi lifted his hands defensively. "I'm sorry, sis. I didn't mean it like that."

Before things escalated, Nikkal leaned over and placed her hand on Tallai's. "Thank you, Tallai, for welcoming us into your home."

Tallai squeezed her hand without a word, and Nikkal felt the tension in the room subside.

Nikkal continued, her voice filled with deep sympathy. "I can't imagine how difficult it's been for you and Baalis the past few years. And I'm sorry that we weren't there for you."

Though Nikkal had not seen Tallai since she and Tobi were married, she knew that Tallai and Baalis had experienced several miscarriages. In fact, they had yet to bear a living child.

"Thank you," Tallai whispered to her. She released Nikkal's hand and wiped several tears from her eyes. She smiled. "Listen, you two make yourselves comfortable while I go out and purchase a lamb for dinner tonight."

"Do you want me to come with you?" Nikkal asked.

"Of course not, dear!" Tallai answered. "You two rest. When Baalis gets back we'll have plenty of time to chat."

Baalis returned before sundown in time for them to eat together. He looked much the same as Nikkal had remembered. He still kept his head shaved, with ritual markings visible on his sideburns and beard. Tattoos covered his arms, neck, and face, as was common for followers of Baal.

After dinner, the four of them sat around the small table, catching up on family history and current events. Nikkal tried to pay attention while Ali squirmed in her arms.

Tired of the struggle, Nikkal set him on the floor. "Go play."

Ali squealed with excitement and crawled off. He soon spotted the idols and darted straight for them.

Nikkal moved to get up and grab him, but Baalis held up a hand.

"Let him be," he chuckled. "Most of them are low quality anyways. Not worthy to represent a god."

Tallai placed a hand on Baalis's. "C'mon love, don't talk like that. You do good work."

Baalis did not respond, but only shrugged indifferently.

"Is business that bad?" Tobi asked.

"Meh, it's okay," replied Baalis. "People are still buying idols, but for the longest time demand has been pretty low, as if everyone has forgotten that the gods even exist."

"Why is that?" asked Tobi.

Baalis shrugged again. "My guess is that it's more about money than anything else. We've had several years of bad harvests, just as you have. The weather has been strange too."

He took a sip of wine. "And of course, this just causes prices to rise, meaning that people have even less to spend on their household gods."

Tobi gestured toward the pile of unfinished idols that Ali was now playing with. "Is that why you have so many?"

Baalis nodded. "For the most part. But thankfully sales have just started to pick back up, which is why I've been busier these past few weeks."

"What changed things?"

"The Israelites," responded Baalis.

Nikkal, whose eyes were on Ali, had been only half-listening to the conversation. But at the mention of Israel, she gave Baalis her full attention. She noticed Tallai react the same way.

"The Israelites?" Nikkal asked.

"Mm-Hmm," replied Baalis. "Have you heard about the recent battle at Arad?"

Tobi and Nikkal both nodded.

Baalis's face turned serious. "When they took the city, the Israelites declared it to be 'Hormah', meaning 'devoted to destruction'. They killed every man, woman, and child. No mercy."

A mixture of sorrow and fear took hold of Nikkal. *The children too?* She looked over at Tobi and noticed his jaw clenched in anger.

Baalis continued. "Now people are starting to panic. They think that Israel is coming for them next and that if they don't seek the blessing of the gods, they'll be destroyed."

Tobi let out a sigh of frustration. "Too little too late, probably. Will the gods even listen? Are they going to protect Jericho?"

"It looks like it," answered Baalis. "The Israelites aren't moving north, at least not yet. Rumor has it that they're headed east, toward Edom and Moab."

Tobi nodded approvingly. "Good, because I'm pretty sure that Edom and Moab could crush them, especially if they work together."

"My thoughts exactly," replied Baalis. "The loss at Hormah—er—Arad, just goes to show how much faith the people of Arad lacked. They had it coming for failing to honor the gods."

He grabbed a piece of lamb from the platter. "The godless destroying the godless. What poetic irony."

Nikkal did not mask her confusion. "What do you mean? Is Israel godless? I thought they had a god."

Baalis spoke as he chewed. "Well, they say they have a god, but I'm not sure it means anything. He doesn't have eyes, ears, a nose, or a mouth."

He swallowed and then let out a chuckle. "He can't see them to protect them, he can't hear them to help them, and he can't speak to them to guide them. So, what good is he?"

Nikkal nodded. *Makes sense. The point of serving the gods was that they actually respond to us.*

"That reminds me," continued Baalis. "Tomorrow there's going to be a special procession through the city in honor of Baal, Asherah, and Moloch, to seek their protection and blessing. I've been helping to sponsor it and hope to make a lot of sales. It'd be great if you guys could attend."

Tobi looked first at Nikkal, who shrugged, and then back to Baalis. "I think we could do that," he replied. "We arrived here ahead of schedule and weren't planning to reach Jebus until the day after tomorrow."

Baalis clasped his hands in excitement. "Great! Trust me, you'll love it. Lots of food, drink, and music. Everyone will be there!"

CHAPTER THREE

Jericho, Summer 1407 BC

NIKKAL SWAYED BACK AND forth with Ali as she, Tobi, and Tallai stood at the edge of Jericho's main road. The noon sun's heat, coupled with the swarming crowd, made Nikkal feel like she could barely breathe. She began to dread ever coming there.

While Baalis had departed early that morning to help setup the parade, the rest of them prepared ceremonial raisin cakes and wine for the celebration. As midday approached, they finished their work and made their way to the center of the city.

Nikkal tried to distract herself by scanning the crowd for her cousin. Even if she were there, Nikkal doubted that she would be able to find her.

Ali grabbed at the cake that Nikkal held in her free hand. She pulled it away from him. "Not yet, sweetie."

He began to fuss and Tallai offered to hold him.

"Thank you," said Nikkal. She handed Ali over to her. He seemed happy and distracted by his new caretaker, at least for now.

Nikkal looked down at the disc-shaped cake in her hand. On it appeared the image of Asherah, Queen of Heaven, mother to Baal and goddess of both love and war. Nikkal had tried her best to depict Asherah accurately, with the goddess riding a lion and holding a serpent in her hand.

She frowned at her own artwork and wondered if Asherah would be insulted. But before she could dwell on it longer, she heard a cheer go up through the crowd.

She strained to see what was happening and soon saw a procession of priests and priestesses moving toward their direction.

"There they are!" Tallai exclaimed. She pointed for Ali.

The sound of flutes, drums, and tambourines filled the air as the crowd around them began to dance and cheer.

Tallai leaned over to Nikkal. "Have you ever been to one of these before?"

"No," Nikkal replied. She had some familiarity with Baal and Asherah, but the Ammonites focused their worship more on Moloch.

Tallai held up the raisin cake in her hand. "So, when the procession gets to us, we break our cakes and throw some of the pieces on the ground. Then we pour out some of our wine as an offering. Once that is done, we can eat and drink as much as we want. The more the better!"

Nikkal nodded and glanced over at Tobi, who held the wine jug. She noticed his eyes widen and then turned to see what had captured his attention.

She gasped in shock. Scantily clad dancers, both male and female, led the procession. Some wore only loin cloths and jewelry, although the jewelry seemed to cover more of their bodies.

Tallai pointed to them. "Those are the acolytes of Asherah."

As they walked, the acolytes made lewd gestures and erotic motions toward the crowd. In return they received joyful laughs and cheers.

Nikkal noticed that several of the acolytes wore multi-colored robes. "Who are they?" she asked.

"They are the Assinu and Kurgarru," replied Tallai.

Nikkal gave her a confused look. *The what?*

Tallai smiled. "Special devotees of Asherah."

Nikkal nodded and turned her attention back to them. She could not tell which ones were women and which were men. Those whose bodies looked feminine wore short hair and carried axes, while those who looked more masculine had long hair and carried mirrors.

"Are they men or women?" Nikkal asked.

"Neither, or both," replied Tallai. "Asherah has the power to change men into women—the Assinu, and women into men—the Kurgarru. The Assinu and Kurgarru have been touched by her and embody her power."

Nikkal watched them interact with the crowd. They not only danced erotically, but on occasion flashed open their robes and exposed their nakedness to those nearby. Several parents in the crowd cheered and held up their children to see.

The Assinu and Kurgarru laughed in response. Not a normal laugh of enjoyment, but an almost maniacal one.

Nikkal caught a glimpse of an Assinu exposing himself to a nearby child. The man had not only been castrated, but every part of his genitals had been removed.

She averted her eyes and moved to block Ali's view. She hoped that the multi-colored people would not see him.

"It's all right, Nik," said Tallai. "The first time is always a bit of a surprise."

Nikkal gave her a look of astonishment, but her sister-in-law's eyes were fixated on the procession. *How can she watch this?*

Tallai's voice seemed distant as she continued to speak. "They plead for Asherah to come and accept their offerings. Listen . . ."

Nikkal strained her ears and soon heard the chants of the Assinu and Kurgarru.

"Lady Asherah! We beseech you!" they cried. "Queen of Heaven eat and drink!"

Tallai tapped Nikkal on the shoulder and pointed. Her voice rose in excitement. "Here comes the high priestess!"

Unable to resist, Nikkal turned her head and let out another gasp.

A young naked woman, seated on a donkey, approached their position. Her only clothing consisted of gold jewelry that wrapped around her neck, arms, and torso. On her shaved head rested a gold crown, and she held a gold cup in her right hand from which she would periodically drink.

Nikkal then noticed an object moving in the woman's left hand. After a moment, she recognized it to be a snake, its brown and gray body coiled around the high priestess's arm. The woman held its horned head in her fingers as it flicked its tongue in and out.

Though Nikkal had seen such snakes before, the appearance of this one made her feel uneasy. And so, she shifted her eyes to a bearded man walking before the high priestess. Naked as well, except for the numerous tattoos that ran across his body, he led the donkey with one hand while holding a scepter in another. Upon his head sat a gold crown similar in style to that of the high priestess.

"Saddle an ass!" the high priestess shouted. "Hitch a donkey! Put on a harness of silver, trappings of gold!"

The priests and priestesses around her shouted back in reply. "He sets Asherah on the back of the ass, on the beautiful back of the donkey!"

Nikkal glanced over at Tobi and observed him gawking at the woman. A wave of jealousy and anger washed over Nikkal. *Stop looking at her.* But he continued.

Tallai's voice disrupted her thoughts. "Baal honors his mother Asherah and leads her on the royal donkey. They celebrate her escape from the underworld and her willingness to help Baal take the throne."

Nikkal looked back at the procession. When it reached their location, the priests and priestesses gestured toward the crowd. "Eat and drink! Eat bread from the tables! Drink wine from the goblets!"

Tallai signaled for Nikkal and Tobi to break their cakes.

Nikkal began to crumble hers and, in imitation of those around her, threw a handful of pieces onto the ground. She saw Tobi do the same before he then tipped over the wine jug and poured out some of the red liquid.

Tobi ate the cake in his hand and took a drink from the wine jug before he passed it to Nikkal.

Nikkal ate and drank. As she chewed, she realized how hungry she was, having not eaten anything since breakfast. Although the cake tasted good, it did not silence the grumbling in her stomach.

When she had finished drinking, she held out the wine jug to Tallai, who gave Ali back to her in return. Tallai then ate her cake and drank deeply.

Nikkal fed a small piece to Ali. At first, he gave her a confused look, but then reached for more.

She focused her attention on him and attempted to suppress the feelings of disgust and jealousy churning inside her. *Why is Tobi not bothered by any of this? Why did he have to keep staring at that woman?*

Nikkal shook her head and told herself that she was being silly. Honoring the gods meant trusting them and doing what they wanted without question. That was the only way to earn their blessing.

She turned to Tallai. "Is it over yet?"

Tallai laughed. "Of course not! The Bull of Heaven comes next." A serious look came upon her face.

At that same moment, an eerie silence settled over the crowd. Only the ominous beat of drums could be heard. Nikkal watched as those around her started to tremble in fear.

A few people cried out. "The bull! The bull!" The rest soon joined in, adding moans of "help us" and shouts of "please, no!" Hundreds of people raised their hands to shield themselves.

Nikkal tried to see through the outstretched arms at what had captured everyone's attention, but only caught glimpses of the object.

Then she saw it. A golden bull standing upon a wooden platform. Four large men carried the platform by means of thick wooden poles that extended out from both sides of it.

Tallai leaned over to Nikkal. "The bull comes to devour our crops, drink our water, and kill our people."

Then, out of nowhere, two individuals ran from behind the bull toward the high priestess. Nikkal could not tell if they were men or women, as they were clothed entirely in black and had their faces concealed by masks formed out of bulls' heads.

"They are the galla, demons from the underworld," Tallai continued. "They serve Moloch, the god of death, who demands payment from Asherah for escaping the underworld. If she does not offer a sacrifice, the bull will destroy the earth."

Nikkal watched them approach the high priestess. With the hand that held the snake, the woman pointed to the bearded man, who then reacted as if betrayed. The galla turned and grabbed the man, tore off his crown, stole his scepter, and dragged him back until he stood before the bull.

Tallai let out a resigned sigh. "Asherah offers her son Baal to take her place in the underworld. As the ultimate victim, he tries to fight the bull, but loses."

The man acting as Baal swung his fists against the galla and postured himself as if he were going to charge the bull.

Nikkal knew that this was just a reenactment, but something about the scene bothered her. *How could she give up her son so easily?*

The sound of wailing broke out among the crowd as the man fell to the ground in front of the bull. The galla then carried his body away.

The people around her cried out. "No! Baal is dead!" Scores of men and women broke down weeping.

Nikkal looked over at Tallai and saw tears in her eyes.

Tallai's voice wavered as she spoke. "Asherah regrets her decision. She calls on Baal's priests and priestesses to come. Together they'll awaken him and restore him to life to defeat the bull, bring us rain, and supply us with crops."

Nikkal watched as another group of priests and priestesses approached. They were all dressed as if in mourning, with faces veiled and bodies cloaked in black.

This new set of priests and priestesses cried out in unison. "Baal is dead!" They moaned and wept with grief. Some of them grabbed handfuls of dust and tossed it over their heads.

The music quickened and the mourners began to convulse. Some started to limp. Others started to shriek. Nikkal felt tempted to move with the music but forced herself to remain still.

When the music reached a crescendo, one of the priests of Baal withdrew a dagger from his cloak. "He cuts cheek and chin! He lacerates his forearms! He plows his chest like a garden! Like a vale he lacerates his back!"

Other priests threw back their cloaks in response, revealing their bare chests, arms, and legs. All of them bore both scars and tattoos upon their bodies, with some displaying fresh open wounds. They then began to cut themselves.

One man ran his blade across his bare chest. Blood flowed out of the gash and down his body as he cackled.

Nikkal instinctively covered Ali's eyes and turned away.

Tallai rested a hand on her shoulder. "They'll be fine, Nik. They do this all the time."

"But why?"

"Don't you know how the story ends?" Tallai sounded surprised at Nikkal's ignorance. "Blood must be shed to bring Baal back to life. If he stays dead, we die. So, we join with Asherah to revive him and save our people. The greater the sacrifice, the greater the blessing."

Nikkal opened her mouth to respond but before she could, one of the priestesses began to shout. "She cuts cheek and chin! She lacerates her forearms! She plows her chest like a garden! Like a vale she lacerates her back. Baal is dead!"

Out of what Nikkal could only guess was her own morbid curiosity, she watched as the woman threw back her cloak and started to cut herself. Nikkal cringed when the woman drew the knife across her bare breasts.

A wave of nausea hit her. "I think I need to sit down."

"Here, I'll take him," replied Tallai. She grabbed Ali just as Nikkal's vision began to swim.

Nikkal sat crossed-legged on the ground and focused on her breathing.

Tobi must have noticed, for he soon knelt next to her. "Are you all right, Nik? Is something wrong?"

She lied to him. "I—I just need to rest a bit. It's the heat."

He handed the wine jug to her. "Here. Take a drink. It'll help."

Nikkal nodded and lifted the jug to her lips. She kept her eyes closed and tried to force the gruesome images from her mind as she gulped.

"Do you want to go?" he asked.

She lowered the jug. "No, I'll be fine."

"All right," he said. He kissed her on the head and then stood back up.

Nikkal took another drink. And then another, each one longer than the first.

Several drinks later—Nikkal did not know how many—a loud cheer erupted from the crowd.

"It's done!" exclaimed Tallai. "Baal must return!"

Nikkal stood abruptly and almost toppled over.

Tobi took hold of her arm as she regained her balance. "Whoa, easy, Nik."

"I'm fine—I'll be fine." She attempted to brush his hand away but missed.

Tobi laughed. "Okay, well let me help you anyways."

He steadied her as they made their way through the crowd. Several of the men and women around them began to kiss and grope each other.

Tallai chuckled. "It's going to be one big party tonight. I imagine many children of the gods will be born."

"What?" asked Nikkal.

"Well," replied Tallai. "Any children conceived during these parades are blessed by the gods. Most of them will be devoted to the gods' service and given special privileges."

Nikkal did not respond, too focused on not falling over as she walked.

Once they returned to the house, Nikkal laid down with Ali until he fell asleep while Tallai prepared the evening meal. Nikkal felt guilty for not helping Tallai in the kitchen, but Tallai insisted that she rest.

By dinner time, and after taking a short nap, Nikkal joined Tobi and Tallai at table. Ali remained asleep, clearly exhausted from the day's excitement.

"Should we wait for Baalis to get back?" asked Tobi.

Tallai shook her head. "No, don't worry about it. On a day like today, I expect he won't be back until late."

They sat down to eat. As Tallai poured the wine, the door opened and Baalis entered.

Tallai nearly dropped the jug. "Baalis! How are you back so soon?"

He beamed with joy. "I sold all my idols today. Every single one of them!"

"Praise the gods!" Tallai replied.

"Yes, congratulations!" said Tobi.

Tallai got up and kissed Baalis. She then gestured for him to sit. "Well, you're just in time for dinner."

"Good," he replied. "I'm starving."

They began to eat as Baalis spoke about his sales.

"I'm going to be busy making more idols now, that's for sure," he chuckled. "Let's hope the demand stays high."

"So, you really sold them all?" Tobi asked.

Baalis raised a finger. "Well, not quite." A smile crept over his face as he reached into his cloak and pulled out a fold of cloth.

He placed it on the table in front of Tobi and Nikkal. "I wanted to give you both a gift in honor of Ali's dedication tomorrow. Go ahead, open it."

Tobi reached out and unfolded the cloth, revealing two pieces of onyx carefully shaped into images of Moloch. Each piece had been carved to resemble a body of a man with the head of a bull. Even the smallest details, such as the eyes and mouth, were clearly visible.

Nikkal picked one up and examined it. "They're beautiful."

"Baalis," said Tobi. "You didn't have to do this. You could have sold these for a decent price."

"I know," he replied. "I've been working on them for a while now. But instead of selling them I wanted to honor you and show how much I admire your faithfulness. It's not a common thing these days."

Tobi got up, walked over to Baalis, and hugged him. "Thank you, brother."

Baalis hugged him back "You're most welcome."

Tobi picked up one of the pieces and admired it closely. "You truly are a gifted stone cutter. I'll treasure this always."

Baalis nodded in respect. "Thank you, Tobi. I appreciate that."

The rest of the evening passed merrily as they ate and drank. It was late when they finally turned in for the night.

"We can take the floor this time, Tallai," said Nikkal. "You've already done so much—"

Tallai raised her hand to cut her off. "No. We insist. You guys take the bed while you're here. No discussion."

Nikkal nodded and settled down onto the mat next to Ali.

She watched as Baalis and Tallai laid down together on their cloaks across the room.

Nikkal closed her eyes and listened to Ali's steady breathing. Sleep came quickly for her, yet it was not restful.

She dreamt again. This time, she stood in an empty room, though she was not back at Old Aliyan's farm. She was in Tallai's and Baalis's house there in Jericho. And just like before, she heard the cries of her son, Ali, coming from somewhere outside.

Determined to get to him this time, she ran out of the house and stopped to see which direction to go. The city sat vacant and dark, as if just before sunrise. The sky grew black as storm clouds began to swirl overhead.

She heard Ali's cries to her left and turned. Where the city wall had just been moments before, there now stood a gate whose metal bars were ornately designed with leaves, fruits, and flowers engraved in gold.

"Ali!" She pushed against the gate. At first, it did not budge. She then leaned in with all her strength and soon created a gap wide enough that she could slip through.

She stopped once she reached the other side. Fear seized her heart. There in front of her appeared the same funnel cloud as in her last dream. The enormous storm swirled in black as lightning flashed within and around it. Ali cried out again. And again, the sound came from within the storm.

Nikkal summoned all her courage and ran into the storm. She covered her face with her cloak as best she could to block the debris. Sand and dust pelted her legs, but she forced them to keep moving. It seemed odd, but she could still hear Ali's cries even above the sound of the whirlwind.

With every step she took, the pain on her exposed skin increased. She glanced out from behind the cloak and saw that she now stood deep inside the whirlwind. Darkness swirled all around her.

As the lightning flashed, she caught a glimpse of a dark figure at the center of the storm. The figure had the appearance of a man, but she could not discern his face. He held Ali, whose cries had now stopped.

Desperation and anger filled her voice. "Give him back!"

The figure did not speak, but merely shook his head.

The unbearable pain forced Nikkal to her knees. She looked at her arms and legs and saw that the searing wind had flayed her skin. Muscles, veins, blood, and bones were all visible.

She tried to scream, but no words came out. She could not breathe. The storm had entered her lungs and were ripping them apart from the inside. Her vision swam, and the last thing she saw was the dark figure. He stood in front of her holding Ali in his hands. The boy was silent and unmoving. *Was he dead?*

Nikkal gasped for air as she sat up. By the pre-dawn light she could see Tobi and Ali still asleep next to her. Across the room on the floor lay Tallai and Baalis, who also did not move.

Nikkal breathed a sigh of relief. Remembering the gift that Baalis had given her, she reached into her cloak and removed the idol of Moloch. Her hand trembled as she held it.

She closed her eyes and sent a quick prayer to the god. *What are you trying to tell me?* The dream had felt so real that, even now, with her eyes shut she could still feel her skin burning.

She concentrated on the cool smoothness of the idol in her hands and, after a few moments, began to calm down.

When she opened her eyes, she saw that Tallai had sat up and was staring at her.

"Is everything okay, Nik?" Tallai's voice brimmed with worry.

Nikkal hesitated to answer, uncertain as to whether to tell the truth or not. But then she felt guilty. Tallai had always been kind to her, even now welcoming her and Tobi into their small home. It would be wrong to lie to her in her own house. Nikkal decided to tell the truth. "I had a dream—a nightmare," she whispered.

"Can you tell me about it?" asked Tallai.

Nikkal nodded.

Tallai motioned to the door with a slight jerk of her head. "How about we get some air?"

Taking care not to wake Ali or Tobi, Nikkal got up and followed Tallai outside.

The early morning streets of Jericho were vacant and quiet, except for the occasional rooster-crow or dog-bark. Nikkal glanced up at the sky. No clouds were in sight.

Tallai remained silent, appearing to wait for Nikkal to begin the conversation. Once Nikkal had gathered her thoughts, she described the dream, as well as the similar dream that had come to her a few days earlier.

After she finished, she turned and looked at Tallai. "So, what do you think? Am I going crazy?"

Tallai shook her head. "No, you're not crazy, Nik. But I think you're being tested."

Nikkal threw up her hands in frustration. "What do you mean, tested? By whom?"

"By Moloch," answered Tallai. "He's testing you to see if you'll be faithful. If you'll go through with the dedication."

Nikkal paused. "I guess that could be it . . ."

"Listen," Tallai continued. "I know you're nervous, but you need to stay on the path. From what you've said about your dream, I think that you're trying to hold on to Ali. But every time you do, it ends up destroying you."

She put a hand on Nikkal's shoulder. "You need to let him go. He belongs to Moloch, not you."

Nikkal felt torn. "I know. I keep telling myself that. But it's hard, Tallai. I love him."

Tallai gave her a sympathetic look. "I know you do. But if you love him, you wouldn't want him to have a life of suffering."

Nikkal shook her head defensively. "But you don't understand. You're not a moth—" She stopped herself, shocked that she would even say that. "I'm sorry. I didn't mean to—"

Tallai held up a hand. "It's all right, Nik, I get that all the time. It comes with the job."

Nikkal tilted her head inquisitively. "What do you mean? I thought that you were helping Baalis sell idols."

Tallai nodded. "I still am, but a few months ago I felt a desire to try to help women in need. Child dedications have been unusually low, and I just thought that if Baalis can use his skills to serve the gods, I should be able to do the same."

"So, you became a priestess of Moloch?" Nikkal asked, still confused.

"Not at all!" Tallai laughed. "I'm just an assistant. I help comfort and encourage those women who make the choice to dedicate their children."

Nikkal's voice filled with excitement. "Then can you be there today for me?"

"Well," Tallai hesitated. "I'm not scheduled to serve until next week. And I promised Baalis that I would help—"

Nikkal took hold of Tallai's hand in desperation. "Please Tallai, I need you there with me. Promise me that you'll come!" She held tight to Tallai's hand, hoping that the physical contact would sway her sister-in-law.

Tallai smiled and nodded. "Okay. I'll be there."

"Thank you so much!" Nikkal threw her arms around Tallai.

As Tallai hugged her back, Nikkal felt hope rise within her. Soon, the nightmares would end.

CHAPTER FOUR

Jebus, Summer 1407 BC

IT WAS JUST AFTER midday when Tallai, Nikkal, Tobi, and Ali arrived at Tophet. They had left Jericho before sunrise and, thankfully, were able to fall in with another group of pilgrims, resulting in an uneventful journey to Jebus.

Never having been there before, Nikkal learned that Tophet was located just south of the city, situated in a small valley called the Valley of Hinnom.

As they crested a hill, Tallai pointed down into the valley. "There it is."

Nikkal held her breath as she looked. A large walled compound, made of stone rather than mud-brick, spanned the width of the valley. It stood at least two-stories high, with walls that nestled up against the hills on either side. Oak trees had been placed strategically to prevent anyone from looking in, although from atop the donkey Nikkal could tell that there were several layers, or sections, to the compound.

Tallai gestured for them to follow the rest of the pilgrims who were headed toward the busy entrance. "Let's get in line quickly. Everyone is going to want to make their offerings and be gone before sundown."

Nikkal's pulse increased as they continued down the valley. *Why am I so nervous? This is something a lot of women do.*

As they approached the compound's main gate, a boy came forward and offered to watch and water the donkey. Tobi agreed and then helped Nikkal to dismount.

Tallai and Nikkal took a spot at the back of the line while Tobi discussed terms of payment with the boy.

Nikkal held Ali tight as she scanned the area. There were vendors lined up everywhere. Some were selling livestock while others offered birds of various kinds. All of them shouted at anyone who passed by or showed the slightest bit of interest.

She kept her eyes moving and soon spotted a young woman leaning against the wall near the entrance. *No, not a woman. More like a girl.* She could not have been more than fourteen or fifteen years old, and yet she held a baby in her arms.

Their eyes met, and the girl hurried toward her. "Would you like a child?" she asked. "Only twenty shekels[1] of silver." She held out the baby to Nikkal.

Nikkal gave her a confused look. "Umm, no thank you. I'm here with my son." She gestured to Ali.

A look of desperation came across the girl's face. "I can't take care of him. You can offer him for both of us and keep yours."

Nikkal stood there speechless.

Panic rose in the girl's voice. "Please!"

Tallai intervened. "I'm sorry, but we don't have any money."

The girl gave Tallai an annoyed look and then stormed off.

As they moved forward in line, Nikkal turned to Tallai. "What was that all about?"

Tallai gestured toward the girl. "Some sell their children so that others can offer them to Moloch on their behalf."

"But why would they do that?" Nikkal asked, astonished.

"Think about it," Tallai replied. "The unmarried and poor can't care for their children. Others have wealth, but few or no children. If you had paid her and then offered her child, Moloch would have blessed both of you. Her, because she offered her child in faith. And you because you helped someone in need."

Nikkal thought for a moment. "But doesn't that cheapen my offering to Moloch, since it wouldn't be my child?"

Tallai shrugged. "Some people have an issue with it, but the high priest is understanding. He says that there are many who can't have children. But that shouldn't stop them from seeking Moloch's blessing."

---

1. One shekel is about a third of an ounce.

Nikkal nodded. Still, the whole idea seemed strange. She looked down at Ali. *Would I do it if I had the money? Should I try?* She shook her head. *No, Moloch would know that I was acting out of fear, not faith.*

Tallai tapped her on the shoulder. "C'mon, we're next inside."

Nikkal snapped out of her own thoughts as Tobi came alongside her and they followed Tallai into the compound.

The courtyard was busier than Nikkal had expected. Numerous attendants and acolytes darted here and there doing various tasks. Some carried musical instruments while others carried incense or candles. On top of this, the sound of birds, goats, sheep, and calves filled the room. The noise and smell of the place threatened to overwhelm her senses.

A young, black-robed attendant who stood just inside the entrance addressed them coldly. "State your name and offer—." His eyes widened in recognition. "Tallai?"

Tallai smiled. "Surprise!"

He laughed. "It's good to see you again. I thought you were off this week."

"I'm here for my sister." She put her hand on Nikkal's shoulder.

"I see," he replied. He glanced down at Ali and then back up at Tallai. "The child?"

Tallai nodded.

"Okay, follow me and I'll get you in right away." He led them through the line.

Nikkal noticed several people shoot angry glances at her as she moved past them. Although she felt somewhat guilty, she was glad to not have to wait anymore. Her nerves were already on edge as it was.

They stopped in front of a metal gate, guarded on either side by two men armed with spears. The gate's bars rose to over six cubits[2] in height. Behind the bars hung a cloth veil that prevented anyone from seeing through into the next chamber. Sewn onto this veil was the image of a bird.

The attendant turned to face Nikkal and Tobi. "All right, what are your names?"

Tobi answered. "Tobimelech son of Aliyan of Rabbah and my wife Nikkal."

"And the child's name?" he asked.

"Ali," replied Tobi.

---

2. One cubit is about eighteen inches.

"Very well. The priestess will be with you shortly." He turned and hurried off.

Nikkal glanced behind her at a young woman holding what looked like a week-old baby in her arms. She rocked her baby with a tense look on her face while her husband, or who Nikkal assumed to be her husband, conversed with another man.

Nikkal locked eyes with the young woman. But instead of receiving an angry stare for jumping to the front of the line, Nikkal only perceived worry and anxiety. She could relate to the woman, and began to wonder if the woman perceived the same feelings in her.

The young woman leaned forward as if to say something to Nikkal, but then Nikkal's ear caught another woman's voice. "Tobimelech, son of Aliyan of Rabbah?"

Nikkal turned to see a middle-aged woman in front of her dressed in black robes embroidered with silver along the sleeves and edges. She recognized them as the robes of a priestess of Moloch.

Tobi raised his hand. "Yes."

"I am Priestess Anat." She nodded toward Tallai. "It's good to see you again Tallai."

Tallai bowed her head. "And you as well, priestess."

Priestess Anat turned back to Tobi. "I am told that you and your wife Nikkal would like to dedicate your son Ali?"

"Yes, that's right," he replied. He gestured for Nikkal to come forward and show Ali to her.

Priestess Anat examined the boy and nodded. "A little older than we prefer, but acceptable." A smile appeared on her lips. "Before we begin the dedication, allow me to go over a few things."

She pointed toward the veiled gate bearing the bird image in front of them. "Since you present the worthiest of offerings, you will be granted access to the seventh chamber, to the seat of Moloch himself."

She paused. "Once we reach the seventh gate, I will go on ahead and see if the high priest is ready for you. Once he is ready, I'll come back and lead you through the final gate. He will say a few words before signaling for you to step forward with the boy."

Tobi and Nikkal both nodded.

She pointed at them. "At that moment, both of you are to come forward without hesitation and present Ali to the high priest. He will receive the boy, bless him, and dedicate him."

For whatever reason, Nikkal winced at the word 'dedicate'. She regained her composure and hoped that Anat did not notice.

Anat drew closer to them and spoke in a soft, but serious tone. "Please remember that at absolutely no point must either of you cry or make noise during the ceremony. Is that understood?"

Nikkal looked down and nodded. Though Anat had addressed both of them, Nikkal felt that the last statement had been aimed at her.

Priestess Anat clapped her hands. "Great!"

The noise startled Ali, who began to fuss. Nikkal reached into her cloak, removed his toy wooden horse, and handed it to him.

Anat smirked. "I'll be back shortly." She turned and went off to speak to the other families in line.

Nikkal watched as Ali played with the horse. It reminded her of a question she had meant to ask Tallai. She leaned over to her. "Why are there so many different animals here?"

"Well," Tallai replied. "There are seven gates here at Tophet, with each gate bearing the image of a different animal."

She pointed to the one in front of them. "The first one is a bird. Those who bring birds may enter the first gate and present their offering to Moloch in the first chamber."

She gestured to the other animals in the room. "A goat is required to enter the second chamber, a sheep for the third, a calf for the fourth, a young steer for the fifth, and a mature bull for the sixth."

She then tilted her head toward Ali. "Only those dedicating children may enter the seventh, and most holy, chamber."

Nikkal nodded and began counting those women who were there with children. Many of them appeared to be alone and very young. Some were with older men, who Nikkal assumed were their fathers. Most of them, like Nikkal, appeared on edge.

She attempted to find the young woman in line behind her before Anat returned, but she had disappeared. Nikkal did not know why, but she desperately wanted to see her, to talk to her. *Where did she go? Did she change her mind?*

"Are you ready to begin?"

Nikkal snapped back around and saw Priestess Anat standing in front of them, flanked on either side by two female assistants that Nikkal had not seen before. They were also dressed in black, although their garb had no embroidery.

Tobi nodded. "We're ready."

Anat smiled. "Then follow me." She signaled to her assistants, who unlocked the gate and opened it. Nikkal held Ali tight as she, Tobi, and Tallai followed Anat on through.

They entered another courtyard similar to the previous one, although a bit smaller. Numerous priests and priestesses worked at small altars to receive those who had brought birds.

Nikkal watched as one priest broke a dove's neck while another squeezed the blood out of a pigeon. The smell of burning bird flesh mixed with incense almost made Nikkal gag.

Priestess Anat and her two assistants guided them forward to the next gate. This one appeared to be identical to the first except that the veil behind the bars depicted a goat.

As she waited for the second gate to be opened, Nikkal glanced behind her and saw several people depart the line and head toward the altars. They all carried birds in either their hands or cages. Those without birds, like Nikkal, continued to wait silently in line.

Nikkal forced herself to remain calm as they passed through the next five gates and subsequent courtyards. All the courtyards looked the same, with the only difference being the image depicted on the veils. It was just as Tallai had told her. She saw a sheep, a calf, a steer, and then a bull. After each gate, more people departed the line and went to the altars in place.

Finally, Nikkal stood before the seventh gate. She noticed several differences from the others. The bars were not dull iron, but were gold, or at least gold-plated as far as she could tell. They were also decorated with gold leaves, fruits, and flowers.

Her eyes widened. *I saw this in my dream!* She then noticed one difference. Unlike the gate from her dream, this one had a veil hung behind it. And sewn onto the veil was the image of a small child.

Nikkal's heart raced as Priestess Anat and her two assistants turned and faced them.

Anat's words were cold and official. "Tobi and Nikkal, you will soon have the honor and privilege of standing before Lord Moloch himself. Be proud of what you are doing. Be encouraged by your faith."

She signaled for her assistants to open the seventh gate. "Please follow me and do exactly as I say. Understood?"

Nikkal saw Tobi nod out of the corner of her eye. She hesitated at first but then nodded as well.

"Excellent, then let us proceed." Anat turned and walked through the gate. This time, her steps were deliberate and ceremonial.

Tobi and Nikkal followed her, while Tallai stayed close behind them.

Once on the other side, Nikkal's heart leapt into her throat. For the first time in her life, she was face-to-face with Moloch.

There, in the middle of the seventh courtyard, stood a large bronze statue, at least ten cubits in height. It had the body of a human and the head of a bull, with a pair of bronze hands extended outward. The statue sat on a stone platform, with three steps leading up to the main dais.

Nikkal's eyes traced the statue from its fingers down to its body. Its palms were turned up, and its arms sloped downward into an opening within the god's belly. A fire had been kindled inside, hot enough to give the statue an eerie orange glow.

Flames belched from Moloch's stomach. Nikkal could feel the heat, even from where she stood. Despite it, Nikkal felt a shiver run up her spine. She pulled her eyes away from the flaming belly of the god and looked around the courtyard.

A row of men with drums and tambourines lined both sides of the path. They provided a slow and steady rhythm that gave cadence to her and Tobi's steps as they followed Anat forward.

And then Nikkal saw him. The high priest of Moloch himself. Dressed in black robes embroidered with gold, he wore a bull-mask over his face. Nikkal gasped upon seeing it. *He looks like one of the galla!* She took a deep breath and forced herself to keep moving.

When they were within ten paces of the high priest, Anat turned around and signaled for Nikkal and Tobi to stop. The musicians then ceased playing, and a foreboding silence fell upon the courtyard.

The high priest spoke, his voice stern and serious. "Tobimelech, son of Aliyan of Rabbah, do you and your wife come willingly and joyfully to dedicate your son Ali to Moloch?"

"We do," replied Tobi.

"And do you acknowledge the authority and power of Moloch over your lives and over the life of your child? That it is Moloch who both gives and receives life?"

"We do," answered Tobi.

The high priest turned toward Moloch and raised his hands. "Lord Moloch," he bellowed. "You require life that you may grant life. Tobi and Nikkal have come before you to seek life, and so I ask that you honor their obedience and receive their son as he passes through the fire."

Nikkal's stomach twisted at the words. She looked at Ali, whose eyes were wide. He stared at her, as if he could sense her anxiety. His knuckles were white as he gripped his toy horse.

The high priest turned back to Tobi and Nikkal and beckoned with his hands. "Bring forth the child."

A voice cried out in Nikkal's mind. *Don't do it!* Surprised by its forcefulness, she did not move until Tobi placed his hand firmly on her back. *No! Stop!* But she allowed Tobi to lead her forward.

Priestess Anat moved to the high priest's right side while her two assistants walked next to Tobi and Nikkal.

The assistant next to Nikkal put her hand on Nikkal's shoulder and whispered. "You're doing great. You're so brave right now. Just keep going."

Nikkal wondered if the woman had noticed her slight hesitation. Then she heard Tallai's voice from behind her. "I'm with you, Nik. It's gonna be okay."

Nikkal did not respond. She began to doubt their words, even Tallai's. *Turn and run!* But she ignored the voice and pushed forward.

They stopped just in front of the high priest, who then stretched out his arms. The eyes behind the bull-mask stared coldly at Nikkal.

Priestess Anat signaled for Nikkal to hand Ali over to him.

Nikkal looked at her son. *I love you, Ali. No matter what.* His eyes remain locked on hers, as if waiting for her to decide what to do. She hesitated for a moment but then felt a nudge from Tobi.

"Go on," he whispered.

Nikkal slowly held out Ali to the high priest. The voice inside her protested. *Do not give him your son!* But she did not listen to it. She was afraid. Afraid of her husband's wrath, afraid of the wrath of the high priest, and, most of all, afraid of the wrath of Moloch.

Impatient at Nikkal's apparent slowness, the high priest snatched Ali from her half-extended arms. The sudden separation startled Ali, who dropped his wooden horse and began to wail.

The high priest, unmoved by the boy's cries, turned and began striding toward Moloch. The musicians started playing their drums and tambourines again, giving pace to the high priest's steps.

Nikkal felt Tobi place his arms around her shoulders to comfort her. But she felt no comfort. The increasing intensity of Ali's cries became unbearable for her. *I can't do this!*

"Wait!" Nikkal shouted. "Please, let me hold him a little longer. Let me just calm him down."

As if scripted, Priestess Anat placed herself between Nikkal and the high priest, blocking her view. "Shh. It's going to be all right, Nikkal. Everything's fine. Please stay calm."

"No!" Nikkal replied. She tried to see over Anat's shoulder. "He's scared! He needs me!" She moved to push past Anat, but Tobi's grip tightened around her shoulders.

"Nik, please," he whispered. "Calm down. He'll be fine."

"No, he won't!" She tried to squirm free from Tobi's grip. When that failed, she gave him a look of desperation. "Please, Tobi, let me go! Let me get him!"

Tobi did not answer.

Her eyes followed the high priest as he ascended the stone steps. When he reached the top, he stopped and glanced over his shoulder back at Nikkal. She sensed intense anger and annoyance emanating from behind the expressionless mask.

The high priest signaled to the musicians, who increased the volume of their playing. He then lifted Ali up and began to speak.

Nikkal strained to hear, but the banging of drums had become so loud that she could not make out the words. Even Ali's cries had become inaudible.

Knowing this was her last chance, she gritted her teeth and lunged forward. The sudden movement broke Tobi's grip and she was free.

"Nik!" he shouted.

She ignored him as she shoved Priestess Anat to the side. The path to Ali lay clear before her.

Then, as if out of nowhere, two men approached her from opposite sides. *Where did they come from?* Before she could react, they took hold of her wrists.

"No! Please!" she begged.

Pain shot up her arms as their grips tightened. She knew that she was not strong enough to break free.

"Wait! Stop!" she cried. No one listened.

Nikkal watched in horror as the high priest placed her son on the glowing hands of Moloch. A cry of intense pain erupted from Ali, so loud that it could be heard even over the thundering of the drums.

"Ali!" she shouted.

She fought to free herself but only received more pain in return. Many different voices spoke to her, including Tobi's. She ignored them all. The only thing she heard were the screams of her dying son.

A wave of nausea and despair washed over her. She wanted to stop watching, but she could not. *What have I done?*

Her vision began to tunnel, and she felt as if she were falling into cold darkness. The last thing she saw was her son's trembling body roll down Moloch's arms into the god's flaming belly. The screaming stopped.

PART TWO

The Woman

CHAPTER FIVE

Rabbah, Fall 1407 BC

NIKKAL STARED DOWN AT the dough in front of her, unable to force her hands to knead it. She did not know how long she sat there, and she did not care.

It had been two months since Ali's dedication, and Nikkal still grieved. How could she not? She had given up her son, and his blood was now on her hands. On top of that, she had broken the rules of the ceremony. *It was all for nothing.*

The rest of her family had tried to comfort her. But they did not know about Nikkal's behavior at Tophet. Only she and Tobi knew, and they did not talk about it. So the family assumed that she simply missed her son. They told her that it was a necessary sacrifice; that her son was better off now and that her future was secure.

But she felt neither security nor peace. The guilt and grief did not lessen, despite her family's words. In fact, she became annoyed when they tried to help her. With Tobi, things were worse. He had become cold and unaffectionate toward her, and in response she had grown bitter and angry with him. *He probably blames me. But he doesn't understand. He can't.*

She heard Naamah's voice and shook herself back to reality.

". . . for baking?" Naamah asked.

"I'm sorry," Nikkal replied. "What were you saying?"

Naamah sighed. "I said, child, is the dough ready for baking?"

"Oh, yeah, I think it is." Nikkal did not move.

"Well, then can you go put it in the oven?"

"Sure," replied Nikkal, her voice distant.

She got up and carried the dough outside. Though the sun sat just above the horizon, Nikkal refused to enjoy its beauty. Instead, she kept her eyes on the ground as she shuffled over to the clay oven.

Naamah had already heated it, one of the several tasks that Nikkal had failed to do that morning. Since Nikkal's return from Tophet, Naamah and Arsay had taken over her responsibilities. Worst of all, they were nice about it. Yet she could tell that their patience wore thin.

She wanted to try to get back to work again. Not only to avoid upsetting her family, but to take her mind off Ali—if that were even possible. And so today would be the day that she would finally bake the bread.

She stooped down and moved to place the soft dough in the oven. She froze as its heat washed over her skin. Images of Moloch flooded her mind.

As she stared into the oven's gaping hole, she imagined herself back at Tophet. She felt the heat of the furnace and heard the screams of her son.

Looking down at the bread, she thought for a moment that she saw Ali. She blinked several times and realized that it was just the dough. But it was all too much for her—too real. *I can't do this.* She burst into tears, dropped the dough, and ran off.

It was not until midday that someone found her in the orchard. As she sat leaning against the trunk of a fig tree, she noticed Arsay approach out of the corner of her eye.

Arsay stopped and stood next to her. Nikkal did not acknowledge her presence, but continued to stare off in the distance.

Arsay did not speak, but instead plucked a few figs and sat down beside her. She then offered one to Nikkal.

Nikkal almost refused but, upon realizing how hungry she was, accepted. "Thank you," she whispered.

They ate quietly, with nothing but the sound of birds and the rustling of the wind around them.

After a while, Arsay broke the silence. "It's really peaceful out here away from all the oblivious men and judgmental in-laws."

Nikkal chuckled but did not speak.

Arsay turned to her. "I'm sorry, Nik. I'm sorry for not being there for you as I should have. I'm sorry for being a bad sister."

Nikkal met her gaze. "You're not a bad sister."

"Yeah, but I wasn't a good one. I let the others criticize you for grieving and I let you become bitter at them. But I don't want that. I want things to get better."

"But how can they get better?" Nikkal looked away as tears welled up inside her. "I've lost my son."

Arsay did not respond.

Several moments of silence passed between them. But just when Nikkal thought that Arsay would leave, she spoke. "When I gave up my firstborn, I felt as you did. I despaired. Despite doing everything right, I thought I had ruined it."

Arsay let out a deep sigh. "But then I realized that I didn't want my child to die for nothing. I needed to trust that the gods would reward me for my sacrifice. And that's the point. Sacrifices aren't easy and if they were then they wouldn't be called sacrifices."

Nikkal shook her head in disbelief. "But why, Arsay? Why did Moloch need my son? Why would he demand that I give him up?" She searched Arsay's face for an answer.

Arsay gave her a sympathetic look. "I know it's hard. But I also know that anything good requires hard work and tough choices. The gods are willing to help us, but we must be willing to do our part first."

She gestured to the trees around them. "And to get life, life must be given. The seed must go into the ground. That's why we sacrifice to Moloch. He's the giver of life to those who give it to him first. If we're faithful to him, he'll be faithful to us."

Nikkal nodded in understanding. But if what Arsay said was true, had Nikkal ruined it by her behavior? She panicked. "What if it didn't work, Arsay? This year's harvest was less than last year's. Beasts and disease have killed a third of our animals. And what if it gets worse?" Her voice trembled as her hand moved to her womb. "What if I don't conceive again?"

Arsay reached out and took hold of her hand. "Listen, Nik, you can't blame yourself for—"

Nikkal snatched her hand away. "But I wasn't faithful! You weren't there, Arsay! You didn't see me ruin the ceremony! You didn't see the way the high priest looked at me!" She began to sob. "How could Moloch not be angry? And how could Tobi not blame me?"

Without warning, Arsay leaned over and hugged Nikkal. They embraced for several moments in silence before Arsay spoke in a gentle whisper. "Things can get better, sis."

Nikkal sniffed. "How?"

Arsay pulled back and looked Nikkal in the eyes. "By making things right between you and Moloch. By showing him that you do have faith and that you're sorry for dishonoring him."

Nikkal gave her a confused look.

"And if you do that," continued Arsay. "I truly believe that Moloch will forgive you, and that Tobi will love you."

Nikkal considered Arsay's words. *Is it possible? Could I ensure that Ali's sacrifice wasn't pointless?*

A determined look came across Nikkal's face. "What must I do?"

The next several days went better for Nikkal than the previous two months. For the first time in a while, she felt hope.

After their conversation among the fig trees, Arsay had instructed Nikkal to send a message to Tallai. Since Tallai worked for the high priest of Moloch, she would be the one to ask about any chance of reconciliation. Nikkal did as instructed by sending Kenaz, their most reliable slave, to Jericho.

A week later, Kenaz had returned and now stood before Nikkal and Arsay, who had ordered him to report to them immediately.

"Well, what did she say?" Arsay asked, her arms crossed.

Kenaz turned to Nikkal and spoke with his typical formality when he served as a messenger. "Your sister-in-law sends you greetings, as does her husband Baalis."

Arsay gestured for him to speak faster.

Kenaz seemed oblivious to her impatience. "She remains in good favor with priestess Anat and the high priest of Moloch, despite the incident. She says that you are welcome to visit at any time, as their house will always remain open—."

Arsay smacked the side of his head. "Get to the point Kenaz, or I will have you beaten! What were her instructions?"

Kenaz winced but showed no signs of anger. He then nodded respectfully to Arsay and turned back to Nikkal. "You are instructed to travel to the Altar of Asherah, just west of Jericho, before the next full moon. There, where heaven meets earth, the goddess Asherah will bring healing and reconciliation between you and Moloch."

He reached into his tunic, withdrew a small clay token, and handed it to Nikkal.

Nikkal took the token and examined it. About the size of her palm, it had a square shape with rounded edges. Its front depicted a naked Asherah, astride a lion, holding a serpent in each hand. Its back contained an image of a palm tree atop a hill, with a full moon hanging above it in the sky.

Her eyes remained fixed on the token as Kenaz continued. "Present that to the servants of Asherah at the next full moon, and you will be granted access to the ceremony of union."

Nikkal looked up at him. "Ceremony of union?"

He shifted his eyes to Arsay, as if waiting for her to explain.

Arsay obliged. "The ceremony of union," she began, "is a celebration of passion and love. The high priestess, as Asherah's representative, is united with Baal, represented by the high priest of Baal. Although she can unite with other gods, and even goddesses."

"Unite?" asked Nikkal.

Arsay nodded. "Through divine intercourse." When Arsay noticed that Nikkal still did not seem to grasp it, she let out a frustrated sigh. "Sex, Nik."

Nikkal's eyes widened. "Oh . . ."

Arsay held up her hands. "Don't worry, you don't have to participate in it. You just have to watch. It's completely voluntary. But to be present at the ceremony is a great honor. The blessing of Asherah rests upon those who attend. It is an act of divine liberation and empowerment."

Kenaz cleared his throat. "There is one more thing."

They both looked at him in anticipation.

His voice turned nervous. "Entry into the ceremony requires a donation of one mina of silver."[1]

Nikkal gasped. "One mina?"

"Yes, my lady." Kenaz replied.

Arsay responded in disbelief. "But that's more than two slaves' worth of silver!"

He stiffened his body in preparation for another smack from Arsay. "That was the lady's instructions."

---

1. One mina is sixty shekels, or about twenty ounces.

Arsay turned to Nikkal. "It's okay. We'll get the money. Just explain the situation to Tobi and I'm sure he'll convince his father to let him borrow what we need."

Nikkal shook her head. "Tobi and I haven't spoken much since the dedication. I think he hates me."

Arsay put her hand on Nikkal's shoulder. "That's exactly why you need to tell him about this. It will give him hope and show him that you're trying to make things right."

"Okay," Nikkal replied. "I'll tell him."

"Good," said Arsay. "Now the next full moon is just over a week away, so we have to leave in a few days."

"We?" asked Nikkal.

"Of course, we!" Arsay laughed. "I'm not letting you travel the roads alone. It's too dangerous."

Nikkal chuckled. "Somehow I don't think that two women travelling together will deter anyone."

"Well, that's why Kenaz will be coming with us." Arsay gestured toward him.

Kenaz eyes widened in surprised. "I will?"

Arsay turned to him, her voice firm. "You will, because if you don't, I'll have Tobi castrate you and then sell you to the highest bidder." She placed her hand on her chin. "You'd make a great eunuch, and the money would help pay for Nikkal's reconciliation. It could be arranged . . ."

Kenaz interjected. "I would be delighted to join you both, if Master Tobi approves."

Arsay smirked. "Oh, he will."

While Nikkal waited until evening for Tobi to return, she considered the best way to speak with him alone. She did not want to hold off until after the evening meal, as he would likely be drunk then, a habit he had formed since Tophet. That meant that she had to find him as he came in from the flocks and fields.

And so, Nikkal worked hard to get her duties done. If she could finish early, she could go out and meet him. She just needed a few moments to talk.

Arsay, fully aware of Nikkal's plan, finished her own work and then began to help Nikkal.

"No need to rush, ladies," said Naamah. "The men won't be in quite yet."

"Sorry, mother," replied Arsay. "I guess we're just hungry."

Naamah looked up at them, a look of excitement on her face. "Oh? Is it perhaps that you are eating for two? Tell me, are both of you pregnant?"

Arsay held up her hands. "No, mother, it's not that. We're just hungry."

"Mm-hmm." Naamah turned back to her work.

Arsay caught Nikkal's attention and nodded to door.

Taking the hint, Nikkal moved to leave. "I just need a bit of fresh air." She departed before Naamah could respond.

The sun blasted Nikkal with its heat as she walked outside. There were no clouds in sight. *Baal has not yet returned, because Moloch won't let him. But I can fix that.*

She rushed out through the gate of the compound and scanned the horizon. A group of men appeared to the northwest, and Nikkal soon recognized Hanun and Peduel, who were running out in front.

She went back into the courtyard and gathered water for the men. Once she had filled several jugs, she carried them out and waited. As she leaned against the compound wall, she reached into her cloak and felt the clay token that Kenaz had delivered to her. Hope rose in her heart.

As the group drew near, one of the men began to run. She guessed that Tobi had recognized her.

"Nik!" Tobi shouted. "Is everything all right?!"

She cupped her hands to her mouth. "Yes!"

He stopped running, but as he drew near, Nikkal could still discern a worried look on his face.

She gestured toward the buckets on the ground next to her. "I prepared water for all of you."

Tobi looked down at them and then back up at her. "Oh, I thought that something was wrong."

Nikkal game him a nervous smile. "No, but I was hoping to talk to you alone."

He hesitated for a moment. "Of course." He turned to Zakar, who was just now catching up. "Zakar, everything is all right. Can you distribute the water and finish up for me?"

Zakar nodded before issuing orders to the rest of the group.

Tobi gestured for Nikkal to follow him, and they walked over to a nearby oak tree, far enough away to not be heard.

When they stopped, he turned to her and crossed his arms. "What did you want to talk about?"

She took a deep breath. "I'm sorry, Tobi. I'm sorry for my behavior at Tophet, and I'm sorry for the way I've treated you ever since. I just, didn't know how to handle it."

She paused to try to gauge his response.

At first, he said nothing. Then he uncrossed his arms and moved toward her. She stiffened, unsure of what he was going to do.

He put his arms around her. "I'm sorry too, Nik."

Her body relaxed at his embrace, and she continued. "I feel like I've ruined everything . . ." She felt tears rise inside her.

Tobi replied with compassion. "Don't say that."

She pulled away and shook her head. "It's true, but I think I've found a way to make it right."

A puzzled look came upon his face. "How?"

"I sent a message to your sister, and she told me that Asherah could help us." She reached into her cloak, pulled out the clay token, and handed it to him.

As he examined it, she continued. "If I attend the ceremony of union at the altar of Asherah in Jericho, then everything will be fixed, and Moloch's wrath will no longer be upon us."

She hesitated for a moment. "The only thing is that gaining access to the ceremony will cost us a mina of silver."

Tobi jerked his head up and locked eyes with her. "A mina?"

She nodded. "I know it's a lot, but it's the only way."

Tobi said nothing, but looked away as if deep in thought. After a moment, he turned back to her. "What does the ceremony involve?"

"Arsay told me that the high priest and high priestess . . ." She fished for the right words. "Reenact the divine union. Those who attend as guests and witnesses to the ceremony receive the blessing."

Tobi nodded and gazed back down at the token in his hands.

She hoped that he would agree. She needed things to be right between them. And if that meant asking for Asherah's help, then so be it.

Several moments passed. *He's going to say no. It's too much money.* Nikkal sighed. "If you don't want me to go, I'm okay with that too." She started to turn away.

"You should," Tobi answered.

Nikkal looked at him with surprise. "Are you sure?"

He handed the token back to her. "Yes. If this is the only way, then we must try."

"But what about the money?" she asked.

"My father will help us," he replied. "He might be old and angry, but he is faithful to the gods. It would please him to know that you're doing this."

"But would it please you?" she asked. Her eyes searched his.

Tobi sighed. "I believe in the gods, Nik. And I believe that this is the right thing to do, however costly it might be."

Nikkal nodded and returned the token to her cloak. She felt relief at Tobi's answer, although a part of her remained uncertain.

"Will you be staying with Tallai and Baalis?" he asked.

She shook her head. "I don't think so. I was hoping to visit my cousin since I didn't get a chance to last time." That was only partially true. The real reason was that she did not think she could handle being back in Tallai's house so soon after Ali's dedication.

Tobi surprised Nikkal by not arguing with her. "Do you need me to go with you?" he asked.

"No," she replied. "Arsay will come with me, along with Kenaz, if you're okay with it."

Tobi seemed taken aback. "Kenaz? But I need him to help work the farm—" He paused for a moment and then smiled at her. "It's all right, I can manage without him. I'd rather have you kept safe. Take Kenaz with you."

"Won't your father be upset?" she asked.

Tobi shrugged. "I'll just remind him that Kenaz is my slave, not his. Besides, if it's in service to the gods, father won't go against it."

Nikkal visibly relaxed. "Thank you."

He put his arms around her and drew her in close. "I love you, Nik."

She hugged him back. "I love you, too."

As they stood there, Nikkal felt both hope and joy creep back into her heart. This time, she would do things right. Then they would have true peace and prosperity.

CHAPTER SIX

Jericho, Fall 1407 BC

THE LINE TO ENTER Jericho crept forward. Fights broke out as many lost patience and shoved their way to the front. A mix of shouts and curses resulted.

Nikkal thanked the gods that she and Arsay were not on foot. While the two women sat securely atop their donkey, Kenaz held the reins with one hand and kept the other near the hilt of his hidden dagger. His head swiveled as he remained vigilant for any signs of an imminent threat. That brought some comfort to Nikkal.

Kenaz nodded toward the gate. "Looks like they called up additional guards."

Nikkal watched as a contingent of soldiers moved through the crowd. With swords brandished, they forced people back into line. A robed man, unarmed and flanked by a pair of bodyguards, walked behind them. He stopped periodically to engage in conversation with those awaiting entry.

Nikkal noticed that some people slipped the man money when he approached them. He would then direct them to the front of the line and into the city.

She looked up at the sky. The sun remained above the horizon. *Several hours until sunset.* Even so, she could afford little delay. The full moon would be tonight, her deadline to reach the Altar of Asherah.

Her hand rested on their bag of silver. She needed the money for tonight's ceremony, not for paying a bribe. Panic gripped her heart as she tried to think of how she might gain entrance to the city.

Within a few moments, the official appeared in front of them. He gave Kenaz a suspicious look. "Where are you from and why do you want to enter Jericho?"

Both Kenaz and Arsay glanced at Nikkal. Since they were staying with her cousin, it only made sense for her to answer the question.

Nikkal cleared her throat and tried to sound official. "I am Nikkal, of the house of Aliyan of Rabbah. We are here to visit my cousin and to worship at the high place of Asherah."

"Who is your cousin?" the man asked.

"Rahab," Nikkal replied.

The man must have recognized the name, as a grin spread across his face. "Rahab?" He moved closer and began to eye Nikkal up and down. "Hmm. I see some of her beauty in you."

He placed his hand on Nikkal's leg and lowered his voice. "My name is Yassib. If you don't want to wait, I can help you get in—for a price."

Without warning, Kenaz stepped in between them. The bodyguards were startled by the sudden movement and readied their weapons. He held up a small pouch. "Would three shekels of silver be sufficient, my lord?"

Nikkal noticed that Kenaz's other hand rested on the hilt of his dagger. She doubted that he would actually use it against Yassib, but the gesture might offer some deterrence.

It worked. Yassib glanced down at Kenaz's hand and, with nervousness, took the pouch from him. "Three shekels should suffice."

After weighing the bag in his hand, Yassib gave a satisfied nod and gestured for them to follow him.

Arsay whispered to Nikkal as they moved out of the line. "Well, that was close."

Nikkal nodded.

When they reached the gate, Yassib signaled for his guards to make a path for them. He then turned to Nikkal. "Please tell your cousin that I look forward to visiting her again soon." He shot Kenaz a resentful look and then departed.

They began to make their way through the city. Although it had only been two months, Nikkal felt amazed at how crowded it had become since her last visit.

Arsay leaned forwarded. "Are you sure you don't want to stay with Tallai and Baalis?"

Nikkal felt a twinge of both anger and sadness at Arsay's question. She fought back the urge to yell and simply nodded. "I can't go back there right now. The memories are still too fresh."

Arsay paused and then spoke again. "Do you know how to get to Rahab's?"

Nikkal hesitated to answer. She had not seen Rahab since her parent's funeral, a few months after her and Tobi's wedding. But even then she had not visited Rahab's house. All she knew was that she still lived in Jericho.

Kenaz must have noticed Nikkal's silence. "I can ask around, my lady. Clearly Rahab is known here, so it can't be too difficult."

"Thank you," replied Nikkal.

They stopped in front of a nearby merchant's stand, and, after a few moments in conversation, Kenaz came away with directions. "He says she runs an inn on the western side of the city. The building is attached to the outer wall."

"How long will it take to get there?" Nikkal asked.

Kenaz looked at the throng of people around them, turned back to Nikkal, and shrugged.

She gestured for him to lead them on.

As they wound their way through the crowds, Nikkal's stomach churned with anxiety. The sun approached the horizon. *Not much time left.*

After about an hour, Kenaz stopped the donkey in front of a two-story building embedded in the city's wall. Numerous individuals, mostly men, were coming and going.

"Is this the place?" Nikkal asked.

"I think so, my lady," replied Kenaz.

Kenaz helped both Nikkal and Arsay dismount before he turned to speak to a nearby boy. After an exchange of words, he handed the boy a few small pieces of silver.

Kenaz grabbed the pack that contained their supplies, including the mina of silver, and slung it over his shoulder. "He'll watch the donkey for us until sunset."

Nikkal nodded and they followed Kenaz inside.

The inn appeared dimly lit and smelled of a mixture of incense and perfume. Nikkal spotted tables, food, drinks, and servers, to be sure, but she soon realized that other activities, besides eating and drinking, took place there.

She glanced to her right and observed a young woman, dressed provocatively, come up to a man seated at a nearby table. After an exchange of words, he nodded, and then she took him by the hand and led him to another room behind a curtain.

"Kenaz," Nikkal whispered, "you said this was an inn."

"It is, my lady. One of the most popular."

"I can see why," she replied.

A woman dressed in scarlet came up to them, flanked by a man who, from his large stature and fierce demeanor, clearly served as her bodyguard.

Nikkal fixed her eyes upon the woman. Her face was beautiful, without flaw, and her body moved with an unmatched gracefulness.

The woman smiled at them as she gestured. "Welcome. My name is Rahab, and I am at your service. Please sit at any of the empty tables or couches and I will have one of my girls bring—"

"Rahab!" Nikkal interrupted.

A confused look appeared on Rahab's face. "Yes?"

"It's me, Nikkal, your cousin!"

Rahab gasped with excitement. "Nikkal! I thought you seemed familiar!" She gave her a hug. "It's been too long, cousin."

Nikkal hugged her back. "I know. I'm sorry I haven't visited."

"Don't be sorry!" Rahab glanced over at Kenaz. "My memory might be bad, cousin, but I know that this isn't Tobi."

Nikkal shook her head. "No, this is Kenaz, one of our slaves."

Kenaz bowed his head to Rahab. "My lady."

Nikkal gestured toward Arsay. "And this is Tobi's sister, Arsay."

Rahab clasped her hands together. "Yes! I remember you as well!" She hugged Arsay and then turned back to Nikkal. "So, what brings you three to Jericho? Will you be staying long?"

Nikkal shook her head. "Perhaps just for a day or two. I'm here to visit the high place of Asherah this evening."

Rahab gave Nikkal a curious look. "Really? What for?"

"Well—" Nikkal began.

Rahab held up her hand. "No, forgive me. It's not my business." She snapped her fingers, and addressed the servant girl who soon appeared next to her. "Please show our guests to one of our overnight rooms upstairs and make sure they are taken care of."

The girl nodded. "Yes, mistress."

Rahab turned back to Nikkal, Arsay, and Kenaz. "Did you bring any animals or other supplies with you?"

"Yes," Kenaz replied. "I paid a boy to watch our donkey until sunset."

Rahab nodded and then spoke to her bodyguard. "Have the animal secured and their supplies brought to their room."

"Yes, my lady," the man replied. His voice matched the seriousness of his face. He grabbed a nearby male servant and went outside.

Rahab gave Nikkal a warm smile. "You have some time before you leave, so please rest a bit. I'll come by and chat with you before you go."

She turned and walked off before Nikkal could reply.

Nikkal attempted to relax, but could not. A blend of fear and excitement set her nerves on edge. As she lay on the bed, she examined the clay token and thought about the upcoming ceremony. *Will this work? Can Asherah reconcile me with Moloch?*

She glanced over at Arsay, who sat looking out the window toward the mountain range west of the city. The setting sun cast a red and orange glow upon the ridge. Rahab must have given them one of her best rooms, to have such a luxury view.

There was a knock at the door.

Arsay stepped back from the window "Who is it?"

"It's Kenaz, my lady."

Arsay walked over and opened the door.

Kenaz entered carrying food and drink. "I figured it would be better to eat in here than in the main hall." He set down the food on a nearby table. "It's crazy down there. Many more people have arrived since us."

Arsay broke off a chunk of bread and handed it to Nikkal.

Nikkal sat up and took it. "Why? What's going on?"

Kenaz gave her a concerned look. "I did some listening and some asking. Ever since the destruction of Arad, more Canaanites are coming here to serve the gods and to ask them for protection."

He paused for a moment. "And not just Canaanites. Amorites, Edomites, and Moabites also. They fear Israel. People keep saying that they are a judgment from the gods."

Arsay spoke, a hint of anger in her voice. "But won't Edom and Moab stand up to the Israelites? Couldn't they just work together and beat them?"

Kenaz sighed. "They probably could. But they won't."

Arsay tilted her head. "What do you mean, Kenaz? I thought Edom hated Israel."

He nodded. "It's true that there is no love between my people and Israel, despite us being distant cousins. Yet word is that Edom and Moab have chosen not to fight them."

Arsay threw up her hands in frustration. "So, what, are they just going to let the Israelites march through their territory?"

He shook his head. "Thankfully, no. They aren't fighting them, but they also aren't letting them pass through. And so, Israel has to go around."

"And then what?" Arsay asked.

"I don't know," Kenaz replied. "If Israel wants to get to the Jordan, they're going to have to eventually turn west into Amorite territory."

"And will the Amorites fight Israel?" she asked.

Kenaz shrugged. "When King Sihon took the throne, he invaded Moab and took half of their land. I bet that's why Moab isn't fighting Israel. They're probably hoping that the Israelites and Amorites will kill each other. Then, when the dust settles, Moab can take back what they lost."

This time Nikkal spoke. "What about the Ammonites? Are they going to fight?" She dreaded the thought of Tobi going to war.

Kenaz shook his head. "Not that I've heard, my lady. The Ammonites have a strong border and are not in Israel's way, so it's unlikely that Israel will attack them. But King Sihon might try to persuade them to help him if he goes to war."

Nikkal nodded. A part of her hoped that Israel would be defeated, that the gods would protect her and her people. Yet, for some reason, she felt that any attempt to resist them would fail—that they could not be beaten.

Her thoughts were interrupted by another knock at the door. Kenaz cracked it open to see who it was and then moved aside to reveal Rahab.

"May I come in?" she asked.

Nikkal smiled. "Yes, of course." She did not know why, but her cousin's presence calmed her.

Rahab entered and addressed Arsay and Kenaz. "May I speak with Nikkal alone?" Her voice sounded serious.

Arsay hesitated, as if caught off guard by the request, but then nodded and signaled to Kenaz. "Kenaz, let's get the donkey ready to go."

"Yes, my lady," he replied. They rose and departed.

When the door was closed, Rahab sat down on the bed next to Nikkal and took hold of her hand. "Cousin, I know it's not my business, but I want to make sure that you know what you're doing."

Nikkal nodded and took a deep breath. "Two months ago, Tobi and I dedicated our son to Moloch. But I ruined the ceremony and dishonored the high priest. As a result, I fear that I brought about Moloch's wrath upon my family." She forced back the tears that welled up inside her.

She then picked up the clay token of Asherah and showed it to Rahab. "But if Asherah can make things right, I must try. I have no other choice."

Rahab took the token in her hands and examined it. "Asherah certainly claims to have great power . . ." For a moment, Nikkal thought her voice contained a hint of mockery.

"Have you been to the high place?" Nikkal asked.

Rahab looked up and gave her a weak smile. "Yes, I've been there many times. But I don't serve anymore. I just focus on keeping the inn."

Nikkal chuckled. "The inn? Is that what you call it?"

A flicker of anger came across Rahab's face. "Sometimes we don't make the best choices when we're young. But we must live with the consequences."

Nikkal studied Rahab's face, unable to discern what she meant. "Haven't the gods blessed you?" she asked.

Rahab shrugged. "You might call it that, although I don't think it'll last."

"Because of their judgment upon us?" Nikkal asked.

"Maybe not theirs . . ." Rahab replied. She stared at the token in her hands.

Nikkal did not know how to respond to Rahab's strange, and cryptic, behavior. She glanced out the window and realized that it had become dark.

"I have to leave, Rahab, or I'll be late."

Rahab snapped out of her trance. "Yes, of course." She handed the clay token back to Nikkal. "I'll have some of my men accompany you to the high place. It's not safe to travel around here at night."

"Thank you."

As Nikkal moved to get up, Rahab grabbed her hand. Her face looked anxious. "Nikkal, don't—"

"Don't what?" Nikkal replied, startled.

Rahab sighed and let go of her hand. "Don't be afraid to change your mind. If something feels wrong, tell my men and they'll bring you back here, okay?"

"I will," replied Nikkal.

Rahab nodded and stood. As she led Nikkal toward the door, Rahab turned to her. "It's okay to have doubts about things, Nik. I often do."

Nikkal did not respond. *Why is Rahab acting like this?*

Rahab looked as if she wanted to say more. But instead she turned and departed.

Nikkal clutched the clay token and followed.

CHAPTER SEVEN

Heshbon, Fall 1407 BC

THE FULL MOON'S LIGHT shone upon the man as he ascended the stone steps to King Sihon's palace. Given the brightness of the evening, he expected that the guards would recognize him and let him pass. When they stopped him, he fought to control his anger.

"Halt," said one of the guards. He held out a spear to block his way. "State your business."

The man spoke through gritted teeth. "I'm Commander Amurrum, you idiot. King Sihon is expecting me."

"Oh—uh—I'm sorry, sir," the guard stammered. He attempted to regain his composure. "You may enter—but you'll have to leave your weapons here."

"What?" Amurrum replied.

"New orders, sir," said the other guard. "From the king himself."

Amurrum considered not complying, but then decided against it. "Fine." He removed his sword and dagger from his tunic and handed them to the second guard.

The first guard pulled his spear back and gestured for Amurrum to continue. "Thank you, sir."

Amurrum walked past them in silence. As he entered the torchlit building, he admired the palace's style—large but without elegance. Few images or decorations lined the walls, just as few rugs or skins covered the floor. *Cold simplicity. Not like Jericho.*

Amurrum passed several servants on his way to the king's hall, all of them careful to bow in respect. They all knew him. He served as chief commander of Sihon's army, with the king as his only superior.

Crossing a hallway, he glanced to his right and spotted the door that led to the king's harem. Two eunuchs, armed and armored, guarded the entrance.

He nodded to them. "Evening, boys."

As usual, they did not respond.

Through the door's opening Amurrum caught a glimpse of one of the veiled women, named Inanna. She gave him a friendly wave that, thankfully, no one else noticed.

Amurrum made no response but just kept walking. The last thing he needed was to have his involvement with Inanna exposed. She was the king's favorite, and for good reason. She also knew it, which is why she had such great influence over both the king and his court.

That is how she had snagged Amurrum. Years earlier, during the celebration of Sihon's victory over Moab, Amurrum had drunk himself silly. When Inanna got him into bed with her, she blackmailed him into maintaining a secret affair. Now, he had no choice but to go along with it.

It had its upsides. She was beautiful, affectionate, and energetic. Still, Amurrum knew the danger. If he ever displeased her, she could just tell Sihon that he had assaulted her, and his life would be forfeit. No trial. No questions. Just death. King Sihon's way.

Amurrum soon arrived at the door to the king's hall. There, waiting for him, stood an older bearded man named Nahash, high priest of Baal and personal advisor to King Sihon.

Nahash, dressed in his standard black cloak of Baal and leaning on a wooden staff, pointed an accusatory finger at Amurrum. "You're late, commander." His voice always reminded Amurrum of a hissing snake.

Amurrum smirked. "Well, if your man had delivered his message right away instead of stopping at every brothel, I might have made it on time."

"Lies," snapped Nahash.

Amurrum shrugged. "Perhaps, but who do you think the king will believe?"

Nahash said nothing but shot daggers at Amurrum with his eyes.

After a moment of glaring at each other in silence, Nahash turned and opened the door to the hall. "He's waiting for you." As he led the way, his staff impacted the ground with every step. Amurrum found it obnoxious.

Once inside, Amurrum looked and saw five unfamiliar men seated at the king's table, with Sihon at the head. They were talking excitedly over a map that had been spread out in front of them.

Even when seated, King Sihon dwarfed the other men around him. Descended from the giants, known as the Rephaim, he easily stood at least six cubits tall, perhaps more, with wrists as thick as a man's thigh and fists as large as a man's head.

Amurrum felt a lump rise in his throat. Being in the presence of one of the last of that ancient race always put a sense of fear and awe in him. He had seen several of their kind, but the two that frightened him the most were King Sihon and his brother Og, King of Bashan.

Sihon glanced up from the table and raised his hand to silence the other five men.

In accordance with protocol, Amurrum knelt and lowered his head. "Oh king, live forever!" He kept his eyes on the floor.

"Rise, Amurrum, and step forward," Sihon commanded. His voice caused Amurrum's bones to shudder.

Amurrum stood and continued toward the table. He stopped in front of an empty chair but made sure not to sit unless the king signaled for him to do so. No signal came. *He's angry with me.*

Sihon grinned and gestured to the other men around the table. "Commander, I would like to introduce you to our newest Midianite allies, chiefs Evi, Rekem, Zur, Hur, and Reba."

Each man nodded to Amurrum as his name was called.

"Allies, my lord?" Amurrum asked.

"Yes," answered Sihon. "For the coming war with Israel. They have pledged both money and troops."

"So, it is true then?" Amurrum replied. "Israel has chosen to invade?"

Sihon chuckled. "Well, not quite." He held up a small piece of animal skin covered in writing and then tossed it to Amurrum.

Amurrum caught it and, after reading it, scoffed. "The Israelites actually expect you to believe that they would pass through your land peacefully?"

"They asked the same thing of Moab and Edom," Sihon replied. "But when they were denied safe passage, they went around. This time there is no going around. If they want to cross the Jordan, they have to come through me. And that's not going to happen."

Amurrum nodded and placed the letter on the table in front of him. A thousand questions ran through his mind, but he refrained from speaking, waiting instead for the king to ask his opinion. He knew Sihon was furious at him for being late and cursed himself for not being more diligent.

The king turned his attention to the men around him. "Gentlemen, in concluding our meeting, let us confirm our covenant together by oath." He signaled to Nahash.

The priest of Baal walked up to the table. "My lords, please extend your right hands over the table, palms down."

The chiefs complied, and Nahash moved their hands so that they were all touching. He then turned to King Sihon. "My lord, please extend your right hand over theirs."

Sihon did. The size of his hand almost covered over the other five.

Nahash then turned toward a large statue of Baal that stood near the hall's fireplace. The statue depicted a bearded man sitting on a throne, with a tall crown upon his head.

"Oh Baal!" Nahash cried. His head flew back, and he raised his arms. "Speak through me that I may bless this covenant of blood!" He began to tremble.

Amurrum noticed that Nahash held his ceremonial priestly dagger in his right hand. Apparently, the rules against having weapons near the king did not apply to the priest of Baal. Amurrum clenched his jaw in anger.

Nahash spun around and faced the table. His eyes were rolled back in his head, and he ceased to tremble.

With deliberate slowness, Nahash ran the blade of his dagger over the palm of his left hand. When the blood flowed, he held his clenched fist over the hands of King Sihon and the chiefs of Midian.

Amurrum watched as Nahash's blood covered Sihon's hand and then ran down onto the hands of the chiefs. The blood then dripped onto the map, landing where the Israelites' last known location was.

Nahash spoke as his hand bled. His voice sounded distant, almost otherworldly. "Evi, Rekem, Zur, Hur, and Reba, do you hereby swear to serve together in unity under King Sihon's banner, to neither attack one another nor refuse aid until Israel is destroyed?"

"We do," they said in unison.

He continued. "And do you, King Sihon, swear to lead, aid, and assist the Midianites, to neither attack them nor refuse aid until Israel is destroyed?"

"I do," replied Sihon.

Nahash pulled back his bleeding hand as he spoke. "This covenant of blood has been sealed. Until the blood of Israel stains the ground, each of you is bound to the other. Whoever breaks this covenant will have his blood and the blood of his children stain the ground. So says Baal."

"Let it be so," they all replied in unison.

Nahash began to tremble again. He let out a piercing cry before his eyes returned to normal. After a moment, he became still and looked at the men around the table. "It is done," he said. His voice sounded tired.

Sihon stood and addressed the five chiefs. "Gentlemen, if you will excuse us, I have a war to plan with Commander Amurrum. Nahash will see you out. Thank you."

The five chiefs of Midian all rose, bowed, and followed Nahash, who now began limping, out of the hall.

As they departed, Sihon picked up a nearby cloth and wiped the blood off of his hand. He then took a drink of wine from a large goblet on the table in front of him.

Amurrum remained standing, knowing that if he sat without permission the repercussions would be terrible.

Once the men had departed, Nahash limped back to the table, still showing signs of fatigue. Amurrum grew annoyed as he watched this faker who claimed to have a connection to the gods. *If I ever get the chance, I'll give Nahash a real limp.*

Sihon lowered his goblet and, noticing it was now empty, gestured toward Nahash. "More wine."

Nahash struck the floor with the end of his staff and a young boy came out of the shadows carrying a pitcher. He was one of Nahash's acolytes, who Amurrum knew was used for much more than just refilling drinks.

Amurrum shuddered at the thought of what the old priest made that boy do.

As the acolyte refilled Sihon's cup, the king looked at Amurrum. "Sit down, commander," he said firmly.

Amurrum complied.

Sihon waited for the boy to finish and depart before continuing. "I don't need any of your excuses. I know full well about your visits to the cult prostitutes. And while you are free to serve the gods, you serve me first, do you understand?"

"Yes, my king," replied Amurrum.

"Good," said Sihon. He took another drink of wine. "Because if you are ever late to answer my summons again, your next assignment will be chief eunuch."

Amurrum nodded. He noticed Nahash grin at Sihon's words. Amurrum clenched his fist under the table. He hated the priest of Baal. It was not so much the strange practices of self-mutilation that bothered him—the gods were to be honored as they required—but it was Nahash's arrogance.

Ever since both men entered the king's service, they had despised each other. Nahash claimed to speak for the gods and to be able to see the future. That often put him at odds with Amurrum when the high priest involved himself in matters of war and strategy.

"With that out of the way," Sihon continued, "what are your thoughts on attacking Israel?"

Amurrum cleared his throat. "My king, I would be concerned about exposing our other borders. We are at peace with the king of Jericho. But if he senses weakness, he might attack us. As for Moab, I imagine they would look for any chance to get revenge."

Sihon nodded. "No doubt that is why Moab denied Israel passage. King Balak wants to use them against us, forcing us to fight and hoping to pick up the pieces after it's all over." The king chuckled. "After what I did to his father, I'm not surprised."

Amurrum nodded. Years earlier he had helped lead Sihon's armies against King Zippor of Moab. Zippor had died at the hands of Sihon in battle, and Sihon had taken half of Moab's land all the way south to the Arnon River. What was left of Moab was now ruled by Zippor's son, Balak.

Sihon gestured dismissively. "But Balak is weak. He won't attack me until he knows he can win. And if he tries anything, I'll take the rest of his land from him after I've dealt with Israel."

"And what about Jericho, my lord?" Amurrum asked.

This time it was Nahash that spoke. "They will not wage war against us." His voice oozed with confidence.

Amurrum shot an angry glance at him. "How can you be so sure?"

"Because it was revealed to me in a vision," replied Nahash. He rolled up his sleeve and revealed fresh cuts going all the way up his arm.

"The gods demand that Israel be destroyed. Those who interfere will be cursed."

Amurrum refrained from answering but turned back to King Sihon. "Okay, but can we trust the Midianites? Moses himself is married to one. How can we be so sure of their loyalty?"

"We can't," replied Sihon. "But I'm not appealing to their loyalty. I'm appealing to their greed and pride."

"How?" Amurrum knew that the kingdom had fallen deep into debt and barely had enough to pay for its own army.

Sihon grinned. "The Midianites hate the fact that one of their own priests not only chose to serve the God of Israel but even became the father-in-law to Israel's leader. That alone might be motivation enough."

He took another drink of wine. "But, when Israel came out of Egypt, they apparently brought much silver and gold with them."

"So, you offered to split the plunder?" Amurrum asked.

"Yes," Sihon replied. "If they agreed to help."

"By attacking Israel from behind?"

Sihon raised a finger. "Not quite. Chaos is very powerful, and distracting, as are beautiful women. Wouldn't you agree, commander?"

"Yes, my lord," Amurrum replied. He began to panic. "But I'm not sure I understand—"

Sihon held up his hand. "Chief Zur, whom you just met, has a beautiful daughter named Cozbi. He plans to propose a marriage between her and an Israelite from the tribe of Simeon. If this can be arranged, we might be able to create division amongst the Israelites themselves."

Sihon pointed to the bloody spot on the map that marked Israel's location. "Once they are divided, our army, along with the Midianites, will destroy them."

Amurrum nodded, relieved. He pointed to the eastern boundary of Sihon's land. "If that is the case, my lord, then I think the best option is to march to Jahaz. It is easily defensible, with water reserves that we can use to resupply before launching a pre-emptive strike."

Sihon looked at where Amurrum pointed, his face thoughtful. "Very well. Gather the troops. I want to leave as soon as possible."

Amurrum hesitated before asking his next question. "My lord, should we inform King Og of our plan?"

Sihon's face turned red with anger. "And why would we do that?"

Amurrum considered his words carefully. "Perhaps he would agree to keep the Ammonites from attacking our rear, just as a precaution."

Sihon did not respond but instead took a long drink of wine. When he finished, he spoke in a low growl. "I have no intention of asking my brother for anything. I don't want his help, and he would never give it."

The fury in his voice subsided. "But I do agree that the Ammonites are a concern, which is why we're going to hire them as mercenaries."

Amurrum gave the king a curious look. He was no expert on finances, but he knew that the king's treasury could not afford foreign mercenaries.

Sihon laughed. "Don't worry. Not with my money. No, with Israel's money. Promise the Ammonites a share of the plunder."

"Ammonite mercenaries . . ." Amurrum said scornfully. Although it could work, he disliked Ammonites. They were unpredictable and undisciplined. Mixing them into the army would be a nightmare.

"But who will lead them?" Amurrum asked.

Sihon leaned forward and grinned. "You will, commander."

Amurrum felt a mix of anger and shame. He did not sign up to lead Ammonites. "But my lord—" he protested. He stopped himself when he saw the serious look on Sihon's face.

"You are my best commander," Sihon replied. "If anyone can put the Ammonites to good use, it's you. And if very few of them live to collect their payment, I would not be heartbroken."

Amurrum nodded in understanding. While he sometimes disliked Sihon's decisions, he respected his ruthlessness. That is why he enjoyed serving him, usually.

Before Amurrum could say anything else, Nahash spoke up. "My lord, before we attack, I suggest we consider hiring Balaam to curse the armies of Israel."

Amurrum fought back the rage building inside him. He had already been shamed by the king, and now this priest of Baal wanted to sow seeds of doubt into their campaign strategy.

To Amurrum's relief, Sihon shook his head. "No, there's no time to send word. And the cost for his services is too high."

"But my lord," Nahash protested, "he's the most feared prophet in the land, perhaps even more so than Moses himself."

Amurrum scoffed. "And we didn't need him to defeat Moab."

Nahash glared back at him. "But if King Zippor had gone to Balaam, we wouldn't be standing here today!"

Sihon slammed his fist on the table. It shook so violently that Amurrum thought it would break in half. "Enough!" he shouted.

The king turned to Nahash. "I'm not hiring Balaam. If I did that, I wouldn't have any money to pay my men!" A determined look spread across his face. "We'll defeat them on the battlefield. My gods were stronger than Moab's, and they'll be stronger than Israel's."

Now it was Amurrum's turn to smile. It felt good to see the priest of Baal humbled in front of him. King Sihon might be prideful, but his pride was in his strength on the battlefield and his boldness as a strategist. *A man after my own heart.*

"Yes, my lord," Nahash muttered. He clutched his staff as if seeking its protection.

Sihon stood abruptly, signaling the end of the conversation. Amurrum stood in response.

"Dismissed," Sihon barked.

Amurrum and Nahash both bowed and turned to go.

"Nahash," said the king. "Have Inanna brought to my chambers immediately."

"Yes, my lord," Nahash replied.

Both men walked out of the main hall in silence. When they approached the intersection that branched off toward the king's harem, Amurrum mocked Nahash. "Will you and your priests be marching with us?"

Amurrum saw a hint of annoyance come cross Nahash's face. "No, someone has to stay here and keep order," the high priest replied.

"Isn't that what Sihon has sons for?" Amurrum asked.

Nahash shrugged his shoulders. "As you may have noticed, the king is a bit more cautious these days. The last thing he wants is some upstart boy usurping his throne while he's gone. His sons will be marching with him."

"And how does he know that you won't steal the throne while he's gone?" Amurrum asked.

Nahash smirked and flashed open his cloak, revealing the ceremonial dagger of the priests of Baal. "The king trusts me, as he should. Which is more than I can say for you."

Amurrum clenched his fists. *You're lucky he does.*

Nahash turned and walked toward the harem's chamber. The two eunuch guards opened the door for him.

"Just be careful not to cut yourself too deeply with that thing," Amurrum replied.

The high priest did not respond but continued walking.

Through the open door, Amurrum caught sight of Inanna again. When she spotted him, he looked away and kept going. He knew that she would not be happy at Sihon's request for her and would probably demand that Amurrum come to her chamber tonight out of spite.

He planned to be unavailable.

CHAPTER EIGHT

Jericho, Fall 1407 BC

THE HIGH PLACE FOR the altar of Asherah resided west of Jericho, along the mountain range that bordered the city. The moon sat high and full by the time Nikkal, Arsay, Kenaz, and several of Rahab's men climbed the winding path.

As they reached a terrace-like area, Nikkal glanced to her right at Jericho. A series of torches were positioned atop the great walls of the city, encircling it in yellow-orange orbs. They cast a warm glow upon the buildings that lined the outer edge. A part of her wished she were back at Rahab's.

The group moved forward and approached several men with torches guarding what appeared to be an entrance to some sort of grove. Palm trees lined the path on either side, their leaves swaying with the evening mountain breeze. Were they welcoming her in or telling her to stay out?

She signaled for Kenaz, who helped her dismount the donkey. "Thank you," she said.

"You're welcome, my lady."

Nikkal looked around and noticed several other pilgrims, both men and women, seated nearby on rocks or mats. Some were resting, some were crying, while others were mumbling to themselves.

Between the guards in front of her stood a priestess, dressed in white robes and donning a close-cropped haircut. As Nikkal drew near, she could see by the torch-light that the woman bore a medallion around her neck bearing the same image that was on Nikkal's clay token. It depicted a naked Asherah, astride a lion, holding a serpent in each hand. On the priestess's forehead was a tattoo of a many-pointed star.

The priestess smiled at Nikkal. "Welcome to the mountain of Asherah, Queen of Heaven. How may we be of service?"

Nikkal stepped forward and held up her clay token. "I am Nikkal of the house of Aliyan of Rabbah. I'm here by Asherah's invitation to attend the ceremony of union."

The priestess took the token from her and examined both sides carefully. She then looked up at Nikkal and nodded. "We've been expecting you, Nikkal of Rabbah. The arrangements have already been made to bring reconciliation between you and Moloch, provided you have brought a donation."

"I have," answered Nikkal. She nodded toward Kenaz, who retrieved the mina of silver and presented it to them.

The priestess signaled to one of the guards, who stepped forward and took it from Kenaz. The guard weighed it in his arms before he nodded affirmatively to the priestess.

"Thank you for your offering," she said. She then looked up and gestured toward the sky. "The moon is full, and Kiyyun is visible.[1] The gods are ready. Are you ready, Nikkal?"

Nikkal took a deep breath and nodded.

"Then please follow me." The priestess gestured to others. "Your companions may wait here. The ceremony will take but an hour or two at most."

Arsay reached out and squeezed Nikkal's hand. "We'll be right here."

"Thank you," replied Nikkal. She turned and followed the priestess.

Torches lined both sides of the grove. They emitted enough light that Nikkal could see numerous rows of date palm trees that formed a natural hedge around the area.

After walking in silence for several moments, the priestess stopped in front of a tent on the left side of the grove. She opened the flap and gestured for Nikkal to enter first. She did, and the priestess followed her in.

The tent inside contained stacks of white robes, along with a large lampstand in the middle that illuminated the area.

"To prepare for the ceremony," began the priestess, "you must be dressed properly." She muttered to herself as she studied Nikkal's height

---

1. Kiyyun is an ancient name for the planet Saturn.

and build. She then turned to one of the piles, picked out a robe, and held it up to Nikkal. "This should do fine."

"Am I to wear this over my clothes?" Nikkal asked.

The priestess let out a chuckle. "No, in place of them. These are the robes of a daughter of Asherah, to be worn in the Lady's presence."

Nikkal nodded and began to undress.

"Don't worry," said the priestess. "Your clothes will be returned to you after the ceremony."

Nikkal handed her own clothes to the priestess and then slipped on the robe. It looked nearly identical to the one the priestess wore, although less ornate. The softness of the robe surprised her, and she had to admit that it felt quite comfortable.

They departed the tent and walked to the other side of the grove toward a much larger tent. The mountain air hit Nikkal and sent a slight chill throughout her body. *How did the priestesses not get cold in these things?*

As they crossed to the other side, Nikkal passed a group of women who wore multi-colored robes. But when she looked more closely, she noticed that they were not women, but men dressed as women. Or were they women dressed as men?

She then recalled the parade in Jericho. "Those are the Assinu and Kurgarru, right?"

"Yes, that's right," replied the priestess, surprised. "While Asherah often takes female form, she cannot be constrained. Her power is such that she can turn a man into a woman and a woman into a man."

The priestess gestured toward the Assinu and Kurgarru as they strode past. "They have made themselves neither men nor women in honor of Asherah. Such is their great faith and devotion to the one who recognizes no boundaries."

Overcome by her own curiosity, Nikkal asked another question. "Do all of them—remove their body parts?"

The priestess did not seem phased by the question. "Asherah welcomes those of all levels of faith. While some will alter their appearance by concealing, others do so by cutting in order to experience liberation and empowerment on a more permanent basis."

Nikkal nodded. She considered asking about what they expected her to do in the ceremony, other than just watch, but decided against it. She hoped that they would not make her shave her head, or worse, cut off her breasts. The thought of that made her cringe.

When they arrived at the second tent, Nikkal smelled the fragrance of cooked meat coming from within.

The priestess held one of the flaps open and gestured for her to enter. "You will now partake of the divine banquet prior to the ceremony. Be sure to answer any questions honestly and to follow all instructions. The priestess here will accompany you from now on."

Nikkal nodded and stepped inside as the flap closed behind her.

Candles lined the tent and cast a flickering glow on its interior. Through the dim light, Nikkal spotted a table in front of her, behind which sat a priestess. The woman wore white robes, just like the rest, but half of her head had been shaved while long black hair flowed down the other half.

"Please sit," she said.

Nikkal sat on the mat in front of her. She searched for the source of the smell and noticed a white-robed girl at the back of the tent stirring a pot. To the girl's right, standing next to a long table lined with idols, stood a boy similarly dressed.

The priestess gestured to a large statue of Asherah seated at the left side of the table. "The great-hearted mistress welcomes you to her table of peace. What is your name?"

"Nikkal."

"Have you attended a ceremony of union before?"

"No."

The priestess nodded. "Have you ever offered yourself in mourning for Baal?"

Nikkal did not understand what she meant. "Umm . . ."

A hint of impatience crept into the priestess's voice as she reworded the question. "Have you ever lain with a man for money?"

Caught off guard, Nikkal paused before shaking her head. "No."

"Thank you. And can you confirm which god you seek reconciliation with?"

"Moloch," replied Nikkal.

The priestess signaled to the boy, who turned and began searching the assortment of idols. He soon found the image of Moloch and placed it on the table opposite Nikkal, facing her. Seeing the black idol's bull head and open arms sent a shiver down Nikkal's spine.

"Prepare the banquet," commanded the priestess.

The girl attending the pot spooned the mixture into two bowls and brought them to the table. She placed one bowl in front of Nikkal and the other in front of the idol of Moloch. Steam rose from the white soup, and Nikkal noticed that it contained small pieces of meat.

The priestess then lifted her hands and addressed the statue of Asherah. "Magnificent Asherah, bless this meal that is set before your servants. A sacrifice of life to bring more life. Mercy and peace are yours. Let this meal be the sign of peace between your daughter Nikkal and the Lord Moloch."

She turned toward Nikkal. "Now, eat with Moloch in the presence of Asherah."

Nikkal lifted the bowl to her lips. She recognized the taste of warm goat's milk. The meat, though quite tender, also seemed to be of goat. When her eyes landed on the idol of Moloch, she grew nervous and lowered the bowl. Half of the soup remained.

"Please continue," commanded the priestess. "Complete peace cannot be achieved unless the meal is complete. If you do not partake of the food and milk of life, you will receive the food and milk of death."

Nikkal complied. It was not the soup that bothered her, but the awkwardness of Moloch staring at her as she ate. After a few moments, Nikkal finished and set the empty bowl down.

"Very good," said the priestess. She signaled for the girl to come over. The girl removed the bowls and then came back with two goblets of wine.

The priestess again raised her hands to Asherah. "Impetuous Lady, we thank you for the meal of peace that you have provided. We now ask that you bless the cup of union, to celebrate the renewal of the covenant."

She turned back to Nikkal. "Now, please drink with Moloch in the presence of Asherah."

Nikkal took the cup in both hands and lifted it to her lips. The wine tasted sweet, although it had a unique flavor of spices that Nikkal could not identify. *Something's wrong.* She lowered the cup.

The priestess's voice became firm. "You must drink the full cup to demonstrate your full devotion to the union."

"The taste is—strange," Nikkal replied. "I'm not used to the spices."

"It's understandable. The cup of union is a unique recipe given by Asherah herself."

Nikkal did not seem sure. *Remember what Rahab said.*

The priestess urged Nikkal to continue. "Do not be afraid. If the union is restored, you will feel peace. If the union is broken, you will feel dread and fear. But we will only know for certain after you have finished."

Nikkal nodded. She ignored the warnings in her heart and lifted the cup to her lips again. The wine warmed her as she drank it down.

After Nikkal finished, the priestess stood. "Well done, Nikkal," she said. She then walked over and held out her hand. "You are now ready to attend the ceremony. Come with me, and I will present you to the Lady under the moon and palm."

Nikkal nodded and took the priestess's hand. As she stood, she felt light-headed. But then a sense of calmness and peace came over her. She breathed a sigh of relief. *Moloch will accept me.*

The priestess led her outside. Nikkal had trouble walking and relied on the priestess to steady her. She had been drunk before, but not by just one cup of wine. It did not matter. She felt too good and too at peace to care about that.

They walked for what felt like forever. With each step becoming more difficult, Nikkal felt a strong urge to lie down. "Are we there yet?" she asked.

As if in answer to her question, they entered a clearing formed by a circle of palm trees. At the center of it stood a large wooden pole, adorned with a variety of shapes and images, topped with an image of Asherah. A stone altar sat in front of the pole, about the length of a man.

By the full moon's light, Nikkal could see that over a dozen people, all in white robes, had formed a circle around the altar. They appeared to be waiting.

Nikkal moved to join the circle of witnesses, but the priestess stopped her. "Hold on," she said.

The priestess then addressed the image of Asherah. "Queen of Heaven, we ask permission to stand before you and your witnesses."

Out from behind the wooden pole came a woman who Nikkal immediately recognized as the high priestess from the parade. But instead of being naked, she wore ornate white robes, embroidered with gold. And though she held no goblet, she wore a gold crown and carried her horned snake in her left hand.

Nikkal did not startle upon seeing the serpent, thanks to the wine she had drank. Still, she averted her eyes from it and instead scanned around for the high priest of Moloch. She could not find him. *Maybe he'll show up after everyone is in place.*

The high priestess stood next to the stone altar, her crown gleaming in the moonlight. "You may enter."

As Nikkal walked forward with the aid of the priestess, the circle of witnesses began to chant. Though their words were indiscernible, the rhythm soothed Nikkal's nerves.

With each step she took, waves of warmth and calmness flowed throughout her body. The night breeze did not bother her one bit. In fact, she began to feel suffocated and had an intense desire to shed her robe.

When she reached the circle of witnesses, she expected to stop and join them. Instead, the circle parted for her, and the priestess led her toward the altar. Nikkal turned her head to saying something, but refrained out of fear of disrupting the ceremony. *No, I must not ruin things again.*

They halted a few steps from the high priestess, who raised her hands and joined them together above her head, as if lifting the snake to heaven.

The chanting ceased.

Lowering her hands with dramatic slowness, the high priestess held the serpent in front of her as she spoke. "We are gathered here under moon and palm to reconcile Nikkal of Rabbah with the Lord Moloch. She has partaken of the divine banquet, and now she will serve as the vessel for Asherah, the Passionate Lady."

Nikkal felt confused. *Wait. Vessel? I'm just supposed to be a witness, right?*

The high priestess signaled for Nikkal to come forward. "Come now and present yourself to the goddess unashamed and unburdened."

The chanting resumed.

As Nikkal went to take a step, the priestess escorting her unfastened Nikkal's robe.

Startled, Nikkal considered protesting. But her mind felt slow. Before she had time to react, she stood naked in the moonlight. Oddly enough, she soon no longer cared. The cool air felt good on her burning skin.

The priestess took hold of Nikkal's arm and urged her forward. Nikkal complied, although her legs seemed like heavy weights as she walked.

Once they reached the stone altar, the high priestess gestured for Nikkal to lie down.

She did not hesitate. It took such intense effort to move that Nikkal welcomed the opportunity to rest. As her hot skin touched the altar, the coolness of the stone rippled along her entire body.

Her eyes stared up at the night sky. The beauty of it awed Nikkal, and she watched the moon and stars spin and jump in front of her eyes as if in celebration. Kiyyun, Moloch's star, danced in harmony with Asherah's moon.

Nikkal's gaze remained fixed upon the heavenly ballet as the high priestess held the serpent over her. "Lady Asherah, see your daughter Nikkal in all her truth, stripped of deception and falsehood. Empower her to be your vessel of union."

The chanting increased and soon synchronized with the dancing of the stars. Even with the snake's presence, Nikkal had never experienced such a delightful event. *This is amazing.*

Out of the corner of her eye, Nikkal saw the high priestess turn and address someone outside the circle. "Lord Moloch, the child Nikkal has been embodied by Lady Asherah's spirit and awaits you. Receive her as an acceptable offering and consummate the divine union."

With great effort, Nikkal turned her head.

A man wearing a bull-mask appeared out of the darkness and strode toward the altar. A loin cloth served as his only clothing. Even without his priestly robes, Nikkal recognized him by his size and gait. It was the high priest of Moloch.

Her heart pounded as she began to panic. *Why is he coming toward me?*

Remembering her own nakedness, she had an impulse to cover herself. Yet her arms and legs would not respond to her commands. Whether from fear, the wine, or both, Nikkal could only watch as the half-bull and half-man beast came closer.

Upon reaching the altar, he stopped and looked down at her. She tried to discern the man behind the mask but found nothing. The eyes were black and lifeless. *Were they a man's or a monster's?* Nikkal focused her attention on the dancing moon and stars. *The ceremony must be over. I know it. Moloch just had to see my faithfulness, and now he'll leave.*

Then, the high priest moved, but not away from her. He began to climb the altar, to climb on top of her. And in that moment, Nikkal understood.

She tried to scream, but barely a whisper of protest escaped her lips. She then willed her arms and legs to move. And although they responded sluggishly, the beast overpowered her with ease.

The dancing heavens were soon blotted out by the dark face of Moloch. When she attempted to look away, she instead caught sight of the horned serpent. It appeared to grin at her as its forked tongue flicked in and out of its mouth.

Nikkal forced her eyes shut. Her head swam and heart raced as chanting voices and beastly grunts filled her ears. She wanted to cry out to someone. But to who? To Asherah? To Moloch? To Baal?

Just then, she thought of the God of Israel. *God of Israel, can you hear me? Do you see me? Will you help me?*

As she repeated these questions over and over in her mind, everything became quiet.

Nikkal opened her eyes and found herself staring up, not at the moon, but at the sun. She heard the sound of running water and turned her head in its direction. A river appeared not too far from her position.

She stood and realized that she still wore the white robes of Asherah. Attempting to get her bearings, she glanced around. Based on the sun's position, she stood on the east side of the river. The river looked familiar, and she guessed that it might be the Jordan. *How did I get here?*

Thunder sounded. Turning to the east she watched as the storm cloud of her nightmares appeared again. As it grew to an immense size, a funnel cloud formed and began moving toward her. For some reason, she did not hear her son's cries.

Fear took hold of her, and she searched for a way to cross the river. But when she stepped into the water, a large creature began to emerge.

The beast that appeared in front of her looked exactly like Moloch, the only difference being that its arms ended in claws rather than hands. She also noticed that its eyes were red, not black, and that blood dripped from its mouth.

It roared at her and came forward. Nikkal froze, unsure where to go. Then she heard it. The sound of a child laughing. It sounded like Ali. But it came from within the storm behind her.

Without hesitating, she turned and sprinted toward the whirlwind. The beast began to chase her, roaring with rage and hunger.

As she approached the storm, she felt the sand and dust pelt her skin. She kept her mind fixed on the sound of Ali's laughter, glad that she could still hear it over the flashes of lightning and peals of thunder.

She gritted her teeth and plunged into the swirling black clouds. Once inside, she heard the beast behind her roar in frustration. Although her skin and lungs began to burn, she kept moving forward toward the sound of her son.

Then she saw him. The same dark figure as before, illuminated by the bright lightning. He held Ali in his arms. But instead of crying, Ali laughed and giggled with joy.

"Ali!" she shouted.

She took another step forward and felt a sharp increase in pain. Glancing down at her body, she noticed that the robe of Asherah had been burned away, along with most of her skin. Pieces of her charred flesh flew off in every direction.

She fought back the pain and called to the figure. "Is he okay?"

The dark figured nodded.

"Can I have him back?"

He shook his head.

She considered asking why not, but already knew the answer. Instead, she asked the only other question that came to her mind. "Who are you?"

The figured pointed at the ground in front of her as four letters appeared to carve themselves in the dirt. Although she recognized the letters, she could not read them, having never learned how.

Nikkal fell to the ground as the pain became unbearable. It hurt too much to move, so she just continued to stare at the letters. They were the last thing she saw as her vision faded to black.

CHAPTER NINE

Jericho, Fall 1407 BC

NIKKAL GASPED FOR AIR as she sat up. She felt a hand on her shoulder and recognized Arsay's voice. "It's okay, Nik. You're all right."

Nikkal coughed hard. Her lungs burned with every breath she took.

"Kenaz, water!" Arsay barked.

A cup appeared in front of Nikkal. She snatched it and began to drink.

"Slowly," said Arsay.

Once the burning sensation subsided, Nikkal took a deep breath and looked around through foggy eyes. "Where am I?"

"Back at Rahab's," replied Arsay.

"How long have I been out?"

"Most of the morning. It's nearly midday." She took the cup from Nikkal and handed it back to Kenaz.

Nikkal glanced down at her bare shoulders and soon realized she was naked. She pulled the blanket up higher. "Where are my clothes?"

"I have them," replied Arsay. She gestured toward the nearby table. "We were just trying to keep you cool. When we brought you back here you were burning up." A worried look came across her face. "I don't know what you ate or drank, but it took a while for it to wear off."

Memories of the previous night flooded back into Nikkal's mind, and she began to sob.

Arsay put her arm around Nikkal and turned to Kenaz. "Kenaz, please give us a moment."

He bowed his head. "Of course. I'll inform the lady Rahab that she is awake."

Arsay nodded as Kenaz departed.

Nikkal spoke between sobs. "How—did—I get here?"

"We waited a while after you went with the priestess," Arsay began. "They eventually brought you out to us wrapped in a blanket. The priestess told us that the ceremony went very well and that you'd be fine."

Nikkal shook her head. "No, I'm not fine."

"What happened, Nik?" Compassion filled Arsay's voice. "What did they do to you?"

Nikkal did not answer. The memories were still too fresh, still too vivid.

Arsay retrieved some bread from the table and brought it back to Nikkal. "Here. You should eat something."

Nikkal tried to take a few bites but did not have much of an appetite. "I still feel so tired."

"Go ahead and rest," replied Arsay. "I'll stay with you."

"Thank you." Nikkal gave her a weak smile. She laid back down and closed her eyes. To her surprise, sleep came quickly. This time, though, she did not dream.

She woke again a few hours later and saw that Arsay had not moved.

"How do you feel?" Arsay asked.

Nikkal rubbed the sleep from her eyes. "Better."

When she opened them again, she spotted the nearby bread. Her stomach growled as she gestured toward it. "I think I'll try to eat something now."

Arsay handed the bread to her and then refilled her cup with water.

"Thank you," replied Nikkal. She began to eat greedily. As she chewed, she forced herself to not think about what happened at the altar of Asherah. "Where's Kenaz?" she asked.

Arsay gestured toward the door. "He's preparing the donkey for travel. We wanted to make sure you were well enough before we left."

Nikkal nodded. When she finished eating, she made as if to stand.

Arsay held out her hands to stop her. "Wait, are you sure, Nik?"

"Yeah."

"Do you want me to help you get dressed?" asked Arsay.

Nikkal shook her head. "No, I can handle it. I just need a few moments."

"All right." Arsay lowered her hands. "I'll tell Kenaz that we'll be ready to go shortly." She stood and headed to the door. Before she departed, she turned back to Nikkal. "Oh, Rahab said she would like to come visit you when you're up. Should I send her in?"

Nikkal hesitated at first, but then nodded. "Yeah, that's fine."

"Okay." Arsay closed the door behind her.

Nikkal sat there in silence. She wanted to go home, but a part of her yearned to stay in bed and shut out the world. She felt torn. *How can I face Tobi after what happened? What do I even tell him?*

She sighed and stood up. Her muscles were sore and a little weak, but after looking over her body, she found no noticeable injuries. It took a little longer than usual to get dressed but, when she finished, she felt better.

Nikkal ran her hands down her tunic to smooth it out. As she did, her fingers bumped against a small object. She reached in and withdrew the onyx idol of Moloch that Baalis and Tallai had given her.

The cold black object stared up at her with lifeless eyes. Anger and shame swelled inside her to a level she had never felt before. She marched to the window and shouted in rage as she flung the idol with all her strength. She did not even bother to look where it landed.

"Feeling better?" a female voice asked.

Nikkal spun around and spotted Rahab standing in the doorway, a worried look on her face.

Nikkal regained her composure. "A little."

"Good." Rahab closed the door behind her and sat down on the edge of the bed. "Because I wanted to talk to you before you leave. Please sit."

Nikkal nodded and sat next to Rahab.

Rahab's voice turned grave. "I know what happened to you."

Tears began to well up inside of Nikkal. "You—you tried to warn me, didn't you?"

Rahab nodded. "It has happened to me and—" She looked away. "And I've also helped to have it done to others."

Nikkal responded with both surprise and anger. "But, why didn't you stop me?"

Rahab looked back at Nikkal with eyes full of regret. "I thought that they'd just have you observe as a witness. That is the usual way." She sighed. "But also, I was afraid."

Nikkal gave her a confused look. "Afraid of what?"

"Afraid of what you would think. Afraid that you wouldn't believe me. And afraid of how others might react if I dissuaded you."

"How others might react?"

Rahab gave a weak smile. "Despite what you may have heard, there are many in this city who don't trust me and who suspect that my loyalty to the gods is wavering."

"But don't you still serve them?" Nikkal asked. She gestured toward the door. "I mean, your inn is much more than an inn."

Rahab let out a sigh. "It used to be just an inn. But, when I turned thirteen, my father entered me into Asherah's service to help pay off our debt. And it worked. Only too well. He never took me out."

"Rahab, I'm s—" Nikkal began.

Rahab held up her hand. "Don't feel sorry for me. I enjoyed it at first. It felt empowering to be the most popular servant of Asherah in Jericho. Every man wanted me. And the money just poured in."

Tears filled Rahab's eyes. "But I'm trying Nik. I don't want that life anymore, not for myself or my family. Yet my father still won't give it up. In the meantime, I do what I can, although I often think it's not enough."

She placed her hand on Nikkal's. "I'm so sorry. I should have kept you from going, whatever the consequences. Please forgive my weakness."

Nikkal squeezed Rahab's hand. "I don't blame you, Rahab." *But who is to blame? Tobi? Me? The gods?* She imagined the Baal worshipers, with their lewd gestures and mutilated bodies. She then pictured Tophet, with her son burning inside Moloch's belly. Finally, she imagined herself on the altar of Asherah, naked and ashamed.

Nikkal spoke with venom. "I hate them. I hate the gods."

To her surprise, Rahab did not seem offended by Nikkal's statement. In fact, she shrugged. "Well, perhaps they're not gods at all. Or at least not worth fearing."

Nikkal stared at Rahab in stunned silence.

Rahab took it as a sign to continue. "As innkeeper, I've seen and heard many things, especially in a city like Jericho." She paused a moment before continuing. "The people of this city are frightened, but not of the gods."

"Then of who?" Nikkal asked.

Rahab lowered her voice to a whisper. "Of Israel. They're coming, and their wrath will be fierce." She let out a resigned sigh. "They're the judgment that we deserve—that I deserve—and nothing can stop them."

For whatever reason, Nikkal attempted to defend her family's beliefs. "But everyone says we're under judgment from the gods, because we haven't been faithful to them."

Rahab shook her head. "No, we're under judgment from the God of Israel. The strange weather, the wild animal attacks, the vicious insect swarms, and the invading Israelites. All of it is our punishment."

Nikkal said nothing.

Rahab continued. "The God of Israel is removing us from the land because of our wickedness. His storm is coming, and all we can do is—"

"His storm?" interrupted Nikkal. "What do you mean? What does he have to do with storms?"

Rahab seemed surprised by Nikkal's sudden question. "Well," she replied, "I've heard that he leads Israel by a storm cloud during the day and some sort of fire at night." She paused in thought. "And rumor has it that when the Egyptians tried to chase the Israelites, a storm hindered their army before they were drowned in the Red Sea."

"I've had dreams of a storm," Nikkal blurted out.

Rahab's eyes widened. "You have? Tell me."

Nikkal shared with her all the dreams that she had experienced, from the first to the last. Rahab sat and listened attentively. Yet when Nikkal mentioned the four letters that had appeared in her most recent dream, Rahab held up a hand to stop her.

"Do you remember what the four letters were?" Rahab asked.

Nikkal nodded.

Rahab took out a small wax tablet and metal stylus from her cloak. She handed them to Nikkal. "Have you ever used one of these before?"

Nikkal shook her head. She had seen such things many times at market, but had never learned how to write.

Rahab placed the wax tablet in Nikkal's left hand and the stylus in her right. "Just form the letters in the wax as best you can."

"I'll try." Nikkal gripped the stylus and pressed it into the wax. She took her time and, after some effort, nodded in satisfaction at her work.

Nikkal then handed the tablet back to Rahab. "I think this is what they were."

The letters were *YHWH*.

Rahab's lips moved as she read over the letters.

"Do you know what they mean?" Nikkal asked.

Rahab shook her head. "I recognize the letters, but I don't know this word. I've never seen it before." She pointed to the tablet. "If I had to guess, it's something related to the God of Israel. Perhaps it's his name. But I'm not entirely sure."

They both stared at the tablet in silence.

Eventually Nikkal spoke. "What do you know of the God of Israel?"

Rahab ran her fingers over the letters again. "Only a few things."

Nikkal leaned in. "Like what?"

"That his ways are not like our ways." Rahab gave her a look of sympathy. "That he does not devour children or ravage women. That he actually defends them."

Nikkal gestured toward the tablet. "Is he merciful and forgiving?"

Rahab sighed. "I truly hope so."

An idea entered Nikkal's mind, and she sprang to her feet. "I know someone who might be able to tell us about this word."

"Who?" Rahab asked.

"My grandfather," replied Nikkal. "He fought Israel forty years ago and took one of their warriors as a slave. If that slave is still alive, he would know about the God of Israel, and what these letters mean."

"Your grandfather still lives in Betharan, right?"

"I think so."

Rahab stood. "Then you should go there, for both of us."

Nikkal nodded. The thought of seeing her grandfather both frightened and excited her. *Would he even remember me?*

There was a knock at the door.

Rahab slipped the wax tablet back into her cloak. "Enter."

Kenaz appeared. As soon as Nikkal saw his face she knew something was wrong.

He bowed his head. "I'm sorry to interrupt. But news has just arrived from Heshbon."

"Go on," replied Rahab.

"King Sihon has not only denied Israel passage through his lands, but plans to launch an attack against them."

"Is Moab or Edom joining him?" Rahab asked.

Kenaz shook his head. "No, my lady." His face turned grim. "But King Sihon is calling on all faithful Ammonites to serve him in battle, promising to pay them well upon Israel's defeat. They are to gather at Heshbon within the next few days."

Fear gripped Nikkal's heart. "Tobi!" She turned to Rahab. "I have to go. I know Tobi. He'll want to fight. I need to stop him."

Rahab nodded. "Yes, go."

Kenaz spoke up. "Everything is ready to depart. Arsay awaits us downstairs."

Rahab turned to Nikkal. "Please take one of my donkeys as well so that none of you need to walk. I'll have my servants ready it right away."

Before Nikkal could answer, Rahab took a ring off her finger and handed it to Kenaz. "Show this to my head servant and tell him what I've said. He'll know what to do."

"Yes, my lady." He bowed and departed.

"But how will we get the animal back to you?" Nikkal asked.

Rahab shrugged. "It will give you a reason to come visit me again."

Nikkal smiled and threw her arms around Rahab. "Thank you for your hospitality."

Rahab returned the hug. "I wish I could have done more."

Nikkal fought back tears as she pulled away. "If I find out anything at my grandfather's, I'll send word, okay?"

Rahab nodded.

Nikkal's anxiety remained high as she, Arsay, and Kenaz traveled back to Rabbah. Although Nikkal had a strong desire to stop at Betharan in search of her grandfather, she feared how Arsay and Kenaz might react. More importantly, she feared that she would not reach Tobi in time to stop him from joining Sihon's army.

Once they entered Heshbon, Kenaz did a quick search for Tobi. Satisfied that he had not yet left home, they continued on the road to Rabbah. After another day of travel, they arrived back at Old Aliyan's farm just before sunset.

Arsay's sons, Hanun and Peduel, were the first to spot them as they entered the compound gate. "Momma!" they both cried out.

"Boys!" Arsay shouted. She dismounted from Nikkal's donkey and welcomed them as they ran into her arms.

Nikkal looked and saw both Zakar and Tobi exit the house and move toward them. Her heart began to pound. She wanted to see Tobi but dreaded what she would say to him. *Should I tell him everything? Should I say anything at all?*

Kenaz dismounted from his donkey and then held out his hand to help Nikkal down.

Her feet hit the ground. "Thank you, Kenaz."

"Of course, my lady."

Nikkal noticed a look of sorrow on his face. She realized that Kenaz knew what had happened to her and that he perhaps blamed himself.

"My lady—" he began.

She held up her hand. "Do not feel guilty, Kenaz. The gods are cruel."

He gave her a confused look.

"Please go and take care of the animals," she commanded.

He nodded, took both reins, and departed.

Nikkal turned toward Tobi and watched as he drew closer.

His eyes met hers, and he smiled. "I'm so glad you're okay, Nik. I heard about King Sihon and was worried about you traveling on the roads."

She smiled back. "They were fine."

He came up and put his arms around her. She stiffened slightly but tried to relax. When he kissed her, she did not fight it, though she did not kiss him back.

Tobi pulled away and looked at her with concern. "Is everything all right, Nik?"

She hesitated. She did not want to lie, but she was not sure she could tell him the truth either. She gave a slight nod. "Yeah, I'm fine. I'm just—tired."

"Okay." He sounded unconvinced.

She allowed him to hold her hand as they walked back to the house, but decided to change the subject. "How have things been here?"

He sighed. "Not good. Many of the trees in our orchard are withering. I don't think it's a lack of water, but some sort of pestilence." He paused. "And we lost one of our field slaves to a lion attack."

"That's terrible!" Nikkal replied. "Was the beast found?"

Tobi shook his head. "No, so we're keeping everyone in groups of two or three for safety. And until the lion is killed, Hanun and Peduel are not allowed outside the compound."

Nikkal nodded. "That's good." She shuddered at the idea of her nephews being mauled by a lion. She had been told that the same thing had happened to her father when he was young, although he had survived the attack.

"But never mind any of that," continued Tobi. He squeezed her hand with affection. "Tonight, we celebrate your safe return." He grinned. "And the fact that you brought back an extra donkey."

Nikkal could tell that he was trying to be funny. But this time she did not feel like laughing. "Rahab let us borrow it."

Tobi nodded. "That's very kind of her. How is your cousin?"

Nikkal shrugged. "She's very busy these days." She left it at that.

Despite the veneer of excitement at dinner that evening, Nikkal sensed a nervousness in the air. No one had yet spoken of Sihon's war with Israel, and no one had yet asked her about the ceremony of union. She watched as everyone simply focused on eating and drinking.

Nikkal stared at the roasted goat meat on the table. Seeing it reminded her of Asherah's banquet, and so she ate nothing. Only Arsay and Tobi seemed to notice her behavior.

Old Aliyan, already half-drunk, raised his cup in a toast. Nikkal braced herself for the words that would come. "I propose a toast to the gods," he began, "for protecting Nikkal and Arsay on such a dangerous journey!"

The rest of the family raised their cups in response as he continued. "And a toast to my daughter Nikkal for having the courage and faith to make that journey!"

Nikkal did not sense any sarcasm in his voice and felt caught off guard by his kind words.

The table toasted and drank.

Old Aliyan downed his cup before slamming it on the table. He then wiped his mouth and addressed everyone again. "Let's pray that Moloch sees our faithfulness and blesses us for it." His gaze shifted to Nikkal. "Are you sure, daughter, that Moloch was pleased with your offering?" He pointed to the family idol on the table in front of them.

Refusing to look at the image of Moloch, Nikkal forced away her rage and gave a slight nod. "That's what I was told."

Old Aliyan seemed satisfied. "Good." He then gestured toward Tobi. "So, you should be well protected in the coming battle."

Nikkal froze. Her eyes met Tobi's. "What?" she asked.

Tobi shot an angry look at his father before turning back to her. "I meant to tell you later, but—I'm going to join King Sihon's army."

"Indeed, he is!" shouted Old Aliyan. "A faithful son to fight the godless Israelites and bring healing to our land!"

Nikkal fought back tears. "When are you leaving?"

"Tomorrow morning," Tobi replied.

"Is anyone else going?"

He nodded. "Just Kenaz." He held up his hands as if to ward off her attack. "We need the money after this year's poor harvest. King Sihon is paying well for every man who joins his ranks."

Nikkal said nothing. *I can't believe this.* She then left the table and stomped off.

Upon arriving at their room, she laid down on the mat. Tears began to roll down her cheeks as she considered all that has happened. She knew Tobi would go fight and she hated him for it.

It did not take long before she heard Tobi enter the room.

He sat next to her and placed a tender hand on her shoulder. "I'm sorry I didn't tell you sooner. I wish my father—"

"It's not your father," she snapped. "I don't want you to go, Tobi."

He sighed. "I know it's hard, but I need to do this."

She sat up and searched his eyes. "Why? Why do you need to?"

"Because the farm is failing, Nik, whether my father realizes it or not. There's no money left. The harvests have gotten worse every year, and even if we sold all our remaining livestock, we would still be in debt."

Nikkal knew that she should care about the farm, but she did not. She only cared about Tobi.

Tobi continued. "The gods are angry with us. We cannot just refuse to stand up to Israel and let the Amorites make all the sacrifices." He softened his voice. "That's why I need to join King Sihon. To show my faithfulness."

"But I don't want to lose you!" Nikkal shouted. She placed her head on his shoulder and wept.

He wrapped his arms around her. "The gods will protect me. We have their favor now, because of you. You've done your part, now it's time for me to do mine."

She could not hold back any longer. "But what if we're wrong?"

"What do you mean?" he asked.

She looked up at him. "What if I don't want their favor?"

He pulled back. "Why would you suggest such a thing, Nik?"

"Because they're evil."

Tobi's eyes widened in shock.

She did not give in to his reaction. She had meant every word.

He shook his head. "You're not thinking right. The gods have given everything to us."

"They've taken everything from us!" she shouted. She buried her face in her hands as another wave of tears washed over her.

Tobi opened his mouth to respond but she went on. "They've taken our son, they've taken our money, they've taken my honor, and now they're taking my husband!"

Tobi's voice became a mixture of anger, surprise, and confusion. "What do you mean, your honor? I thought that you only had to watch."

She stared straight at him. "They stripped me naked, Tobi! Forced me on the altar, and he—he took me!"

Tobi's voice wavered. "Who did?"

"Moloch!" She let herself fall back down on the mat. Her body convulsed with sobs of pain, shame, and rage.

She never noticed Tobi leave the room. Alone, she cried herself to sleep.

CHAPTER TEN

Rabbah, Fall 1407 BC

NIKKAL WOKE AS THE first rays of dawn streamed through the window. She reached over and felt the spot where Tobi should have been. It was empty.

When she went downstairs, she found him in the main room, packing his supplies. Despair crept into her mind as she realized that he would not be swayed from his decision. *He's going to go no matter what I say.*

He must have sensed her arrival, for he stopped and spoke. "I'm going to fight, Nik, but I hope you'll accompany me to Heshbon."

She did not answer.

He turned and looked at her with sadness in his eyes. "It would mean a lot to me if you did."

She wanted to yell, to scream at him, but she remained silent. A thought then entered her mind, and, after a moment of reflection, she nodded. "I will."

Tobi seemed relieved. "Thank you, Nik."

Nikkal began to pack her own supplies. Yes, she would go to Heshbon with him, but she would not be coming back to Rabbah, at least not anytime soon. She would travel to Betharan to find her grandfather, alone.

Once they finished, Tobi retrieved his shield and spear, and they went out into the courtyard. Kenaz stood waiting for them with his spear in hand and shield on his back.

He gave her a look of surprise. "Will you be coming with us, my lady?"

"Only to Heshbon."

He nodded. "Then I'll prepare one of the donkeys for travel."

"Bring me Rahab's," Nikkal commanded. "I'll go on to Jericho from Heshbon and return it to her."

Kenaz bowed and headed to the stable.

Tobi looked at her with concern. "By yourself, Nik? That's a far distance on a dangerous road. How will you get back?"

She waved her hand dismissively. "I'll be all right. I know the road well. Besides, I'll be safe with Rahab. Come get me after the battle, okay?"

He hesitated for a moment but then nodded. "Okay."

By late-morning they were ready to depart. Old Aliyan had insisted on a proper send-off, and so he called the household to come out and say good-bye to the three of them.

Zakar walked up to Tobi and grasped his hand. "You take care, little brother. Don't get yourself killed."

"I'll try not to," Tobi replied.

Nikkal did not appreciate the humor. She understood that Zakar, as the eldest son, needed to stay behind to oversee the farm. But still, his words bothered her.

Zakar stepped back and made room for his father.

Old Aliyan came forward holding an ornate-looking khopesh and presented it to Tobi. "This sword, son, has been in the family since our ancestors came to this land. It once tasted the blood of the Zamzummim. Let it now taste the blood of the Israelites."

Tobi bowed his head and received it. "Thank you, father. I will bring honor to you and to the gods."

Old Aliyan nodded and then kissed Tobi on the forehead.

Less formal goodbyes were then exchanged between the rest of the household. Nikkal's farewell to Zakar, Naamah, and Old Aliyan were mutually cold, given the fact that the whole house had heard Nikkal's blasphemous shouts the previous night.

When it was time to say goodbye to Arsay, Nikkal paused. Although her sister-in-law had heard the same words, Nikkal knew that Arsay understood. She had been with her after the altar of Asherah and probably felt guilty for encouraging Nikkal to do it in the first place.

Nikkal hugged her. "Goodbye, sis."

Arsay hugged her back, but Nikkal could tell that she seemed unsettled. "I'm sorry, Nik," she whispered.

"Don't be," Nikkal replied. "You've been a good sister." She pulled away and gave Arsay a weak smile. "If I don't see you again for a while, you take care of yourself, all right?"

Arsay furrowed her eyebrows in confusion, but then nodded.

Nikkal signaled to Kenaz, who helped her onto the donkey. This would be her third time departing Rabbah. She had not wanted to go the last two times. This time, she could not wait to leave.

As they made their way out of Rabbah, they found themselves joined by other Ammonites who answered Sihon's call for soldiers. Nikkal recognized some of the men, as well as a few of the women who traveled with them.

They arrived at the outskirts of Heshbon by early evening. Despite it being the location of King Sihon's court, it had never grown to the size of a city like Jericho, although it remained larger than Rabbah. Yet the recent influx of soldiers and suppliers had ballooned the population to several thousands. The change, even from the previous day when Nikkal had last come through, seemed dramatic.

Tobi turned to Kenaz. "We need to check-in with Sihon's commanders if we hope to get paid."

Kenaz nodded. "They'll probably be near the king's court." He pointed through the mess of tents and make-shift shelters in front of them. "Once we get closer, I can check in while you find a place to camp."

"Sounds good," replied Tobi.

They began to weave their way through the maze of people and animals, which reduced their speed to a crawl.

Looking around, Nikkal spotted numerous altars that had been erected to Moloch, Asherah, Baal, and a host of other gods. Soldiers and non-combatants alike were lined up to offer sacrifices. When she observed several black-robed men cutting themselves, she averted her eyes in disgust.

They then passed a variety of tents for both male and female prostitutes, with soldiers coming and going. Several of the available prostitutes called out to Kenaz, Tobi, and even Nikkal. Though she avoided eye contact, she shuddered upon hearing the shameless sounds that bombarded her ears.

As sunset approached, they found a somewhat open spot where several other Ammonite mercenaries had set up their tents.

"I'll ask about who we are to report to," said Kenaz. He walked off toward the direction of King Sihon's palace.

Nikkal helped Tobi unload the supplies and secure the donkey to a nearby tree. Tobi used the same tree to help support their tent. Once erected, it appeared large enough to sleep three, though Nikkal expected them to be cramped.

Despite Tobi's presence, Nikkal did not feel safe. The place was chaotic. Drunken and lustful soldiers, when they were not harassing nearby women, often fought each other over the smallest offense.

Tobi handed her a dagger. "Here, take this. Just in case."

She hesitated. Weapons made her nervous. Still, given the situation, she took it and tucked it away in her cloak.

Tobi looked around as if scouting for danger. Appearing satisfied that they would not be bothered, he held the tent flap open for her.

"Thank you." Nikkal entered and unrolled her mat. Sitting down, she let out a sigh of relief.

Tobi leaned his spear and shield against the nearby tree and joined her. After setting up his bed, he took a long drink from his wineskin and then offered some to Nikkal.

She adamantly shook her head as memories of Asherah's table entered her mind.

He gave her a worried look and put the skin away. He then retrieved the family sword from his pack and began to examine it.

Nikkal bit her lip. She and Tobi had barely spoken to each other the entire day. Soon he would depart, and they might never speak again. She did not want to leave him like this. *I need to say something.*

She took a deep breath. "Tobi."

He looked at her but did not respond.

"I'm—I'm sorry for how I acted last night. I shouldn't have shouted."

He lowered his sword with a sigh. "I—I don't know what to think any more."

"About what?" Nikkal asked.

"About everything. About us."

Nikkal stayed silent, afraid of what she might say.

He continued. "What you said about the gods, about Moloch, is unforgiveable."

Anger kindled inside her. "But I wasn't lying about what happened to me." *Does he think I'm making it up?!*

He shook his head. "I just can't believe that Asherah or Moloch would allow that. I'm not saying it didn't happen. But maybe those priests and priestesses weren't really obeying Asherah—"

"Were they obeying Moloch when they burned our son alive?" Nikkal spat.

Tobi looked down and stared at the blade in his hands. "I don't know," he muttered.

Nikkal threw up her hands. "Well, all I know is that I tried, Tobi. I tried to make it right. I ate the food of Asherah, and I drank her wine. I was told that there would be peace, but there is no peace. That same man, the man who killed our son, he raped me, right there on the altar of Asherah!"

She began to sob. "And Asherah blessed it. I tried to cry out, but no one helped me. No one rescued me. They all just watched . . ."

Tobi said nothing. He just kept his eyes on his sword. But Nikkal knew he could hear her.

She wiped the tears from her eyes. "Listen. I love you, Tobi. And I want to be with you. But I can't serve the gods anymore. They're cruel. They take and do not give."

The next words stuck in her throat, but she forced them out. "If that means that you are no longer pleased with me, then . . ."

He gave no reaction.

They sat there in silence. It only broke when Kenaz returned.

The tent flap parted, and Kenaz's face appeared. "We've been assigned to Commander Amurrum. More importantly, King Sihon is going to address the troops now. We should attend."

Tobi nodded and got up. Before he left the tent, Tobi glanced back at Nikkal with tears in his eyes and then departed.

Out of curiosity, Nikkal held open the tent flap and watched. She had no intention of getting closer, but hoped that she might still see something.

In the distance she spotted a giant of a man standing on the steps of the palace. She assumed him to be King Sihon. Sihon's two sons, slightly shorter, stood next to him.

Nikkal had never seen King Sihon, nor his brother King Og. But she knew the stories. Growing up, she had been told about a race of fearsome giants who had dwelled in the land. While most of them had been slain by the time the Amorites and Ammonites arrived, some had remained and intermarried with the new occupants. The result was men like Sihon and Og.

Through the torchlight that line the palace, she tried to gauge Sihon's size. He must have been at least two heads taller than Tobi, who himself was tall for an Ammonite.

As Nikkal stared at King Sihon, her spine tingled with fear. But it was not his size that frightened her. He had an air of cruelty about him. Rumor had it that both he and his brother were so merciless that, if one was ever in danger, the other would not lift a finger to help.

King Sihon raised his fist. "Soldiers!"

Nikkal flinched at his voice.

He paused until the camp quieted. "As you've heard, Israel is now at our border, promising to behave peacefully if we let them pass through to the Jordan." He mocked. "They are fools to think that we would believe them."

The crowd of soldiers laughed.

Sihon's voice became stern, angry. "You also know that Moab and Edom have refused them passage as well. But instead of fighting the Israelites as they should have done, they now try to use them against us, to destroy us!"

He waved his hand in contempt. "They are cowards! Unable to attack us on their own, they want Israel to do their dirty work for them!"

The crowd of soldiers responded with angry shouts and murmurs.

Sihon let them continue for a bit before he signaled for them to be silent. His voice then turned somber. "Even my own brother, Og, refuses to join our righteous cause. He is afraid, as all cowards are."

His voice rose in determination. "But fear not, my brothers, for we will not face Israel alone. The gods are with us. We will march upon the Israelite camp, and we will destroy them. Silver, gold, livestock, women, and children will all be yours for the taking!"

The soldiers cheered with excitement.

Again, Sihon waited a moment before he quieted them. "And after that," he continued. "After we pour out the blood of their children as a drink offering, we will deal with Moab and Edom once and for all."

He drew his sword and raised it high. "I, King Sihon, have taken the lands of Moab by my own hand, and by my own hand I will destroy the Israelites! Forty years ago, they saw the giants of this land and hid in the wilderness. Soon, they will see yet another giant, and be destroyed!"

The soldiers cheered and began to chant. "Sihon! Sihon! Sihon!"

King Sihon smiled as he lowered his sword. He made a show that he wanted to speak but waited for his troops. They took the hint and quieted themselves.

Sihon held out his arms in a gesture of magnanimity. "So tonight, my brothers, eat, drink, and be merry! Seek the favor of the gods! Show the God of Israel that he does not rule here. He is not the god of this land and never will be!"

A defiant cry erupted from the crowd as swords and spears were held high.

This time Sihon did not try to silence his troops, but shouted over them. "Fill your bellies and your beds, for tomorrow we will send the Israelites back to the wilderness from which they came! Tomorrow, we go to war!"

The resulting cheer forced Nikkal to cover her ears. She watched as King Sihon stood there, grinning as he received the adoration of his men. The thought of Tobi marching in that man's army gave her a sense of dread.

She closed the tent flap and sat down.

After a few moments, Tobi and Kenaz returned. Their faces bore a look of seriousness, and she wondered if they cheered as much as the rest.

Nikkal resolved to try to sleep as Kenaz and Tobi prepared their gear. She planned to depart early before the army woke up and while the roads were still somewhat safe. Hopefully, she could slip away without Tobi noticing.

But sleep did not come to her. Too many anxious thoughts ran through her head. *Does Tobi still love me? Will he divorce me? Should I just run away and not come back?*

Once the men had finished readying their equipment, Kenaz departed the tent while Tobi laid down next to Nikkal. He did not speak, but rolled over so that he faced away from her.

Nikkal forced herself to think of something other than Tobi. Instead, she thought about Betharan, her grandfather, and the God of Israel. All of it brought a sense of both excitement and nervousness.

Yet, despite her best efforts, her mind kept returning to the coming battle. *Will Sihon win? Will Tobi survive? Do I even care?* As she reflected on this, she realized that she wanted the Israelites to win. But, at the same time, she did not want Tobi to die. *I do still love him.*

Nikkal considered praying to the God of Israel. She had only done so once before, but that was in a moment of desperation. She remembered now that he had no ears, eyes, or mouth. *Does that mean he is mute, deaf, and dumb? Did he even hear me last time?*

Unsure, she decided to try anyways. "God of Israel, please spare Tobi's life," she whispered.

She felt Tobi's body move. His head popped up. "What is it, Nik?"

"What do you mean?" she replied.

"Oh, I heard you say my name. I thought you were talking to me."

The last thing she wanted was to tell her husband that she just prayed to his enemy's god. "No, it's nothing."

She felt his eyes upon her. *Should I tell him?*

Tobi sighed. "Listen, I know things haven't been good between us lately. But I just want to say—" He hesitated. "Good night." He then laid back down.

She did not respond. Tears welled up inside her and she forced them back. He chose the war over her. He chose the gods over her. *He does not love me.*

Nikkal felt more determined to leave now than ever before. She decided to not even bother resting, but to just wait for Tobi to fall asleep. For a while she laid still, until Tobi's breathing steadied into a calm rhythm. Then she got up, careful not to disturb him.

She grabbed the few things that she needed. But before she exited the tent, she realized that Kenaz was still missing. Had he not come back? Had he deserted? *Good for him if he did.*

The cool night air filled her lungs as she closed the tent flap behind her. Silent darkness had settled upon the camp, except for a few smoldering fires here and there. By the dim light she found Rahab's donkey and crept toward it.

As she began to untie the reins, she heard Kenaz's voice off to the side. "Are you going to leave now, my lady?" he whispered.

She turned and spotted him on the ground a few steps away. How had she not seen him? "You scared me Kenaz," she replied. Realizing how suspicious she looked, she changed the subject. "Why are you out here?"

He got up and gestured toward the donkey. "I wanted to make sure no one stole the animal. But I also wanted to give you and Master Tobi time alone."

She nodded. *That was kind of him. Though I wish my time with Tobi had gone better.* "Well," she replied, "I'm sorry to have woken you." She hoped he would just go back to sleep and let her depart in peace.

Kenaz stood there in silence. She knew he waited for an answer to his question.

Nikkal sighed. "Yes, I'm leaving now. I can't sleep and I want to go before the camp wakes up."

"You're going to travel all the way to Jericho by yourself, after no rest?" Kenaz asked. She could tell that he suspected something.

For a moment she thought about chastising him, putting him in his place as a slave. He had no business questioning her. Yet she felt sympathy for him. He might be a slave, but he had served her family well. Even now, he joined a war that he might not believe in. He fought because he had to, not because he wanted to. *He's been loyal. I can trust him.*

Taking a risk, she decided to tell Kenaz the truth. "I'm going to see my grandfather at Betharan." She paused, waiting for a reaction, but Kenaz just stood there.

She continued. "I'll go to Jericho eventually to return the donkey to Rahab, but I want to see him first. It's been too long."

Kenaz nodded. She wondered if he knew that there was more to it than that. If he did, he did not ask. "May I at least help you get going?" he asked.

She nodded, and he untied the donkey for her. After he helped her up, he handed her the reins. "Safe travels, my lady. May the gods be with you."

She did not reply. As he went to lie back down, she considered that this might be the very last time she spoke to him. "Kenaz?" she whispered.

He quickly turned to face her. "Yes, my lady?"

"I need you to do something for me."

"Anything."

"Please don't tell Tobi where I went until after the battle. I don't want him to be distracted or worried."

He gave her a curious look. "Does that mean I should tell him the truth, that you'll be at your grandfather's?"

"Yes," she replied. "You can tell him the truth, when the time comes."

He bowed his head.

"And Kenaz, please keep him safe."

He bowed even lower and placed his hand over his heart. "I will protect him with my life, my lady."

"Thank you." She fought back tears. "You've been good to us, Kenaz. I'll miss you."

"And I you, my lady," he replied. She sensed genuine sorrow in his voice.

As she guided the animal away, she glanced back at Kenaz, and then to the tent where Tobi slept. For the third time in her life, she sent a prayer to the God of Israel.

CHAPTER ELEVEN

Heshbon, Fall 1407 BC

NIKKAL MADE SURE TO take it slow and steady as she worked her way through the camp. She knew that if drunken soldiers woke up to find a woman travelling alone, it would not go well for her. By the time she escaped the outskirts of Heshbon and reached the road to Jericho, dawn's light appeared on the horizon.

She patted the donkey on its neck. "Now we need to pick up the pace." As the animal entered a trot, the first rays of light shone upon the road in front of her. She breathed a sigh of relief when it appeared empty. For now, at least, she would not have any trouble.

Since encountering late-arriving soldiers remained a possibility, Nikkal made a point to get off the road as soon as she saw any traveler approach. Twice she had to act, both times leading the donkey off into the brush and having it lie down. In each case, those who passed by were not soldiers and either did not notice Nikkal or did not care about her.

By mid-morning, she approached the town of Betharan. Despite passing through it three times in the past year, she still could not remember the location of her grandfather's house. The only thing she knew was that he did not live in the immediate vicinity of the town.

She considered her options. If she went to the inn, the chance of running into less-than-savory characters increased. So instead, she hoped to find someone outside, ideally a woman, who could help her.

To her relief, Nikkal soon spotted a middle-aged man sitting with his back against a tree. He appeared to be sleeping and did not react to her approach. As she drew closer, she realized that his leg was wrapped in bandages and that a wooden stick lay on the ground next to him.

She halted the donkey a few steps in front of the man. "Good morning, sir."

The man opened his eyes and looked up at her. "Spare some silver for a lame man?" His voice sounded hoarse and desperate.

Though her heart stirred at his request, she realized that she had forgotten to bring any money with her. She had not needed it when she travelled with Tobi, who always handled such things.

She shook her head. "I'm sorry, sir. I don't have any silver."

A momentary flash of anger came across his face. "Well then. Be on your way." He closed his eyes.

Nikkal's voice turned desperate. "Please sir. I really don't have any money. I'm just trying to look for a man named Shalim. Can you tell me where he lives?"

His eyes shot open at the mention of her grandfather's name, and he stared straight at her. Yet he said nothing. The silence soon became awkward and Nikkal considered finding someone else.

Then, he spoke. "Why do you want to see that crazy old man?"

Unsure of how much information to disclose, Nikkal gave a vague answer. "I'm stopping here for business on my way to Jericho. I just have a few questions for him."

The man paused and then grinned. "Are you sure you have nothing to offer me?"

She shook her head. "Please sir, just point me in the right direction. If I find him, I'll ask him to pay you for your trouble."

The man shrugged. "Fine, have it your way."

Using both his stick and the tree as support, the man stood. "Shalim lives just south of town, a short walk from here through the brush."

He balanced himself with his crutch and pointed with his free hand to a nearby tree line. "If you head that direction you'll find a footpath just wide enough for your animal, but you might want to walk to avoid getting hit with the low branches."

Nikkal followed his finger until she discerned a small gap in the trees. "I see it." She urged the donkey forward as she kept her eyes on the path's entrance.

Remaining at his tree, he continued to talk to her. "If you keep following the footpath, you'll eventually come to a clearing. That's the edge of Shalim's property."

Once she reached the path and dismounted, she looked back toward the man. "Thank—" she began to say, but he had disappeared. She glanced around for a moment but found no trace of him. The only sounds were of chirping birds and the steady breathing of the donkey.

She turned and entered the brush. The footpath was barely visible, but now that the sun had risen, she could follow it if she paid close attention. She felt a sense of vague familiarity as she went. Perhaps she had walked this path with her father many years ago. Either way, she felt certain that the stranger had not lied to her.

"I should have asked him his name," she muttered to herself. Maybe her grandfather knew him. Or maybe she could just return to the same tree later. Regardless, she would find a way to pay him back.

As she went on, Nikkal thought about what would happen when she saw her grandfather. Should she just tell him who she was right away? Or should she wait to see if he recognized her? *What if he does not want to see me?* Nikkal had not considered that as an option, but she doubted he would react like that.

The sound of snapping twigs came from her right. She stopped and looked for its source, only to see a deer bounding away. She breathed a sigh of relief and felt for her dagger under her cloak. It was still there.

"Would you like some company, my lady?" a man's voice spoke.

Startled, she scanned around and, at first, saw nothing. Then a man came out from behind a tree in front of her. It was the same crippled man from the town.

He hobbled onto the path, stopped, and leaned on his crutch. "The road is quite dangerous."

The hair on the back of Nikkal's neck raised. *How did he get in front of me?* Determined not to panic, she maintained her poise and spoke calmly. "Oh, I appreciate your kindness, sir, but I'll be fine."

She pointed at his crutch. "Besides, you've done enough for me already. I wouldn't want to burden you any further."

He laughed as he discarded the crutch and began to walk toward her. All signs of him being crippled disappeared. "Well, I think I'll tag along anyway."

She turned to run and found two more men appear out of the trees behind her, one on the right and one on the left.

Drawing out her dagger, she faced the not-so-crippled man. "Please. Leave me be. I have nothing."

"I wouldn't say that," he grinned. "The donkey itself is worth a decent amount." His grin widened. "And as for you—well, we'll get to that . . ."

He looked at the dagger in her hand and then drew out a sword that had been concealed by his bandages. "Drop the dagger, and perhaps we'll let you live."

She tightened her grip on the blade. Her heart raced as he crept closer. "Get back!" she shouted.

He shook his head. "Stubborn, aren't you? As I said, have it your way." He signaled to the two men behind Nikkal. They both came at her simultaneously.

She turned to the man at her right and, without thinking, lashed out with the blade. It caught him in his forearm, and he cried out in pain.

The other man came up from behind and threw his arms around her, pinning them down. She tried to break free but could not escape his grip.

The not-so-crippled man raised his sword to her throat. The point of it dug into her flesh. "Drop. The dagger. Now."

She let the blade fall to the ground.

He nodded to the injured man. "Now, since you injured my friend here, you're going to take care of him first—"

Thwack! The man's grin disappeared from his face as he dropped his sword and went limp.

When he fell to the ground, Nikkal saw that an arrow protruded from his spine. Several steps away stood a man holding a bow. The hood of his cloak and the foliage of the brush concealed his features.

The bowman quickly notched another arrow and drew it back, aiming at the man Nikkal had injured.

The one holding Nikkal pulled out a dagger and held it to her neck, using her as a human shield.

The bowman spoke sternly. "I recommend you both leave now."

The men looked at their dead leader and then back up at the bowman.

The man holding Nikkal spoke up. "If you shoot, I'll kill her."

"Then both of you will die," the bowman replied. "But it doesn't have to be that way. You can both live if you let her go."

The two men looked at each other again and then, with a nod of his head, the man holding Nikkal withdrew his knife and pushed her forward. Both men then turned and fled back into the brush.

Without averting his eyes or relaxing his stance, the bowman addressed Nikkal. "Move forward quickly along the footpath to my right. Stay out of my line of sight. They might change their minds and try to attack."

She bent down, picked up her dagger, and led the donkey just as she was instructed. As she drew near the bowman, she turned to him. "Thank—"

"Keep going," he interrupted. "Follow the path and do not look back. I'll find you when I know it's safe."

She nodded and kept moving. She tried to keep track of how long she walked, but the shock of her recent encounter distracted her. *If he had not shown up . . .*

The brush began to thin out and soon Nikkal found herself in a clear area. Forcing herself to think about where she was going, she remembered what the not-so-crippled man had said and began to look for some sort of structure or dwelling. Then she spotted it. Off in the distance stood a two-story walled compound. She did not recognize it but figured it might be a good place to start looking for her grandfather.

"Are you lost, young lady?" a voice asked from behind. She turned and saw the bowman step out of the brush and walk up next to her.

"I'm—not sure," she replied.

"Well, someone like you shouldn't be travelling out here alone. This place is full of wild beasts and wild men."

She nodded, distracted by his voice. She had not noticed it earlier, but now he sounded familiar.

"But thank the Lord I was already out hunting when I found you." He pushed back the hood of his cloak, revealing the face of a well-tanned and wrinkled man in his sixties. That surprised Nikkal, as she had not expected him to be as old as he was given his quick movements.

The bowman shrugged. "It's too bad the deer got away, though. We'll have to find something else to eat for dinner."

Nikkal studied him. Both his beard and hair were grey, but his eyes still displayed a strong sense of vitality. Beyond that, they seemed just as strangely familiar to her as his voice.

"So," he continued, "where are you headed?"

Realizing that he waited for her to answer, she snapped back to reality. "I'm looking for a man named Shalim."

"Oh?" the man said. He gave her a curious look. "I see." His brow furrowed deep in thought, as if trying to recall an old memory.

"Grandfather?" Nikkal asked.

His face lit up with a mixture of joy and bewilderment. "Nikkal? Is that you?"

She nodded and threw her arms around him. Tears came to her eyes as he returned the embrace.

"Praise the Lord it is you!" he said.

He pulled away and placed his arms on her shoulders to look at her. "My goodness, you're all grown up!"

"You too," she replied, pointing to his grey beard.

"Ha!" he laughed. "Yes, I suppose I am."

He gestured toward the house. "Come on, let's get inside. Your grandmother will be so happy to see you."

Nikkal nodded. As she reached for the donkey's reins, her grandfather stepped up and grabbed them first. "Here, let me take care of that," he said.

"Thank you," she replied.

He chuckled. "There is so much we have to talk about."

She smiled at him. "I know."

They then turned and walked to the house together.

That evening, Nikkal found herself at table with Shalim and her grandmother, Ishara. Her grandfather had insisted on having a feast in celebration of Nikkal's arrival, and asked Ishara to prepare a young calf for dinner. Nikkal had offered several times to help with the meal, but each time she was told to sit and rest.

Nikkal shifted in her seat as she waited. The cushion made her feel awkward, and she smiled at the irony of it. A few months ago, she had to get used to the new Canaanite fad of sitting at a high table. Now she needed to go back to reclining at a low one.

"Is everything all right?" Shalim asked.

Nikkal nodded. "Yes, I just have to get used to sitting on the floor to eat again."

He gave her a curious look.

"Oh," she continued, "the latest trend from Jericho is eating at a high table. My family just got one and I've spent the last few months getting used to it."

He shook his head. "Yes, Jericho and its trends. It's hard to keep up with them these days."

Nikkal nodded.

Ishara walked over and set the dish of roasted calf onto the table.

"It looks delicious," said Shalim.

Nikkal nodded in agreement. She did not realize her level of hunger until she saw the food. And so, as soon as Ishara sat down, Nikkal reached for a piece of meat.

Shalim lifted his hands and bowed his head. "Let's give thanks."

Nikkal caught herself and pulled her hand back. Uncertain as to what she needed to do, she decided to copy her grandfather's posture.

"Lord God," Shalim began. "We thank you for bringing Nikkal to us safely. We praise you for your goodness and for your many blessings. We give thanks now for this food before us and ask that you nourish us with it. Amen."

Nikkal felt confused by the prayer. She looked around the room and found no image, idol, or statue. *Who was he praying to? And why did he end the prayer like that?*

Shalim must have noticed the puzzled look on her face. "Does your husband's family not pray, Nik?"

Nikkal nodded. "They do, but only in the presence of their god."

Shalim grinned. "We do the same."

Nikkal scanned the room again. "Where is he?"

"He is everywhere." Shalim gestured in all directions. "He is always present, always listening."

That made no sense to Nikkal. "But how do you know who to talk to, or where to send your words?"

Shalim paused for a moment before speaking. "If your god is limited in his ability to hear, then he's not much of a god. You would never know if your words were loud enough, or if he was even paying attention. And if you're not a good speaker, he could become bored with you."

His voice turned serious, yet gentle as he leaned in. "But the true God hears us when we are least able to speak and when it seems like no one is listening."

The words caused a shiver to run down Nikkal's spine. She recalled her cry for help at the altar of Asherah when she first prayed to the God of Israel. There had been no statue of him in sight, no idol present. Yet she felt as if he had heard her.

She nodded. Shalim then gestured for her to begin eating.

With eagerness, she took a bite of the meat in front of her. Her grandfather had been correct. It was delicious.

For several moments no one spoke, as Nikkal focused on satiating her hunger. But once her stomach felt full, she broke the silence. "Why do you say 'amen' at the end?"

Shalim smiled. "Do you not know what that word means?"

"Oh, yes, I do. It means 'truth', but I never heard anyone use it at the end of a prayer like that."

Shalim nodded. "It's a custom of the Israelites, to remind them that their God is truthful and trustworthy."

Nikkal said nothing. Even though she knew that her grandfather followed the God of Israel, it still made her nervous to talk about it. Feelings of both fear and curiosity flowed through her.

Her grandmother broke up the tension. "How long will you be staying with us, dear?"

Nikkal had not even thought of that. "I—I'm not sure . . ."

Ishara nodded. "Well, we always keep an upstairs room ready for visitors. So, it's yours as long as you like."

"Thank you," replied Nikkal.

"And how is your husband—?" Shalim began. He paused. "Forgive me for not knowing his name."

Nikkal flashed a weak smile. "It's all right. His name is Tobimelech. But everyone calls him Tobi."

"Tobi." Shalim nodded. "And how is he?"

"He's fine." She knew that she did not sound convincing.

"Will he be joining us?" Shalim asked. "I truly hope so."

Ishara gave Shalim a look.

Nikkal felt tears build up inside her. "Tobi and I—" She began to cry.

Ishara went over and placed her arms around her. "It's all right, child."

Her grandmother's embrace helped relax her, and she began to tell them everything. Through the sobs she recounted Ali's death at Tophet, her rape at the high place of Asherah, and Tobi's enlistment in King Sihon's army.

Upon finishing her story, Nikkal felt a weight lift from her shoulders. She had needed to talk to someone. Still, she felt unsure of her rash openness and bit her lip as she waited for her grandparents to respond.

Shalim spoke first, his words soft and gentle. "You've been through a lot, Nik, but you're safe now. We're here for you."

Nikkal nodded. "Thank you," she whispered.

Ishara sighed. "It's been a long day, and you must be tired." She stood and gestured for Nikkal to follow her. "Come, let's get you some rest. We can talk more tomorrow."

The mere mention of sleep caused Nikkal to become aware of her exhaustion. Sleep would be welcome. As she moved to follow Ishara, a question popped into her mind, one that she did not want to wait until the morning to ask.

She turned to Shalim. "Grandfather?"

"Yes?"

"What do the letters *YHWH* mean?"

His eyes opened wide. "Why do you ask?"

She hesitated at first but then answered. "I've seen them in my dreams, well, nightmares really."

He paused before his voice turned solemn. "The word is pronounced 'Yahweh', and it is the personal name of the God of Israel. It means 'He Who Is.'"

More questions flooded her mind as she pondered his response. But before she could say anything else, her grandfather stood. "Good night, Nik. We'll talk more about this tomorrow."

She nodded. "Okay. Good night." She turned to follow Ishara.

That night, Nikkal dreamt again. This time, she found herself standing in her grandparent's house, alone and in the dark.

She heard a rumbling outside and ran out the door and into the open air. The sky to the east turned black, and she again stood frozen as the funnel cloud formed in front of her as in the past.

A low growl came from behind. Nikkal spun to face it. From the west, arising out of the Jordan River—or at least what she thought was the Jordan River—were three figures.

Nikkal recognized the first as the Moloch-like creature from her last dream. Yet this time it walked on all fours rather than on two legs.

The second figure, a woman, sat astride the creature. She seemed identical to the priestess of Asherah. Yet instead of being covered in gold jewelry, she was covered in blood and filth. She held a bowl of steamy, milky, liquid in one hand and a cup of wine in the other, cackling with hideous laughter as she rode the beast toward Nikkal.

The third figure was that of a man, tall, regal looking, and wearing a twisted crown on his head. His left hand held the reins that controlled the beast. He looked like King Sihon, though a more grotesque and deformed version.

A wicked sneer come across the man's face. "Come back to us, Nikkal! We miss you!"

Nikkal felt a deep sense of dread at the approaching figures. As if she were observing some wicked spectacle, the beast growled, the woman cackled, and the man mocked.

"There's no escape," he said. "You belong with us!"

She glanced over her shoulder at the black whirlwind to the east. It remained in the same spot. Seeing it also stirred up fear within her, but it seemed to be different sort of fear. More like awe. She felt drawn to it.

The three figures were almost upon her now. The man reached out his right hand to grab Nikkal's arm.

She turned and bolted toward the storm cloud. Though she did not look back, she heard the three figures scream, shout, and roar with anger. She had made her decision. She would rather die in the storm than be with those three monstrosities.

Shutting her eyes, she plunged headfirst into the funnel cloud. And as before, her skin began to burn.

She opened her eyes and saw the dark figure in front of her. He held Ali, who slept peacefully in his arms.

"You're him, aren't you?" she shouted.

The figure pointed at the ground. She saw the letters *YHWH* appear before her in the dirt.

She dropped to her knees in pain. Her lungs felt as if they were on fire.

"You are 'He Who Is'?" she asked.

The figure nodded.

She looked at Ali. "Is he safe with you?"

He nodded again.

Nikkal struggled hard to speak. "Can I stay with you?" She expected him to shake his head, but he did not.

Instead, the dark figure lifted a finger and pointed behind her. Fighting through the pain she turned her head and looked through the small gaps in the storm at the three malevolent figures outside. They appeared to be waiting for her eagerly, cackling and begging for her to come out.

She shifted her eyes back to the dark figure.

He stood there, as if waiting for an answer.

She shook her head. "No, I don't want them." The words had come easy, and Nikkal realized that the burning inside her lungs had lessened.

Taking a risk, she said the next thing that came to her mind. "I don't know you, but—I want to."

A bright explosion hit Nikkal as the dark figure transformed into a figure of blinding light. Unable to bear it, Nikkal shut her eyes and placed her hands over them.

Warmth and peace flowed over her, overwhelming her to the point that she began to weep uncontrollably. She collapsed onto the ground. Yet instead of it being cold and hard, it felt soft and warm, like a blanket.

She sensed the figure approach her and stiffened her body, unsure of what he would do. She dared not open her eyes, afraid that they would melt in their sockets. Yet when his hand touched her shoulder, all the fear within her washed away.

A man's voice whispered in her ear. "Nik, wake up."

CHAPTER TWELVE

Betharan, Fall 1407 BC

SHE FELT A HAND on her shoulder. "Nik, wake up." The voice sounded like her grandfather's.

Nikkal startled and sat up. At first, she did not know where she was, but then looked around and remembered.

"I didn't mean to scare you," said Shalim. "I heard you shouting and so I came as quick as I could. I thought you were being attacked."

Nikkal rubbed her eyes. "No, I'm all right."

"Are you sure?"

She nodded.

Shalim let out a sigh of relief. "Well, I'm glad it was just a nightmare." He turned to leave. "Breakfast is ready for you when you come down. But take your time."

"Grandfather?" she asked.

"Yes?"

"I saw him. In my dream."

His face turned serious. "Who, Nik?"

"He Who Is," she whispered.

Shalim's eyes widened. "Are you sure?"

She nodded.

"Was that the first time?" he asked.

She shook her head. "I've been dreaming of him for a while, but I didn't know it was him until now. I always thought that it was someone else."

Shalim stroked his beard. "Hmm." He then smiled at her. "Let's chat about it after breakfast."

When Nikkal arrived downstairs, the table had already been set with a plate of fruit and cheese. Ishara finished preparing the bread, while Shalim reclined on a cushion reading from something that looked like an animal skin.

Ishara glanced over at her. "Good morning, dear."

"Good morning, grandmother," she replied.

Nikkal sat down opposite Shalim just as he folded up the skin and tucked it into his tunic.

Ishara placed the fresh bread on the table and sat next to her husband.

Nikkal delighted at the smell and felt an urge to begin eating. But before she reached for a piece, she looked at her grandfather.

He smiled and then signaled for Ishara and Nikkal to join him in prayer.

Nikkal closed her eyes and bowed her head as she listened to her grandfather's words.

He spoke with reverence. "Almighty God, Lord of heaven and earth, we thank you for this day and for this food. We pray that you would bless this food and enable us to serve you this day. Amen."

"Amen," Nikkal replied.

As they began to eat, Nikkal thought of the numerous questions that she still wanted to ask her grandparents, not only about the God of Israel, but also about her father. *There's so much I don't know.*

Her grandfather must have noticed her demeanor, for he broke the silence with a chuckle. "The last time we ate together, besides last night, was when you were just a few years old."

He gestured toward the place where Nikkal sat. "Your mother sat in that very spot, holding you on her lap."

Nikkal smiled. "I don't remember that."

Shalim laughed. Yes, you were quite young. Now you're married! The years have been swift."

He held up a finger. "By the way, I'm curious as to how you met Tobi. When I eventually found out that you'd gotten married, I knew nothing else about your husband, not even his name."

Nikkal shrugged. "It's no amazing story. Father got involved in the salt trade between Rabbah and Jericho. One day, he did business with Tobi's father, who had an obsession for all things Canaanite. They made a deal, and I ended up betrothed to Tobi. A Canaanite daughter-in-law."

"Sounds quite romantic," he replied.

Nikkal laughed. "Yes, I suppose it was."

After a moment, Shalim sighed, and his smile faded. "So much has happened, and I've missed it all." He then became silent, as if his mind were in a different place, a sorrowful place.

She leaned forward. "Grandfather, what happened between you and my father?" She felt a twinge of regret at asking such a direct question, half expecting that her grandfather would respond with anger.

But he did not. Instead, his eyes locked onto hers. "What happened between us started forty years ago. He was a boy at the time, but it was when Israel first came out of Egypt. Are you familiar with the story?"

Nikkal nodded. "The Israelites attempted to invade Canaan but were defeated at Arad, right?"

"That's right," Shalim replied. "Your father, grandmother, and I were living in the hill country of Canaan when Israel attacked. Us, along with some Amalekites and Amorites living nearby, went out to fight them. I wanted to win glory and plunder, and so I joined up as an archer."

Shalim shook his head. "How naïve I was back then—" He paused in thought. "Anyways, when we faced the Israelites, I was certain we would lose. They had the numbers and the high ground."

His voice turned serious. "But something was wrong. The Israelites seemed weak, uncertain. We beat them easily and drove them back. And in the end, I captured one of their wounded soldiers and kept him as a slave."

Nikkal's voice rose in excitement. "I remember father mentioning him several times."

Shalim nodded. "Yes, Emet, a faithful and hardworking slave, from the Israelite tribe of Simeon. What did your father say about him?"

She shrugged. "He never had anything nice to say. At one point I heard him mention that we were cursed because of him. That all our troubles started because you kept him and didn't sell him."

Shalim sighed. "Yes, I figured that's what your father would say. In a way he was right. Getting rid of Emet would have made things easier for me."

"What do you mean?" Nikkal asked.

"Well, Emet first acted like a typical captured soldier. He wanted to die from his wounds, and so he resisted our attempts to heal him."

Shalim let out a short laugh. "But I wasn't going to lose my war spoils. I wanted to at least get him well enough to sell him. But when he healed, something changed in him. He began to serve us willingly and honestly, without complaint. It was strange."

He then gestured toward Ishara. "In fact, your grandmother was the one who convinced me to keep him rather than sell him. We had just moved to Betharan and needed honest labor more than we needed fast money."

"Why did you move?" asked Nikkal.

Shalim let out a slight chuckle. "Opportunity."

Nikkal gave him a curious look.

"You see, King Sihon had just taken the throne and invaded Moab, capturing half their lands. And when he established his capital at Heshbon, I decided to buy property near the main road between it and Jericho."

"Was my father happy about moving?" Nikkal asked.

"Not at first," replied Shalim. "But he got over it. Things started to go well for us. We made connections over the years with people in Jericho, Heshbon, and Rabbah, and secured an engagement between your father and mother. We honored all the gods, as good Canaanites should."

He paused and looked at Ishara. "But one day that all changed."

"What happened?" Nikkal asked.

This time it was Ishara who spoke. "Your father, around fourteen at the time, was working in the fields when a young lion came and attacked him. Emet heard the screams, fought off the lion, and rescued your father."

Tears welled up in Ishara's eyes. "Your father ended up bitten and bloody, but alive. Emet tended to his wounds and prayed over him daily."

Nikkal nodded. "Father told me about this, although he left out the part about Emet rescuing him."

Shalim sighed. "He also probably left out the fact that this was when we first learned about the God of Israel." He pulled out the animal skin from his tunic.

Placing the skin on the table in front of her, he then pointed to the writing on it and began to read aloud. "Hear, O Israel: The Lord our God, the Lord is one. You shall love the Lord your God with all your heart and with all your soul and with all your might."

She looked down to where his finger rested on the word *YHWH*.

Nikkal pointed to it. "He Who Is."

Shalim nodded. "After the attack, I asked Emet why he had put him-self in danger to help the man who would one day be his master. He told me that God had made him our slave for a reason."

He folded up the animal skin and put it away. "Emet explained that, at first, he had been bitter and in despair, hoping to die from his wounds. He was angry at God for Israel's defeat. But then he realized that Israel had deserved to lose, and that his slavery was punishment for his sin."

"His sin?" asked Nikkal.

"Mm-hmm," Shalim nodded. "Apparently, God had commanded them not to invade Canaan yet and that if they did, he would not be with them. When they tried anyway, they lost."

"So, God abandoned them?" she asked.

Shalim held up a finger. "Disciplined them. Emet told me that soon after being captured he repented of his disobedience and asked God for wisdom. When it became clear that he would live, he understood that he needed to be a faithful servant right where he was." He then placed his hand on Ishara's. "And who would have thought that it would one day re-sult in your grandmother and I becoming followers of the God of Israel."

Nikkal nodded. *So that's how it all began.* She then decided to ask the one question that puzzled her the most. "Why did you choose to fol-low him?"

Shalim grinned. "Before we get to that, let's take a walk. I need to stretch my legs."

He turned to Ishara. "Is there anything you need help with before we head out?"

She shook her head. "No. Just make sure you get everything done before sundown."

"All right," he replied, getting up from the cushion. He gestured for Nikkal to follow him. "C'mon, Nik."

The farm was larger than Nikkal had imagined. When she had first ar-rived, she had only seen the front of property. The stone wall, along with several tall trees, had obscured the other side. But now that she saw the rest of it, she realized how successful her grandfather must have been.

As they walked, he showed her a small fenced-in area for several sheep, a stable for oxen, a vegetable garden, and a grove of about a dozen olive trees. He also pointed out several structures attached to the main house that she had not noticed before.

She marveled as they went. "How are you and grandmother able to maintain all of this?"

Shalim laughed. "We don't. Or, at least, we don't by ourselves." He gestured toward one building on the right side of the house. "We have a family that lives there, a husband, wife, and their little girl. You should be able to meet them today when they return from their trip."

He then turned and pointed to a mud-brick structure attached to the left side of the house. "And that is the sleeping quarters for any so-journers looking for work and a place to stay. We offer a meal and a bed, while they offer any labor that they can provide."

"Do people stay a while?" she asked.

He shrugged. "Sometimes we have folks stay for a day or two. Others stay longer. There are many who come for work during planting or harvesting season. If they stay until the work is done, they are allowed to keep some of the produce as an additional payment for their labor."

"The extra help must make things easier," replied Nikkal.

He sighed. "It's still a lot of work, and I'm not as young as I use to be. So, I've tried to focus on less demanding and less dangerous enterprises."

"Like what?" Nikkal asked.

He made a sweeping gesture with his hand. "We used to have a decent herd of cattle that would graze in the open. But it has become harder to keep them from being stolen or killed."

"My family has been having similar problems," she replied.

He nodded and pointed to several fences and walls that surrounded the property, some of which were in serious disrepair. "I've tried to protect the property and the animals as best I could. But it's easier to focus on improving and cultivating the land rather than trying to keep large herds."

Nikkal spoke up. "Is that why grandmother reminded you to get everything done before sundown? Because of the danger?"

Shalim chuckled. "No, that's because tonight, when the sun goes down, begins the day of rest."

"What?" she asked in frustration. Nikkal already had so many questions. Now more were being piled on.

Her grandfather stopped walking and took the animal skin out of his tunic. He held it in front of her and pointed to the ten rows of letters underneath the top line. "The Israelites call these the Ten Words, or Ten Commandments."

She nodded in interest.

He pointed to each row as he spoke. "We are to have no other gods, make no idols, speak no blasphemy, honor the Sabbath, honor our parents, commit no murder, commit no adultery, commit no stealing, bear no false witness, and covet nothing of our neighbors."

She considered each of those commands. Some of them sounded quite reasonable while others made no sense.

He then moved his finger to the fourth row. "The Sabbath is the last day of each week. It is a day where we rest from our labors and give thanks to God. That begins at sundown tonight." He put the animal skin away and resumed walking. "And so, today we work so that tomorrow we may rest."

Nikkal stood there deep in thought. *A day without working? Every week? I wonder what that's like.* Realizing that her grandfather had continued on ahead, she rushed to catch up.

After several moments in silence, they arrived at a lone cedar tree. There, at the base of it, sat a pile of smooth stones that had been stacked up into a mound.

Shalim stopped and looked down at them. His face filled with sorrow.

Nikkal noticed the change in his demeanor. "What is it, grandfather?"

He pointed to the rocks. "This is Emet's grave. The twelve stones represent the twelve tribes of Israel."

So, he is dead. She placed a hand on his shoulder. "I'm so sorry. How—when did it happen?"

He gripped her hand. "Almost a year ago he became ill and, despite our best efforts, never recovered. We weren't sure what it was, but Emet knew."

"He knew?"

Shalim turned and looked at Nikkal. "Emet said that his generation had been cursed by God, and that they would die before God brought Israel out of the wilderness. So, forty years after his capture, his life would end."

"Do you believe that?" Nikkal asked.

Shalim nodded. "There's no other explanation. He had been perfectly healthy. And not long after I buried him, I found out that Israel had come out of the wilderness and defeated the Canaanites at Arad. That confirmed it for me."

Nikkal watched as her grandfather knelt and placed a hand on the stones as he spoke. "Emet was a good servant and a good friend. He was like a brother to me."

Shalim then took out the animal skin and beheld it as he spoke. "Just before he died, he gave me his copy of the Ten Commandments. He said that when the armies of Israel arrived, I should show it to them and they would spare my household."

Nikkal considered his words. *Would God really spare them? He didn't spare Arad.*

Shalim let out a sigh and stood up. "It's amazing to see how God brings good out of evil and turns his enemies into his friends."

Nikkal shook her head "I—I don't see it, grandfather. I don't know how to see it." Feelings of anger, shame, and despair bubbled up inside her.

He gave her a look of empathy. "Nik, your people—our people—are under judgment. We have done—are doing—terrible things. We've done some of those things, and some of those things have been done to us. But we have a choice. We can either seek refuge and hope in false gods or in the one true God of Israel."

"But how is he any different than the other gods?" she asked.

Her grandfather's voice grew firm. "The gods of the Canaanites and Ammonites are cruel, demanding life and offering death. They have eyes but do not see, ears but do not hear, and mouths but do not speak."

The words struck Nikkal. She remembered how Baalis had mocked the God of Israel for not having a physical mouth. *The irony of it.*

Shalim continued. "But the God of Israel offers life and demands that we die, die to ourselves, die to our sins. He formed our eyes and so he sees us, he formed our ears and so he hears us, and he formed our mouths and so he speaks to us."

Though she stood silent, her mind raced with different thoughts. Yet one stood out from the rest. *He was there, Nik. He saw you on the altar. You were not alone.*

Shalim held up the animal skin to her. "These are the words of God. So, you must choose, Nik. You must choose whether to hold onto your anger, your bitterness, and your despair. But if you do, know that you are choosing Baal, Moloch, and Asherah, the ones who are not gods."

She nodded in understanding. *I don't want to serve them. Not anymore.*

His voice turned gentle. "Or you can choose to repent of your own sin and forgive those who have sinned against you, including Tobi. If you do, know that you are choosing the God of Israel, the one who is and the one who forgives."

The idea of forgiveness, real forgiveness, appealed to Nikkal. *Yes, I want that. I need that. But what will it cost?*

"That's what happened to me." Shalim gestured to the pile of rocks. "Emet showed me my sin. It took years for me to realize it, but when I did, I knew what the right decision was."

Nikkal looked down at the ground. She still felt uncertain. "But what if I lose him, grandfather? What if I lose Tobi? What if he hates me?"

When he did not answer right away, she glanced up and saw tears in his eyes. "You must count the cost," he replied. "Loving the Lord with all of your heart might mean you are rejected by everyone, including those you love."

"Like my father did to you?" Nikkal asked.

He nodded. "You had already been born when your grandmother and I became followers of the God of Israel. And even though your father had come to accept Emet's worth as a slave, he thought that Emet had overstepped his bounds by seeking to pull us away from the gods of our people."

"My father refused to follow your decision?"

He sighed. "Yes. And it didn't help that others began to shun us, affecting our business and livelihood. Your father soon became angry and bitter."

Nikkal nodded. She recalled how heated her father always got whenever the topic of her grandparents came up in conversation. *It all makes sense now.*

Shalim shook his head in sadness. "I tried to tell him that Emet had not deceived me. But he would not hear it. And so, he took you and your mother and left for Heshbon. That was the day that I lost my son, my daughter-in-law, and my granddaughter." He fell to his knees and wept.

Nikkal knelt and embraced him, not realizing that she had also begun to weep. How long they stayed like that, she did not know.

When her grandfather's sobs subsided, he lifted his head and looked at her. "Nik, even though I lost that which was most precious to me on that day, I also gained something more valuable than I could ever imagine."

She remained silent, hanging onto his every word.

He held out the Ten Words. "I gained a peace and a joy that I'd never had before. I received mercy, freedom, and life. All of it was undeserved and none of it will ever be lost."

Nikkal gazed down at the animal skin. *Yes, I want that, no matter if I lose everything.* Tears filled her eyes as she placed her hand on it. She then looked up into her grandfather's face and smiled. "I've made my choice."

That evening, joy and laughter filled the dinner table. Nikkal learned that her grandparents always hosted a Sabbath feast for anyone staying on their property. Though there were few in attendance that evening, it nonetheless remained a feast.

The young family that lived with Nikkal's grandparents had returned before sundown and joined them at the table. The man's name was Hadad, and he helped both produce and sell olive oil for Nikkal's grandparents. He and his wife, Ashima, and their little girl, Liluri, had just returned from a business trip in Jericho.

During the first part of the meal, after introductions had been made, the topic of conversation centered around the olive oil business and the upcoming harvest. Nikkal spent the time listening, along with making silly faces with Liluri, who had taken an immediate liking to Nikkal.

Nikkal considered asking if Hadad and Ashima knew her cousin, Rahab. But, considering Rahab's line of work, she decided it would not be appropriate, especially given Liluri's presence.

When the conversation came around to the topic of Israel, Nikkal's ears perked up.

"Word around Jericho," said Hadad, "is that King Sihon's army is headed to Jahaz."

"Makes sense," replied Shalim. "It's a strategic border town. Has he encountered the Israelites yet?"

Hadad shook his head. "Not that I've heard. But they'll probably meet soon enough."

Shalim stroked his beard. "Well, we should expect refugees and wounded soldiers to pass through in the days and weeks ahead."

Hadad nodded. "We'll be sure to stay here with you and Ishara to help care for those in need and to protect against any dangers. Although, if Israel loses, I don't expect we'll see many refugees."

Shalim spoke with confidence. "They won't lose. Not this time." He sent Nikkal a look of genuine concern. "But we will pray for the soldiers on both sides, and we will care for anyone who comes to us in need."

Nikkal gave a smile of appreciation to her grandfather. He knew how difficult it was for her. She still loved Tobi and wanted him to be safe. But most of all, she wanted him to know the truth about the God of Israel.

Shalim gestured for everyone to join him. "Let us pray."

Nikkal closed her eyes and listened as Shalim led them in prayer. As her grandfather spoke of the coming battle, her thoughts turned to Tobi. "God," she whispered. "Please watch over him."

PART THREE

The Man

CHAPTER THIRTEEN

Road to Jahaz, Fall 1407 BC

TOBI TOOK A QUICK drink from his waterskin. It felt close to empty, so he limited himself in order to conserve as much as possible for the upcoming day's march. He thanked the gods that it would only take a few more hours to reach Jahaz, the border town between King Sihon's territory and the wilderness. There they could resupply, find the Israelites, and destroy them. At least, that was what they were told.

As he sat on a boulder next to Kenaz, he glanced around at the other men in his company. Most were preparing to depart, while some continued to eat and drink. Yet all remained quiet, as if a spirit of dread had come over the entire army.

"What do you think, Kenaz?" Tobi asked.

Kenaz gave him a puzzled look.

Tobi gestured to the demoralized men around them.

Kenaz shook his head. "We should have stayed longer at Medeba, my lord."

Tobi nodded in agreement.

Two days earlier, they had departed south along the King's Highway from Heshbon in high spirits, though many of the men still felt the effects from the previous night's festivities. It did not help that they then marched all day in what could only be described as unusually hot conditions, given the time of year.

They stopped at Medeba to gather more soldiers and supplies. Some of Sihon's commanders advised him to keep the army there for several days until the hot spell passed and cooler weather arrived. The king decided against it, thinking that they could make Jahaz in one day. But the brutal heat, coupled with an unexpected dust storm, force them to stop halfway.

"Do you think it will pass soon? The heat?" Tobi asked.

Kenaz shrugged. "Don't know for sure. But that's not what scares me."

Tobi knew exactly what he meant. The terrible heat had only been the beginning of their misfortunes.

The previous evening, several men in search for food thought that they had come across some wild honey. Instead, they found themselves attacked by a swarm of those deadly wasps that Tobi had heard about. Though he did not see the insects, he got to know how real they were when he saw the welts on those who returned to the camp. And not all of the men returned.

But then it got worse. In the middle of the night, several male lions attacked a group of men as they slept. Some had been dragged off while others were severely injured. None of the lions were killed and none of the missing men were found. Tobi, like many others who were awakened by the commotion, had a hard time going to back to sleep.

While the losses from these events were only a fraction of the army, the men had been demoralized. Bad omens with lack of sleep seemed to them a recipe for disaster.

Kenaz held out his waterskin to Tobi. "Would you like some of my water, my lord?"

Tobi shook his head. "No. You keep it. You need it as much as I do."

Kenaz nodded and put his waterskin away. "It's only morning and yet it feels so warm. I think it'll be another hard day of marching."

"Well," Tobi replied, "let's pray that the gods help us get to Jahaz quickly."

Kenaz lowered his voice. "I don't know if the gods have any power, here or there."

The response shocked Tobi. He looked at Kenaz with concern.

Kenaz did not meet his gaze but stared off toward the direction of Jahaz. "The land seems to fight against us, my lord. King Sihon's own land . . ."

Tobi considered the gravity of Kenaz's words. He was right, and he was probably not alone in his opinion. Still, he appeared to be the only one willing to say it.

A sense of fear and doubt entered Tobi's heart. *Is the land really against us? Could we lose the battle?* He had not considered that outcome. Sihon's army was strong and included a large contingent of chariots. Word among the troops was that the Israelites fielded only about twenty thousand men, roughly half the size at Sihon's disposal. And Israel apparently had no chariots. *How could we not win with those numbers?*

Tobi turned his thoughts to Nikkal. When Kenaz informed him that she had departed in the middle of the night, Tobi had been angry. He had wanted to see her before the army marched, at the very least so that they would not part ways on bad terms.

Tobi reached into his tunic and pulled out the small onyx statue of Moloch. Turning it over in his hand, he considered sending some prayers to Moloch, to ask for the god's protection over Nikkal and over the army. But he did not feel like praying right now.

Instead, he put away the idol and took out another object, Ali's small wooden horse. Tobi had retrieved it at Tophet after his son's dedication, although it pained him to look at it. He had kept it hidden from Nikkal, knowing that it only would have upset her more.

As he examined the toy, a wave of sadness washed over him. He felt conflicted. He missed his son but feared missing him too much. For if he did, he might incur Moloch's wrath. *Still, maybe I should've told Nik I had it.*

Shouts drew Tobi's attention and he put the horse away. Looking up, he saw his commander, Amurrum, leading a procession of unarmed men. The men, bound as prisoners, were being driven forward by several guards toward the center of the camp.

"Ammonites," Kenaz whispered.

Tobi nodded as he recognized some of the men who had walked with them from Rabbah.

Commander Amurrum stopped in front of the king's tent. "My lord!"

After a few moments, King Sihon appeared, both annoyed and angered. "What's going on, commander?"

Amurrum knelt. "O king, live forever. I have found several Ammonites attempting to desert."

"That's a lie!" shouted the first bound man. "We were searching for food and water!"

"Quiet!" Amurrum stood, turned, and hit the man in stomach. The man groaned as he doubled over.

"Are you certain they were deserting?" Sihon asked.

Amurrum nodded "Yes, my lord. A few of them confessed after being caught."

The Ammonite who had been hit spoke again between coughs. "That's because you tortured them!"

Amurrum struck the man in the face.

The man fell to his knees as blood dripped from his mouth.

"As I said," Amurrum continued, rubbing his knuckles, "they confessed."

Sihon's words were stone cold. "Then do what must be done." He turned and went back inside his tent.

Pleas for mercy arose from the other Ammonite deserters, some of whom fell to their knees. Yet no one came to their defense.

Amurrum drew his sword and walked toward the man he had struck, who had just regained his feet.

But instead of begging for his life, the man stared defiantly at the king's tent. "The gods have abandoned you, Sihon! The land has turned against you! Stop before it's too—"

Amurrum's sword sliced his throat. As blood began to pour out of the wound, the man made a gurgling sound and then collapsed onto the ground.

Tobi watched in horror as Amurrum moved down the line, slaying each man in turn. No amount of begging or shouting slowed him. At the end of it all, about twenty Ammonites lay dead.

Amurrum wiped his sword clean and addressed the nearest soldier. "Pile their bodies at the back of the camp as a warning to the others."

The soldier nodded and then pointed to Tobi and Kenaz. "You two, come help me with this!"

Without hesitation, Tobi and Kenaz complied.

As they passed by Amurrum, the commander held up his hand to stop Tobi. "You an Ammonite?" he asked.

"Yes, sir," Tobi replied.

Amurrum looked him up and down. "Awfully tall for one. Did your mother go whoring after the Rephaim?"

Tobi did not answer.

Amurrum drew in close. "Will you desert too, I wonder?"

"No, sir," Tobi replied.

"We'll see." Amurrum pointed his sword down at the dead man next to him. "If you try to run, I will not hesitate."

Despite being a hand length taller than Amurrum, Tobi felt small and weak. He nodded in understanding.

"Get to work, Ammonite," Amurrum spat. He turned and walked away.

Tobi reached down to grab the first body as Kenaz came up to help.

More shouting occurred, this time coming from the direction of Jahaz. Tobi glanced up to see a runner sprinting toward their direction.

Everyone nearby, including Amurrum, stopped what they were doing.

"My lord!" the scout shouted. He halted just outside of Sihon's tent.

This time, Sihon came out with his sword in his hand. "What is it now?"

The scout, still trying to catch his breath, spoke as if in a near panic. "Israel—is at Jahaz."

"That's impossible!" Sihon replied. "Are you sure of this?"

"Yes, my lord—around twenty—maybe thirty—thousand men."

A concerned look spread across Sihon's face "Any chariots?"

"No, my lord."

The king paused for a moment. He then let out a defiant shout. "Fine! Israel thinks they can occupy Jahaz and prevent our resupply. But they don't have the strength to hold it."

Sihon turned toward the troops and raised his sword. "Men, it looks like Israel is in a hurry to fight us! I guess they'd rather die sooner than later. Well, let's not keep them waiting! Break camp and move out!"

The area came alive as Sihon's commanders began to bark orders.

Tobi, still holding onto the body, looked at Amurrum for instructions.

Commander Amurrum shrugged. "I guess it's your lucky day, Ammonite. Get your gear and prepare to march. Leave the dead."

Tobi nodded. He looked down one last time at the man's face. He did not know his name, but he decided that if he made it back to Rabbah he would find out who the man's family was and inform them of what had happened.

He released the body and ran back to the boulder to retrieve his spear and shield. Confirming one last time that his family's sword remained secure in its sheathe, he and Kenaz formed up with the rest of the men.

It took less than an hour for everyone to move out. Tobi and Kenaz's unit made up the immediate right flank of Sihon's army, with the two men positioned next to each other several rows from the front.

The hasty departure and quick pace caused Tobi to temporarily forget about the unfortunate events of the previous two days. Yet the intolerable heat, coupled with the threatening shouts of the commanders, soon drove his mind back to a demoralized state. He needed to talk to someone.

Tobi whispered to Kenaz. "Why are we marching so fast? Is Sihon that worried about Israel holding Jahaz?"

Kenaz kept his eyes on the man in front of him. "I believe he's more frightened than we think."

Tobi wiped the sweat from his eyes. "At this pace, we won't have the strength to fight when we get there."

He saw Kenaz nod out of the corner of his eye.

A murmur spread throughout the ranks. Tobi took advantage of his height to see what the commotion was all about. There, within sight, stood the town of Jahaz. It sat in a valley between two ranges of hills, and served as a sort of gateway between the wilderness and King Sihon's lands. Such a position, coupled with the town's underground springs of water, made Jahaz strategically valuable.

"Keep moving!" shouted the commanders.

Tobi leaned over to Kenaz. "It's Jahaz. We made it."

Before Kenaz could reply, Tobi felt a gust of wind come up from the south. Hot sand and dust blew into the faces of the men. Using a combination of his cloak and shield, Tobi tried to block the debris.

"The wind shifted . . ." Kenaz muttered.

Tobi did not respond. He gritted his teeth and did the best he could to keep pace with the other men. After a while, the wind died down. Tobi took the opportunity to glance out from behind his shield. And for the first time in his life, he saw the army of Israel.

The Israelites had formed up in rows, similar to Sihon's army. Both ends of Israel's army were tucked up against the hills to protect them from any flank attacks. As far as Tobi could tell, the scout had been accurate. The Israelite army appeared to be half the size of Sihon's army and contained no chariots.

Tobi's bowels felt as if they had turned to water when he looked out upon Israel's warriors. He remembered what he had heard about the battle of Hormah, and how the Israelites had killed every man, woman, and child there. *How could they murder children?* He then heard his own voice in his mind. *But isn't that what you did to your son?*

Before he could argue with himself, he turned his attention to the rhythm of voices and music coming from the Israelite ranks. *They're singing.*

At first, the noise of the wind and the shouts of Sihon's commanders prevented Tobi from making out the words. Yet, with each step forward, the voices became clearer, until at last Tobi could discern the lyrics.

> ... The Lord is my strength and my song,
> and he has become my salvation;
> this is my God, and I will praise him,
> my father's God, and I will exalt him.
> The Lord is a man of war;
> the Lord is his name ...

As Tobi drew closer to the singing Israelites, he had to strain to hear the orders of Commander Amurrum.

"Stay in line!" Amurrum shouted. "No gaps! Keep moving!"

Tobi then heard Sihon's booming voice. "Chariots, forward!"

He glanced to his right and watched as Sihon's war chariots surged forward toward Israel's left flank. They kicked up large clouds of dust as they gained speed. After a few moments, the dust settled, and Tobi saw that many of the chariots had slowed and lost their cohesion. Some even appeared to have stopped.

"What are they doing?" Tobi muttered.

"Huh?" Kenaz asked.

Tobi opened his mouth to reply but struck his foot against a rock and stumbled. As he recovered his balance, he noticed that dozens of other men had done the same thing, with several having fallen to the ground.

The army slowed to a crawl as the soldiers tried to reform their ranks.

"Get up! Keep moving!" shouted Amurrum.

Tobi scanned the area in front of him. "It's the rocky terrain. The chariots can't keep speed or formation."

"Neither can we," replied Kenaz.

Tobi did not respond but glanced up over the ranks to see how the chariots fared. Arrows and stones shot forth from Israel's front lines, striking several horses and drivers. His blood ran cold as the first screams of wounded men reached his ears.

Just when the chariots attempted to counterattack, a strong gust of wind kicked up and blew dust into the face of Sihon's army. Tobi shielded his eyes but strained his ears. He heard a shout of triumph rise from the ranks of Israel, followed by more screams from the chariots.

As soon as the gust died down, Tobi popped his head out again to scan the battlefield. Most of Sihon's chariots were in chaos, with many of them driverless. One group of remaining chariots reorganized themselves and tried to drive straight into Israel's ranks.

Tobi's jaw dropped when the horses reared up and refused to charge. As a result, the drivers were exposed to attack and were soon mowed down by a storm of arrows, stones, and spears.

"By the gods . . . ," said Tobi.

"What's happening, my lord?" Kenaz sounded desperate.

Tobi shook his head in disbelief. "The horses won't move forward. They're afraid."

"And not just the horses . . ." Kenaz muttered in reply.

Although he agreed, Tobi said nothing. Instead, he looked over at the center of Israel's army, where the music seemed to be loudest.

The words of the Israelites filled his ears.

> . . . Now are the chiefs of Edom dismayed;
> trembling seizes the leaders of Moab;
> all the inhabitants of Canaan have melted away.
> Terror and dread fall upon them . . .

Just then, Tobi caught sight of what appeared to be a gold-plated box. Dozens of musicians, dressed in strange garb, surrounded the object. He focused his vision and noticed that two winged creatures, also made of gold, sat on top of the box. "Is that their god?" he asked.

"What?" Kenaz replied.

But before Tobi could answer, Commander Amurrum's voice erupted. "Shields up!"

A wave of projectiles came out from Israel's ranks toward Sihon's infantry. Instinctively, Tobi raised his shield over his head.

Thud!

The sound of stones and arrows upon wood rippled throughout the ranks. Dozens of men cried out and fell to the ground.

"Slingers! Archers! Return fire!" Sihon shouted.

Taking a risk, Tobi uncovered his head to see the results. As soon as he did, he despaired. With Sihon's arrows and stones mid-flight, a heavy gust of crosswind forced many of the projectiles to veer off target and fall to the ground.

Tobi could not believe his eyes. *How could the winds have changed like that?* He looked up and noticed a dark cloud hovering high over the army of Israel. The sight of it made him shiver.

The gust died down as Israel launched their return volley.

Tobi ducked behind his shield again. More thuds, screams, and cries. He forced himself not to look.

"Spearmen, charge!" Sihon shouted.

His commanders repeated the order to their companies.

"Keep close ranks!" barked Commander Amurrum.

Tobi felt the mass of men around him surge forward. Some of the soldiers stumbled and fell, but Tobi and Kenaz kept their footing.

When they were within a few steps of Israel's front line, an Israelite trumpet sounded. Shouts of "for the Lord!" filled the air as the Israelites rushed to meet Sihon's army.

The two groups collided to the sound of splintering wood, hacking flesh, and screaming men. Arrows and stones continued to come in sporadically, but most landed behind Tobi's position. His stomach twisted itself in knots when he realized that he stood only three rows from the front. *It'll soon be my turn.*

As he watched men from both sides fall, it became clear that the ratio of losses was far from even. Despite Sihon's advantage in numbers, the Israelites were causing much more damage than they were receiving.

Movement on a hill behind Israel's army caught Tobi's attention. He glanced up and spotted several men standing at the top. One of them appeared to be holding a staff in the air.

Tobi squinted. "What the—?"

Someone shoved him forward. Tobi barely avoided falling over several dead bodies that littered the ground. His delay caused a space to open between him and the row in front.

"Move forward, Ammonite! Close that gap!" Commander Amurrum shouted.

Tobi rushed to obey.

Just as he got back into position, the soldier in front of him took a spear strike to the neck and fell. Tobi stepped forward and found himself face to face with the Israelite spearmen. Kenaz kept close to him, attempting to maintain cohesion.

The mass of men behind him lurched forward again, forcing Tobi to engage with the warrior. He struck out with his spear, but the Israelite's shield blocked it. For several moments, Tobi traded spear thrusts with the Israelite. Neither gained an advantage at first, but Tobi felt himself tiring.

As if aware of this, the Israelite came at Tobi with renewed vigor. When Tobi attacked with his spear, the Israelite deflected it downward and then used his legs and shield to break it.

Tobi dropped his broken spear shaft and reached to draw his sword. But before he could, the Israelite thrust out his own spear toward Tobi's chest. Tobi moved to block the attack but failed to fully deflect it.

The Israelite's spear caught him in the side. Tobi screamed in pain and instinctively pulled back, clutching his wound.

Kenaz moved to help him. "My lord!" He dropped his own spear and led Tobi away from the front line. The next row of Sihon's army moved in to fill the gap.

Tobi despaired. *We can't win. The Israelites are too strong. Their god is with them.*

Commander Amurrum, who stood several rows back, began to force his way toward Tobi's position. "What are you doing, Ammonite? Get back and fight!"

Tobi opened his mouth to reply, but before he could say anything a bellow of rage erupted from King Sihon.

All the nearby soldiers, including Israelites, turned and watched the giant king, in full armor, charge straight into Israel's ranks. Sihon roared like a lion as he swung his huge sword left and right, cleaving several Israelite soldiers. Those that were not cut down were bowled over by his massive frame.

Sihon's royal guard, including his two sons and several chariots, tried to keep pace with him, but the king surged forward like a madman, as if determined to reach the golden box in Israel's midst.

But the Israelites did not seem phased by the sudden outburst. Soon after Sihon began his attack, a trumpet sounded and all the Israelite soldiers near him disengaged and fell back.

King Sihon paused and shouted in triumph. "Come on! Come fight me you cowards!"

Another trumpet blast sounded, and this time a hail of arrows and stones poured into Sihon's location from the Israelite slingers and archers closest to his position.

Due to his sheer size, most of the projectiles hit him. He shouted in pain and frustration as stones pummeled him and arrows stuck into his body. Although his armor ensured that none of the hits were lethal, the intensity of the attack stumbled him, and he dropped to one knee.

A shout rose from the Israelite spearmen as they launched a counterattack. The sudden reversal caught Sihon's army off guard and soon King Sihon found himself isolated and surrounded by Israelite soldiers, each hacking and slashing at him as they swarmed past.

With a final cry of rage, King Sihon fell to the ground and did not rise. The royal guard, including both of Sihon's sons, were also overtaken and killed.

The Israelite army shouted in triumph as Sihon's army wavered. Small groups of men began to disengage and flee.

The commanders, including Amurrum, attempted to hold things together, screaming at their own men and striking at them to get them to stay in line.

Tobi took his hand away from his wound and saw that it was covered in blood. He felt lightheaded and weak. When he looked up at the battle, he noticed that the front lines of Israel were nearing his position. The sound of battle grew dim in his ears, and he froze.

Kenaz pulled him by the arm. "My lord, the battle is lost. We need to go!"

Tobi snapped out his trance and nodded. With Kenaz's help, they pushed toward the rear. Chaos erupted as more of Sihon's army began to break and run. Tobi realized that it would soon be every man for himself.

Once they were clear of the main body, Kenaz pointed to a nearby chariot headed toward them. The driver was slumped over.

Kenaz let go of Tobi. "Wait here, my lord." He jumped in front of the horses with his arms out until they stopped. He then turned to Tobi. "Get in, quick!"

Fighting to stay conscious, Tobi stumbled over and stepped onto the chariot platform. He used his free hand to push the driver's dead body out.

Kenaz followed him in and grabbed the reins.

Commander Amurrum's voice thundered. "Ammonite! Get back here!"

Tobi turned and saw Amurrum racing toward them, sword brandished.

Kenaz handed Tobi the reins. "Go, my lord! Don't wait for me!" He stepped down from the chariot just as Amurrum reached their position.

Amurrum stopped and pointed first at Tobi and then at Kenaz. "I knew you'd desert us, Ammonite. You and your Edomite slave."

Kenaz drew his sword. "Commander Amurrum. The battle is over."

"It's not over until I say it's over!"

Kenaz signaled to Tobi. "Get out of here! Go!"

Tobi snapped the reins and felt the chariot surge forward. It took great effort not to pass out as pain shot through his side.

Tobi glanced back and watched as Amurrum launched a ferocious attack against Kenaz. The Edomite blocked many of the blows, and even managed to make some good counterattacks, but Tobi could tell that Amurrum was the stronger warrior.

Amurrum soon found an opening and exploited it, knocking Kenaz's sword from his hand. As the commander moved to land a killing blow, a wave of panicked soldiers crashed into them and kicked up a mass of dust.

For a moment, Tobi could not see either Kenaz or Amurrum. All he could hear were screams and shouts. He pulled on the reins to slow the horses. "Kenaz!" he cried out.

Tobi considered turning the chariot around, but then Kenaz appeared, sprinting toward him. He soon reached the chariot and pulled himself onto the platform.

Out of the chaos behind them, Tobi heard the shouts of Commander Amurrum. "Ammonite! You and your slave are dead! By the gods, I'll kill you both!"

Kenaz grabbed the reins from him. "You drive too slow, my lord." He sent the horses into a gallop.

Tobi continued scanning behind them, worried that Amurrum would appear at any moment. But he never came.

As they gained distance, Tobi watched as Sihon's army melted away. Thousands of men fled in all directions as the Israelites cut down those that could not escape.

He sighed and slumped down on the platform. *It's over.*

Kenaz placed a hand on Tobi's shoulder. "My lord, don't you die on me!"

"I just need to rest a bit, Kenaz," Tobi replied. He leaned his head back against the chariot wall and closed his eyes. "But I don't think I'll make it to Rabbah. It's too far, and I'm too tired . . ."

"We're not going to Rabbah, my lord."

Tobi opened his eyes and gave Kenaz a curious look.

Kenaz smiled nervously. "We're going to Betharan, to see your wife."

"Betharan?"

"Yes, so you need to stay alive for me, all right?"

Tobi nodded and closed his eyes again. "I'll do my best . . ."

CHAPTER FOURTEEN

Betharan, Fall 1407 BC

NIKKAL WORKED THE SOFT dough with her hands while Ashima and her daughter, Liluri, sat with her, kneading their own batches. While Nikkal enjoyed the smell of fresh baked bread, she preferred the scent of uncooked dough, especially once it had been fully leavened.

Although Nikkal had only been at her grandparent's home for a few days, it had been a time of peace. Now that she had abandoned the old gods and placed her trust in the God of Israel, she felt as if a heavy burden had been lifted off her. The guilt of Ali's death, the shame of offering herself before Asherah, and the anger she felt toward Tobi no longer dominated her thinking. In addition to all of that, the nightmares had ceased.

She set the dough aside to give it time to rise before baking, and then turned toward Ishara. "I'll start on the next round." She moved to collect the necessary ingredients for another batch.

Ashima nodded. "Yes, I think two or three more would be good."

As Nikkal mixed the ingredients, her mind turned toward Tobi. For the past few mornings, the women had made extra loaves of bread to provide to those refugees and soldiers fleeing the most recent battle. Word had reached them of King Sihon's defeat at Jahaz. It had been a slaughter, with thousands dead including Sihon and his sons.

Preparing food for the expected influx of people had been good for Nikkal, although it did not stop her from worrying about Tobi. *Is he still alive? If so, will he come here? And if I see him again, what will I say?*

Nikkal sat down and began to knead just as Ashima helped Liluri finish her batch. They locked eyes, and Nikkal at once knew that Ashima sympathized with her concerns.

Ashima turned to her daughter. "Go on outside, dear, and help Ishara with the ovens. You've done well."

"Okay, momma," Liluri replied. She grabbed her doll that she had laid on the table. But before she ran off, she turned to Nikkal and waved. "Bye, Nikkal."

Ashima held up a finger. "How should you address her?"

Liluri bowed her head. "Oh, I mean, 'my lady.'"

Ashima nodded with approval. "Good girl."

Nikkal waved back. "Goodbye."

Liluri ran outside.

Once they were alone, Nikkal turned to Ashima. "You don't have to call me that. You barely know me."

Ashima smiled as she began to knead another batch. "God commands us to honor authority. You'll one day inherit this farm, and we'll serve you just as we serve your grandparents."

The words reverberated in Nikkal's ears. She never considered what would happen when her grandparents died. Her father had been their only child, with her as their only grandchild.

She let out a nervous chuckle. "I don't know the first thing about managing an entire farm. And without a husband . . ." A sense of fear gripped her as she considered what life would be like as a young widow.

Ashima placed her hand on Nikkal's. "No matter what happens, we're here for you, my lady. All we can do is trust in God."

Nikkal gave her a weak smile but said nothing. She could tell that Ashima spoke with sincerity. Nikkal had been relieved when she had learned that both Ashima and her husband, Hadad, had also become followers of the God of Israel through their relationship with her grandparents. Besides that, she knew nothing else about them.

Taking advantage of their time alone, Nikkal decided it was as good a moment as any to learn. "Ashima, how did you and Hadad end up coming here? Were you already married when you met my grandparents?"

Ashima chuckled. "That story is an interesting one, to say the least." She paused for a moment. "But it might surprise you that I was once a temple prostitute in service to Asherah."

Nikkal raised her eyebrows.

Ashima shrugged. "I know, even I'm surprised by it now. But I was. And by age fifteen I had conceived Liluri. In a panic, I wanted to end the pregnancy. But I didn't want to wait to dedicate her to Moloch, and so I went to the marketplace in Jericho in search of the herbs I needed."

"And what stopped you?" Nikkal asked.

"Ishara did. She saw me in the marketplace and, by God's providence, introduced herself. She knew who I was and what I was doing. But instead of letting me go on like that, she offered me a place to stay, along with an opportunity to work for her and Shalim on the farm."

Nikkal paused her kneading and looked up at Ashima. "What about your family? Did they agree to that?"

Ashima laughed. "My parents tried to keep me at the temple. Prostitution was way more profitable than farming. But I didn't want to do it anymore. I didn't want to kill my child or raise her in that environment."

Nikkal nodded and resumed her work. "And what about Hadad, was he the father?"

Ashima shook her head. "No. He had already been working for your grandparents for several years as a slave, having been sold to them to pay off his debts."

"How did you two come to be married, then?" Nikkal asked.

"Well, at first, he kept his distance. His own mother had been a prostitute, and so I think he wanted to avoid any reminders of that."

"Was he a follower of the God of Israel when you met him?

"Yes. And I had just become one also. We got along very well, but he still did not want to marry me." Ashima nodded in the direction of the door. "But when Liluri was born, something changed."

"What was it?" asked Nikkal.

Ashima shrugged. "I'm not entirely sure. But I think Shalim helped nudge him in the right direction. Either way, Hadad and I were soon married, and he adopted Liluri as his daughter."

"Does he want to have more children?" Nikkal asked.

Ashima grinned. "He does, and, Lord willing, it won't be long until the child arrives."

Nikkal gasped. "Oh wow! That's wonderful! How far along are you?"

"It's still very early, I just found out myself."

"Does Hadad know?" Nikkal asked.

"Mm-hmm. I told him a few days ago." She paused. "But we don't want to tell Shalim and Ishara quite yet. We've—well, we've lost several children, and it's just too hard to go through the cycle of celebrating and mourning. So, we'll wait another month or two."

Nikkal nodded. She felt awkward that Ashima had confided in her, but she guessed that being a stranger made it easier to talk to, in a way. She had thought the same about Arsay and Tallai when she first met them. Of course, they still served false gods, and had helped Nikkal do terrible things. Ashima had been like them, and yet she now served the God of Israel.

"Ashima," Nikkal began, "when—how, did you end up becoming a follower of Yahweh?"

Ashima chuckled. "Well, when I arrived here, I had been wrestling with God for some time, unsure of my identity."

"Your identity?" Nikkal asked.

"Yes," Ashima replied. "You see, Asherah claims to give her followers new identities. Men can become women, and women can become men. Women can become warriors and men can become spinsters. And neither of them needs to be constrained by fatherhood or motherhood."

"Do you get to choose your own identity?" Nikkal replied. "Or does Asherah choose it for you?"

Ashima shrugged. "A good question. Probably both. According to the teachings of Asherah, all of your feelings come from Asherah's spirit. I never desired to become a man or a warrior. But I wanted men to want me. That gave me power over them. The power of Asherah."

"So, by quitting your service to Asherah, you were giving up on that power?"

"Yes, that's right," replied Ashima. "That's what I struggled with. But, with Ishara's help, I soon realized that God, as creator, gets to say what I am and am not. He gives me identity. So, for me to choose my own identity is not freedom, but slavery to my passions."

Nikkal nodded. "My family told me that giving up Ali would free me. They said that I should delay being a mother in order to earn more money for my future children." Her voice turned sorrowful. "I believed them and thought I could control my future by serving Moloch."

Ashima gestured to the dough in front of her. "God is the one who formed us. Our duty is to trust him and obey his word. That's what I had to learn. Asherah teaches that marriage is slavery for women. But I've never been more free than when I've been under authority, first to God and then to my husband."

Nikkal glanced down at her own dough and considered Ashima's words. *It all sounds so new to me, but I know she's right.* When she looked up, Ashima pointed to her loaf. "Is yours ready?"

"I think so," Nikkal replied.

They carried their leavened dough outside and found Ishara and Liluri watching over the ovens. Ishara helped them swap out the cooked loaves with the uncooked loaves. "Is that the last of them?" she asked.

Ashima nodded.

"All right." Ishara pointed to several nearby baskets. "You can put the finished ones in those."

As Nikkal began, she heard Shalim's voice from the woods. "Hello, ladies!" he shouted.

Nikkal turned and saw Shalim and Hadad walking out of the tree line. Shalim waved to them while Hadad carried a dead deer on his back.

The two men exchanged words. Hadad nodded and went off to dress the deer while Shalim continued walking toward the women. As he drew close, he pointed to the baskets. "Are they all filled and ready to go?"

"Almost," replied Ishara. "One more batch to go."

"Good," said Shalim. "I'll get the ox cart ready so Hadad and I can get these to the village and be back before sundown."

Nikkal spoke up. "Please let me come with you. I want to help."

Shalim seemed as if about to refuse, but then his face softened, and he nodded. "All right. But you must stay close to me. Things could get out of hand quickly."

She nodded. "Thank you, grandfather."

Sympathy filled Shalim's voice. "Nik, even if we don't find Tobi, he knows you're here. If he's alive, he'll find us."

"I—I know." She prayed to God that he would.

A few hours later, Shalim, Hadad, and Nikkal, armed with several baskets of bread, approached the town of Betharan. Their two oxen pulled the cart at a slow and steady pace.

The town now bustled with activity since Nikkal had last seen it. She observed several large groups of people coming from the east, many of whom carried their belongings with them. The number of beggars, both sick and lame, had also increased. As for wounded or fleeing soldiers, Nikkal spotted none yet.

They stopped the cart near the main road and began offering bread to those who appeared to be most in need. Nikkal stood in between Hadad and Shalim, who both carried weapons in their tunics.

It did not take long before people started coming up to the cart. Nikkal feared that a mob would form, but Hadad and her grandfather seemed unconcerned.

As people approached, Shalim and Hadad made it clear, through their speech and body language, that any attempts to harm them or steal the bread would be resisted. With each person, Hadad and Shalim asked questions and confirmed that the individual was either sick, injured, or a refugee. If so, Hadad and Shalim signaled for Nikkal to hand them bread.

Nikkal watched as a man, woman, and child approached Shalim. After Shalim exchanged a few words with them, he nodded to Nikkal.

She handed the man a loaf of bread.

"Thank you," he replied.

"Where are you from?" she asked.

"From Heshbon." He broke off a piece of bread and handed it to his wife, and then broke off another one for the child, a small boy.

Nikkal grew nervous. "Heshbon? Has it been taken?"

The man shook his head. "Not yet. But they say that the Israelites cut off King Sihon's head." He placed his hands over the boy's ears. "They also say that when the city falls, all of the men, women, and children will be massacred."

Nikkal did not know how to respond, so she changed the subject. "Have you seen any surviving soldiers on the road?"

He took a quick bite of bread. "A few. But most of them are fleeing north to Bashan, to seek protection under Sihon's brother, King Og."

Another family came up to Nikkal, and she realized that she needed to end the conversation. "Thank you." As the man and his family departed, she retrieved another loaf from the basket.

By the time the bread had all been distributed, sunset approached. Dozens, if not hundreds, of people had passed through Betharan, and Nikkal felt exhausted.

She felt grateful that no mobs had formed, and that no violence had occurred. There were still folks on the roads, but as evening approached Nikkal observed that there were less women and children and more young men and soldiers.

Shalim turned to her. "Let's go." He gestured for Hadad to help him prepare the cart. They both worked in silence, and Nikkal could feel their sense of urgency.

She sat in the cart next to the empty baskets and began to scan the area. "There are more soldiers on the road," she whispered.

"Yes," replied Shalim. "Not all of them will be fleeing the battle. There are men who stay behind hoping to take advantage of the chaos, knowing that many husbands and fathers have gone to war."

Hadad spoked up. "And others will be looking for isolated and wounded soldiers to capture and sell into slavery."

Nikkal nodded and rested her hand near the hidden dagger she carried.

Once they departed, she breathed a sigh of relief. It did not take long before the town had disappeared and Nikkal could no longer hear anything but the cart as it crept along the path. Her hand slowly drifted away from her dagger.

With night now upon them, Hadad lit a lamp to guide the path for the oxen.

The soft light and the rhythm of the cart's slow and steady movement soothed Nikkal, and she soon felt her eyes close. But before she could fall asleep, the sound of rapid footsteps reached her ears. It seemed to come from behind them.

She lifted her head. "Grandfather?" she whispered. "Do you hear that?" In the lamplight, she could see that he had.

He nodded. "Someone is coming. Must have followed us from the town." He retrieved his bow and notched an arrow to the string.

Hadad stopped the cart and drew his own bow as well.

The steps grew louder, and were coupled with the sound of breaking twigs and moving branches.

Shalim shouted into the darkness. "I am Shalim of Betharan, and you are entering my property! Speak your name in peace or turn back at once!"

The pace of the footsteps slowed, and Nikkal soon heard the sound of heavy breathing.

"Shalim?" a man said weakly.

Nikkal recognized that voice. "Tobi!" she shouted.

Shalim dropped his bow and gestured toward Hadad. "Hand me the lamp."

"Tobi!" Nikkal repeated.

Shalim moved the lamp so as to light up the path behind them.

Two men then appeared out of the darkness, and Nikkal recognized them as Tobi and Kenaz. Kenaz supported Tobi, who appeared to be severely wounded.

Tobi's eyes found hers and he smiled. "Nik," he whispered.

Shalim stepped down from the cart. "Hadad, help me please."

Hadad ran over and, with Shalim, aided Kenaz in loading Tobi onto the cart.

Nikkal knelt beside her husband as her eyes filled with tears.

Kenaz fought hard to catch his breath. "He was—struck by a spear."

Shalim passed the lamp to Nikkal. "Hold this for me."

She took it right away and watched as Shalim and Hadad examined Tobi's wounds.

"Has he received any care?" Shalim asked.

Kenaz shook his head. "No. No time. We started out on a chariot but had to continue on foot when we encountered bandits. The chariot belongs to them now."

Shalim nodded.

Hadad leaned in and sniffed the wound. "The bleeding seems to have stopped. The biggest concern now will be fever."

"All right," replied Shalim. "Let's get him back to the house." He looked at Nikkal. "Watch over him. If he stops breathing, let me know."

Nikkal nodded.

Kenaz sat down opposite Nikkal while Shalim and Hadad got the cart moving again.

As they continued along the path, Nikkal felt as if the oxen were slower than ever. She held Tobi's hand and began to pray aloud. "Lord—"

She paused, unsure of how to continue, or what formula she should use. Then she considered how her grandfather prayed and used that as an example. "Thank you for bringing Tobi to me. You've protected him in battle and brought him this far. Please save him. Please don't let him die. Amen."

By the lamplight she noticed that Tobi watched her as she prayed. She did not know if he had been listening, but his eyes did not leave hers.

She felt him squeeze her hand.

Once they arrived back at the farm, everyone moved with a purpose. Shalim, Hadad, and Kenaz carried Tobi to Nikkal's room, where his old clothes were removed and his wounds were attended.

Hadad had been correct in his assessment that the wound had begun to fester. Ishara showed Nikkal how to clean and dress it using vinegar and honey.

Shalim then prayed over Tobi. His prayer seemed heartfelt and genuine, and Nikkal believed that her grandfather wanted Tobi to live, even if he remained loyal to the old gods.

When Shalim finished the prayer, he turned to Nikkal. "We've done all we can. The rest is in God's hands."

She nodded.

"Do you want someone else to stay with you?" he asked.

She shook her head. "No, I'll watch over him. You all should get some sleep."

Shalim nodded. "Well, if his condition worsens, come get me."

"I will."

As he moved to go, Nikkal turned to him. "Grandfather?"

"Hmm?" he asked.

She walked over and hugged him. "Thank you."

"Of course, my dear." He hugged her back.

Shalim then gestured for everyone else to follow him out.

Nikkal soon found herself alone with Tobi. It had been a long time since she had spoken to her husband in private. Now, it seemed, that even if she tried to speak, he might not hear her.

She checked his breathing. It seemed steady. But when she placed a hand on his forehead, his skin felt warmer than normal.

After extinguishing the lamp, she laid next to Tobi and kept her hand on his chest. She measured the pause between each breath and prayed that they remained the same.

Very soon, though, she drifted off to sleep.

When she woke, she sat up, alarmed that she had slept so long without checking on Tobi. Dawn had not yet arrived, so she put her hand on Tobi's chest and leaned in to listen. He still breathed.

She let out a sigh of relief.

"Nik?" Tobi whispered.

She squeezed his hand. "I'm here."

"Where am I. What happened?"

"You're at my grandfather's, in Betharan. You were wounded . . ."

He attempted to sit up but cried out in pain and laid back down.

She put her hand on his chest. "No, don't move. You need to rest." She touched his forehead. Still warm. "You have a fever."

His voice cracked. "I'm, I'm thirsty."

"I'll get you some water." She retrieved the waterskin that her grandmother had left for her and lifted it to Tobi's lips. "Here."

He grasped it with his hands and began to squeeze.

"Slow down," she replied.

He coughed a little as he finished. "Thank you."

They laid together in silence. Nikkal did not know what to say, or even if Tobi wanted to talk anymore.

Just when she thought that he had fallen back asleep, he spoke. "It was a slaughter."

She did not respond.

He continued. "Everything was against us. The land, the weather, the animals, even the rocks themselves. It was as if—as if the gods had no power." His voice started to waver. "Somehow, I knew we'd lose. Deep down I knew it—but I kept going. And then it was my turn, but I couldn't win. They were too fast—too strong—and the singing . . ."

"Singing?" Nikkal asked.

"Yes. Beautiful but terrifying. With trumpets—and their God right in the middle of them."

Tobi's statement caught her off guard. From what she knew, the Israelites did not have any idols or images of God. "God was among them?" she asked.

"It felt like he was. But it didn't look like a god. It was a gold box, with winged creatures on top. They were pointing at something. But there was nothing there." He began to sob. "I was wounded, and I ran—like a coward I ran. I couldn't fight. I was so scared . . ."

Nikkal felt tears in her eyes and drew herself closer to Tobi.

His body shivered as he spoke. "Commander Amurrum tried to stop me. But Kenaz fought him—helped me get away."

She hugged him tight. He did not push her away.

As he sobbed in her arms, she felt a renewed love for him. Closing her eyes, she sent a silent prayer to God that he would open Tobi's. *I want to be with him, Lord. But, more importantly, I want him to know you.*

CHAPTER FIFTEEN

Heshbon, Fall 1407 BC

THE SUN HAD NEARLY disappeared over the horizon when Amurrum stumbled through the door of the barracks. He had made it back to Heshbon. Finally, after several days and nights on foot from Jahaz, he could rest.

The soldiers in the barracks were startled at his sudden entry. They drew their swords and looked ready to attack until the one nearest the door spoke. "Commander Amurrum?" he asked.

Amurrum nodded. "Water—" he croaked.

The soldier turned to the other men. "You heard him. Water. Now!"

The men rushed to comply.

Within moments, Amurrum was handed a waterskin. He snatched it up and lifted it to his mouth. After several moments of gulping, he tossed the empty skin back to the soldier who had given to him. Still fighting to catch his breath, he turned to the soldier near the door. "Report."

The soldier bowed his head. "Sir, we heard that the army was destroyed, and that King Sihon is dead."

Amurrum nodded. "And?"

The soldier grew nervous. "And we've tried to gather the remaining men to mount a defense of the city. It's chaos, sir. Most are fleeing west to Jericho. Some are going north to King Og. But others are talking of setting up their own kingdom here at Heshbon."

"Have any other commanders made it back?" Amurrum asked.

"No, sir. You're the only one so far."

Amurrum nodded. "Inform the men that I'm taking command of the city for its defense. Any who are caught fleeing or refusing to fight are to be executed without hesitation. Do you understand?"

"Yes, sir."

Amurrum sat down at a nearby table. "Now, give me food and wine and leave me. I'm not to be disturbed."

The soldier bowed his head. "Yes, sir." He then signaled to the other men in the room to move.

The men handed bread and a wineskin to Amurrum before departing the barracks.

Now alone, Amurrum smiled to himself knowing that he had made it back before anyone else could set themselves up as warlord. *It'll take some work, but soon I'll have things under control.*

He took several bites of bread and then a long drink from the wineskin before closing his eyes. Images of the battle at Jahaz filled his mind. The relentless Israelites, the death of the king, and the retreat of the Ammonites. He cursed them all under his breath, especially the one Ammonite. *What was his name again? Oh yes, Tobimelech.*

If it had not been for Tobimelech's Edomite slave, Amurrum would have killed him, taken the chariot, and gotten back to Heshbon a lot sooner. The thought of it angered him, but not enough to overcome his exhaustion. As he drifted off to sleep, he comforted himself with a thought. *If I ever find that Ammonite, I'll kill him, his slave, and everyone else he cares about.*

It was late morning when he finally woke up. He scanned around and saw that the barracks remained empty. A feeling of panic took hold of him. *How long have I slept? What if the men have abandoned me?*

He went over to a nearby basin of water and splashed some on his face before rushing outside. As soon as he opened the barracks door, he let out a sigh of relief. Two soldiers stood guard, one on either side.

Startled, the men snapped to attention. "Sir."

Amurrum studied them both. Young and inexperienced. *Men like this won't be enough to hold off the Israelites.* He shoved that issue aside and chose to focus on one step at a time. "Any news?" he asked.

The guard on the right nodded. "Sir, your orders are being carried out. We've setup several patrols to try to keep the peace and to round up any stragglers. But I was told that you are to go to the palace right away."

Amurrum made his annoyance clear. "By whom?"

"Queen Inanna, sir," the guard replied.

Amurrum nodded and glanced toward the direction of the palace. "Hmm." *Word of my return travels fast. Still, there may be an opportunity here.*

He turned back to the guard. "All right. I'm headed there now. But I want twenty of our strongest soldiers to secure the palace entrance and not let anyone in or out without my permission."

The guard bowed his head. "Yes, sir." He then turned to go.

"Wait."

The guard stopped.

"Any word on High Priest Nahash?" Amurrum asked.

The guard shook his head. "No, sir."

"Fine. If he is found, I want him arrested on sight. Do you understand?"

"Yes, sir!"

Amurrum dismissed him with a wave of his hand. Once the guard had departed, Amurrum made his way to the palace. He felt good. Visions of being crowned king entered his mind. *And why not? I've earned it.*

He nodded to a patrol of soldiers in the street. They returned the greeting and stood at attention as he passed by.

Although the city seemed calm, signs of looting were still visible. Broken jars and overturned carts lay everywhere. Amurrum assumed that most of the looters were already gone, having taken everything of value. *That's going to make it difficult to raise another army.*

As Amurrum passed by several houses, he spotted women and old men peering at him through their windows. He wondered how many able-bodied men remained in the city. If there were not enough to mount a defense, he might have to give up on his dream of ruling Heshbon.

When he approached the palace doors, he was not greeted by the normal guards but by several eunuchs who normally protected the king's harem.

"Commander Amurrum?" one of them asked.

"Yes," he replied.

"The queen awaits you. Please follow me."

Amurrum nodded and followed the eunuch inside. As they walked through the halls, Amurrum noticed the eerie quietness of the palace. He turned to the eunuch. "Where is everyone? Where are all the servants?"

The eunuch's voice turned sullen. "News of the king's death reached us two days ago, when the first fleeing soldiers arrived. That's when everything fell apart. The guards abandoned their posts. And several of Sihon's wives fled with their servants. We were barely able to prevent the palace from being ransacked."

They reached the intersection that led to the king's harem. But instead of turning right toward it, they turned left and mounted the steps to the upper floor and into King Sihon's private chambers.

Amurrum grinned. *If all goes well, they'll be mine soon.*

When they reached the chamber doors, the eunuch turned to Amurrum. "The queen was elated to hear that you lived and had made it back." He then opened the doors and gestured for Amurrum to enter.

Amurrum looked in and spotted Inanna standing at the window. She wore a royal gown of blue and green and appeared to have a nervous, even frightened, look about her.

When she saw Amurrum, her face lit up with joy. Yet, probably out of habit, she spoke with a cold formality. "Welcome, commander."

Amurrum remained equally cool as he entered. "My lady."

She turned to the eunuch. "Leave us. We are not to be disturbed."

The eunuch bowed low. "Yes, my queen."

Amurrum waited in silence for the eunuch to depart. As he stood there, his eyes traced Inanna's olive-skinned body and he felt his yearning for her rise within him. He had always found her beautiful, but now she could no longer blackmail him. In a way, that made her even more attractive.

He smiled at her. *Now she needs me. Now I have the power.*

As soon as the door shut, Inanna ran to Amurrum and threw her arms around him. "Thank the gods you're alive." She kissed him.

He kissed her back.

After a few moments she pulled away and placed a hand on his worn tunic. "You look terrible."

He shrugged. "Sorry. I didn't have time to change."

She nodded and then walked over to a nearby table that contained a wine jug and several cups. She poured a drink for both of them. "I would offer you some of my late husband's clothing, but I'm afraid they wouldn't fit." She laughed at her own joke as she handed him a cup.

He nodded. "Thank you."

She offered up a toast. "To the gods," she said, before pouring some of the wine onto the floor.

"To the gods," he replied, mimicking her action.

They both then drank together in silence.

Inanna turned to the nearby window and looked out upon the city. "So, how did it happen?"

Amurrum knew what she meant, but took a moment to decide how best to tell the story. "At the height of the battle, your husband charged into the midst of Israel's army, hoping to cause a panic, just as he had done against King Zippor of Moab. But this time it didn't work. Israel repulsed the attack and killed him."

She nodded but did not look at him. "And how did you manage to escape?"

Amurrum clenched his jaw. *Is she suggesting that I abandoned the king?* He took a long drink of wine before answering. "I led the Ammonite mercenaries. After your husband's death, they began to break, and I tried to keep them from fleeing. Once I realized that it was too late, I had no choice but to retreat."

She nodded again. A hint of suspicion entered her voice. "And why did you come back?"

Amurrum drained his cup, set the empty goblet on the table, and walked up to her. "I came back to defend this city, as the king would have wanted."

Inanna turned and looked at him. Her eyes indicated a hint of disappointment.

He knew what answer she wanted. *And I will give it to you, for a price.* He reached out and took hold of her hand. "But more than that, I came back for you."

She smiled and kissed him passionately. He did not have to fake interest, for at that moment the desire for power and pleasure merged in Amurrum's mind.

Afternoon had arrived by the time Amurrum forced himself to get out of the bed. He had been kept there not only by the enthusiastic affections of Inanna, but also by the fact that it had been the most comfortable bed he had ever slept in.

He cursed himself for his laziness as he gathered his clothes. The time for rest and reward would come later. Knowing that he still needed to secure a crown, he began to dress in haste.

Inanna rolled over and faced him. "Where are you going?"

"To make sure you're safe."

Her voice turned accusatory. "Or to make sure you become king?"

He looked over at her and shrugged. "Why not both?"

She did not reply.

Amurrum finished securing his sword to his tunic before turning to her. He could see the anger on her face. "Listen," he began, "if I'm going to be with you, I don't want to be some consort or plaything."

She scowled at him. "The prince consort is a high honor. Besides, the people won't accept you as king, not without my support."

He struck back. "And how long do you think you'd last without my protection? Your eunuchs can't stop Israel from taking the city."

"Can you?" she asked.

The words stung. He opened his mouth to reply but a knock came to the door.

"What is it?" Inanna barked.

"My queen," replied one of her eunuchs, "there is a disturbance at the palace entrance. High Priest Nahash as arrived."

A look of panic came across Inanna's face, but her voice remained calm. "Thank you, I'll be right there."

After waiting a moment to ensure that the eunuch no longer stood near the door, Amurrum spoke up. "It's all right. I've ordered his arrest on sight. As long as I'm here, you're safe."

She jumped out of the bed and began to dress. "He knows about us, Amurrum, he knows!"

"No, he doesn't—he couldn't." But in that moment, Amurrum doubted his own words. He shook his head. "It doesn't matter. I'll deal with him myself. Even if he knows, it'd be worse if he saw us together."

She stood and stared at him with fear in her eyes.

Amurrum walked up and put his hands on her shoulders. "We can talk about whether I'm prince consort or king later. Either way, I'm not going to let some arrogant priest of Baal stop us."

She nodded and smiled. "Okay." She kissed him once more before he turned and walked out.

Upon reaching the bottom of the stairs, he approached two eunuchs who stood guard. He nodded to them, but they did not acknowledge him in return. One gave him a look of disdain as he passed by.

Ignoring their lack of respect, he continued to the main entrance. As soon as he exited, he saw that a rather large crowd had gathered on the palace steps. Many were shouting at the twenty soldiers that stood in their way.

Scanning the area, Amurrum spotted the black robes of High Priest Nahash and his fellow acolytes standing at the head of the mob, their backs turned to the soldiers as they excited the crowd. *So, you decided to show yourself.*

He walked toward the crowd, stopping just behind his line of soldiers. As he did, Nahash and the other priests turned to face him.

The high priest of Baal leaned on his staff and pointed a bony finger at Amurrum. "There's the usurper now!"

"It's good to see you too, Nahash," replied Amurrum. "I'm surprised you came."

Nahash smiled. "Surprised? Why? I've been given charge of the administration of this city in the king's absence."

"The king is dead, Nahash, and you are hereby relieved of your duties." Amurrum dismissed the high priest with his hand. "I suggest you depart now before I have you arrested for treason."

"Under whose authority?" Nahash spat.

"The queen's," replied Amurrum. "I now serve as commander of her armies. This city is under military control and your actions are unlawful."

Nahash turned to address the crowd. "You see! This man would make himself king! He abandons our king on the field of battle and leaves him to die, and then comes back here and moves into the palace!"

The crowd murmured with anger.

Amurrum concealed his nervousness as he spoke. "Lies, Nahash! I stood by the king to the very end and have returned to protect this city. I am here now only by the queen's command."

A wicked grin came over Nahash's face. "The same queen who you've been bedding for years, right?"

Before Amurrum could respond, Nahash addressed the crowd again. "I've seen the evidence! I've spoken with the harem guard! This man swore an oath of loyalty to his king and yet seduced the queen behind his back. And she enjoyed it!"

Nahash gestured toward Amurrum. "It's because of this man that your king is dead. This man dishonored the king's bed, abandoned the king in battle, and now seeks the king's throne. Treason I say! Treason!"

The crowd lifted their hands in defiance and shouted. "Treason! Treason!" They began to draw closer to the line of soldiers.

Amurrum shouted to his men. "He lies! Arrest him! Arrest Nahash!"

Several of the soldiers glanced at Amurrum with uncertainty on their faces. They did not respond to his command.

Amurrum drew his sword and prepared to give the order again but stopped when he heard Nahash let out a horrible cry.

Everyone nearby turned and watched as the high priest began to tremble. His eyes rolled back into his head, revealing nothing but white. As if it were coordinated, he and the other priests pulled up their sleeves, drew out their daggers, and began to gash themselves. Blood trickled onto the ground.

Nahash then lifted his hands to the sky and shouted in a voice that could only be described as demonic. "Baal speaks! 'Treason' he says! Treason!"

Still in his trance-like state, Nahash turned to the crowd. "The gods have abandoned you because your king has been abandoned!"

The crowd cried out in despair.

Nahash trembled again as his eyes returned to normal. After pausing a moment, a maniacal look came across his face. Turning to Amurrum's soldiers, he held up his staff. "Baal demands justice! Baal demands sacrifice! Those of you who are loyal to King Sihon must stand with Baal now or be destroyed! Decide!"

Of the twenty soldiers in front of Amurrum, all but six stepped forward and joined with Nahash.

Nahash lifted his hand, now covered in his own blood, and pointed at Amurrum and his six men. "Take them for Baal!"

"Inside!" Amurrum shouted as the crowd surged forward.

The seven of them were able to enter and bar the door just before the first person had reached them. The palace door soon shook with angry pounding.

One soldier turned to him. "What—what do we do, sir?"

Amurrum pointed with his sword down the hallway. "There's a secret exit in the back. C'mon, let's go." He began to lead them through the palace but stopped at the steps leading up to the king's chamber.

He signaled for them to go on ahead. "Keep going until you get to the king's dining hall. Under the main table is a rug covering a wooden door. It leads to an underground tunnel. I'll meet you there. Go!"

The six soldiers continued as Amurrum ran up the stairs. The eunuch guards were nowhere in sight. *That's strange.*

He panicked when he saw that the door to the king's chamber had been opened. As he rushed through it, the two eunuch guards attacked him.

The first guard came in high and from the left with his sword. Amurrum ducked and then struck out with his own sword, catching the man in his thigh.

The second guard had been standing near the king's bed and now charged straight toward Amurrum.

Amurrum lunged to the side just in time. The eunuch tried to match Amurrum's movement but lost his balance and crashed into the wall.

Amurrum rose and launched a ferocious counter-attack. The man with the wounded leg tried to shift his weight to avoid getting struck but was too slow. Amurrum ran his sword right across the man's abdomen.

The other eunuch got up and lunged at Amurrum a second time. Both men collided and fell to the floor.

The impact caused Amurrum to drop his sword, so he shifted his mindset to hand-to-hand combat. Taking advantage of his experience and training, he slipped the eunuch's grasp and slid his arms around the man's neck. But instead of choking him out, Amurrum squeezed and yanked with all his strength until he felt a snap. The man fell limp.

Catching his breath, Amurrum retrieved his sword and scanned the room. "Inanna!" he shouted.

There was no reply.

He considered the possibility that she had escaped but then spotted her lying on the bed. Running over to her, he soon realized that he was too late. Her naked body lay stretched out on the bed, covered in blood. Deep gashes ran down her face, chest, arms, and legs.

Amurrum's stomach twisted in a mixture of grief and anger. *Her own eunuchs turned on her. Nahash . . .*

He stood there and stared at her body, unsure of what to do. His dreams of becoming king were shattered. There was nothing for him here.

A loud crash and the sound of triumphant shouting reached his ears. The mob had broken through the door. He was out of time. Amurrum ran from the room, down the stairs, and toward the dining hall.

He considered making one last stand in order to kill as many of them as possible. He could probably take out a good number, but doubted that he could get to Nahash. The only choice was to live, for now.

He entered the dining hall and saw that his soldiers had found the hidden tunnel and entered it. Amurrum climbed down after them and, before closing the secret door, swore an oath to the gods that he would get revenge on everyone who had wronged him.

CHAPTER SIXTEEN

Betharan, Fall 1407 BC

It took a week before Tobi could get out of bed. On the fifth day after his arrival, his fever had broken, and he began to recover. Now, about two weeks later, he had regained almost full mobility, although his side still felt sore whenever he exerted himself too much or stayed in one position for too long. That is why he had decided to get up early.

Tobi looked over at Nikkal. She remained asleep, of which he was thankful. Ever since coming to Shalim's, he had felt a distance between them. *She's changed, that's for sure.* He suspected that she had abandoned his family's gods. Not knowing yet how to process that, he chose for now to avoid any awkward conversations.

Attempting not to wake her, he got up from the mat and began to dress in the dark. It took longer than usual to do it without making noise, but he succeeded.

He crept down the ladder to the first floor of her grandfather's house. Given that the sun had not yet risen, he expected it to be dark, but it was not. Lamplight illuminated the main room. Entering, he found Hadad and Kenaz gathering supplies and weapons.

Kenaz noticed him first and bowed his head. "Good morning, my lord."

Tobi ignored the greeting but sought to satisfy his curiosity. "What are you guys doing?"

"Going hunting," replied Hadad.

Tobi gave a curt nod. Although he did not mind Hadad, he felt annoyed that he and Kenaz had become friends. While Tobi recovered in his bed, Kenaz served on the farm in any way he could. He and Hadad, both having experienced lives of slavery, soon bonded. As a result, Tobi feared that Kenaz would come to like this place more than Rabbah.

"You're welcome to come too," continued Hadad.

Tobi felt torn. He hated the idea of watching as Hadad continued to pull Kenaz away from him. But he also wanted to do something different, something fun. Since regaining his mobility, he had helped Shalim with simple tasks, such as harvesting olives. The first rains had not yet come, so plowing and planting were not an option.

Tobi shrugged. "Sure, I'll go." *Anything is better than what I've been doing.*

Shalim entered the room carrying his bow and stopped when he saw Tobi. "Oh, good morning, Tobi."

Tobi gave a single head nod. "Shalim."

"Will you be joining us on the hunt?" Shalim asked.

"I guess so, but I didn't pack anything."

Shalim chuckled. "Don't worry about it. We've got enough for everyone." He tossed a bag to Tobi.

Tobi caught it as Shalim listed its contents. "A wineskin, a waterskin, and some bread."

Tobi nodded. "Thanks." He shouldered the bag.

Shalim then held up a bow. "Do you know how to use one of these?"

Tobi shook his head. "I'm only familiar with swords and spears. I never learned to shoot."

Shalim offered the bow to Kenaz. "What about you? Can you shoot?"

Kenaz shrugged as he took it. "It's been a while, but I'll try."

"Wait," said Tobi, "you know how?"

Kenaz nodded. "From before I was a slave. But I'm probably rusty."

Tobi felt himself turn red with embarrassment and anger. "So, am I to just carry everyone's food and water?"

He expected Shalim or Hadad to laugh, but neither of them did. Shalim just turned, grabbed a spear that was leaning against the wall, and handed it to Tobi. "Here, take this."

Tobi raised his eyebrows in confusion as he grabbed it. "How am I going to get close enough to kill a deer with this?"

This time, Shalim chuckled. "There's more than just deer out there. Besides, your job will be to flush out the game. As you move, the animals will head toward us, and we'll take the shots."

Tobi still did not understand. "If the animals are going to run from me, why do I need a spear?"

Shalim picked up his pack. "Just in case."

Before Tobi could ask another question, Shalim gestured toward Hadad and Kenaz. "You two ready?"

They nodded, and the four of them departed in silence.

Outside, the sun's rays were just creeping out over the horizon. From what Tobi could see, no clouds were visible.

Hadad looked up. "I don't think it will rain today."

Shalim stopped and let out a sigh. "I know. I'm glad to go hunting but we need the rain. He paused for a moment. "God will provide. We must trust in him." As he continued walking, he signaled for them to follow.

Tobi observed Shalim as the group approached the tree line on the northern edge of the property. When Tobi first arrived, he thought that Shalim would be angry or hostile toward him. But instead of ridiculing Tobi about the battle of Jahaz or belittling the gods of the Ammonites, Shalim had just focused on caring for him. And the care seemed genuine. It all made Tobi feel awkward. *Why would a traitor treat me so well?*

Out of nervousness, he shifted the spear in his hands. Memories of the battle of Jahaz entered his mind. He had not held a spear since then, and now he found himself marching toward another battle, although a somewhat different one. A battle not against man, but against nature.

Attempting to distract himself from reflecting on his own cowardness, he turned his mind to Nikkal. *Do I still love her? What if she really is a traitor like her grandfather?* If that were true, he was not sure if he could stay with her. In some ways it would be easier to just leave her and move on. *I can't even remember when I had last lain with her.*

Tobi, annoyed at his own thoughts, decided to pass the time a different way. He glanced over to his left at Hadad and asked the first question that came to his mind. "So, Hadad, where were you raised?"

Hadad seemed taken aback by the sudden question, but soon replied. "Jericho."

"Do you still have family there?"

Hadad shook his head. "I have no one else. My family is here." Hadad's eyes remained on the tree line in front of them.

Tobi assumed that Hadad had no desire to talk, and so decided to abandon any attempts at further questioning.

Yet Hadad continued. "I'm a child of the gods, as they say. When my mother was of age, she celebrated the annual mourning for Baal by offering herself to a stranger. She conceived and, when I was born, she named me Baal-Hadad."

"Baal's thunder," remarked Tobi.

Hadad shrugged. "Or Baal's hammer, depending on who you ask. But either way, in reality I was a boy with no father."

Tobi's heart sank as he listened. He had heard the stories. According to tradition, every woman, at least once in her life, had to serve as a prostitute during the month of mourning. Any money she earned would be dedicated to the goddess Asherah, or Inanna, as the Akkadians had called her.

"Are you familiar with the annual mourning for Baal?" Hadad asked.

Tobi nodded. "I was told it came from the Akkadians to the east, who mourn for Tammuz instead of Baal. We Ammonites adopted only parts of the tradition. For example, we allow women to shave their heads rather than offer themselves. That's what my sister did when her time came."

Hadad did not seem impressed. "Such an option is not permitted in Jericho. To truly honor Baal requires you to become a victim like him."

Before Tobi could reply, Hadad continued. "Anyways, I was a terror growing up, and soon found myself on the streets. I began stealing, and then drinking, and then stealing so that I could keep drinking. Eventually, I was caught and sold into slavery to pay off my debts."

"What about your mother?" Tobi asked.

Hadad shrugged. "No man wanted to marry a woman with baggage, especially baggage like me. So, she did the only thing she knew and became a common prostitute. It was only later, after I had been enslaved for several years, that I found out that she had gotten sick and died."

Tobi felt like an idiot for asking. "I'm so sorry . . ." They walked a bit more in silence before Tobi mustered the courage to ask one more question. "So, how did you come to be here?"

They entered the tree line and Tobi strained his ears as Hadad reduced his voice to a whisper. "I was a rebellious slave, beaten regularly for disobedience. I was sold several times, but never for enough to pay off my debts. One day, traveling through Betharan, I mouthed off at my latest master and was nearly beaten to death for it."

"Oh . . ." replied Tobi.

Hadad let out a soft chuckle. "It was for the best. Shalim happened to also be there that day. Seeing my sorry state, he offered to buy me. I've been here ever since."

"And I still can't get rid of him," replied Shalim.

All of them laughed, but Shalim lifted his hand to quiet them. "All right, let's keep it down now." He signaled toward the left as he began to whisper. "Hadad, you and Kenaz take left. I'll take the right."

Hadad and Kenaz both nodded and began to move stealthily.

He then turned to Tobi. "You go straight ahead slowly. We'll shoot whatever you flush out. If it comes toward you, stand your ground and level your spear. We'll do the rest."

Tobi nodded and tightened the grip on his weapon.

As the men spread out, Tobi crept forward. The sun had now risen, although the trees blocked much of the light.

Tobi periodically glanced to each side. At times he could spot Hadad, Kenaz, and Shalim through the trees. They kept a safe, but calculated distance, with bows at the ready.

As he continued forward, he thought about what Hadad had said. He had always been told that the children of the gods were to be honored and celebrated. Yet that clearly had not happened with Hadad.

He considered his own people and their worship of Moloch. Moloch was their king, as his very name meant. And as king he always claimed the firstborn as his, blessed and chosen by him. Ali had been Tobi's firstborn. *And I gave him to Moloch.*

A deep feeling of sorrow and regret washed over Tobi at the thought of his son. *Hadad had been fatherless, and now I'm childless.* His thoughts were interrupted by the rustling of the brush in front of him. He stopped in his tracks.

There, not far away, came a grunting sound. Within a few short moments, the grunting turn into a growl.

Tobi readied his spear just as a wild boar charged out of the thicket, squealing in anger as it rushed toward him.

He heard shouts from Hadad and Shalim but could not make out what they said. Time seemed to slow down as the distance between him and the brownish-gray beast shrunk.

Tobi froze, unsure of what to do. A part of him wanted to stand firm with his spear, but another part told him to drop it and run.

The enraged animal drew closer as the squeals grew louder. Tobi's heart raced and, in a moment of panic, he dropped the spear and ran.

Shouts came from the other men, but Tobi could not hear them. All that mattered was escape.

He pumped his legs as fast as he could. Glancing over his shoulder, he saw that the boar was nearly on top of him.

Just then, Tobi's foot caught a tree root and he stumbled. Unable to regain his balance, he hit the ground hard and cried out as the impact shot pain into his old wound. Bracing himself for the boar's attack, he curled up into a ball and shut his eyes.

A squeal of pain erupted from the boar.

Tobi looked up and saw that an arrow stuck out of the animal. Yet still, it kept charging, its eyes wide with panic. Only a few steps separated the boar's tusks from Tobi's body.

Another arrow came in from the other side and hit the boar, knocking it to the ground. Then a third arrow landed.

The boar let out a weak squeal of pain as it lay panting on the ground. Soon the breathing lessened, and then it stopped.

Kenaz arrived first at Tobi's position. "Are you all right, my lord?" He held out his hand.

"I think so." Tobi took it and stood up.

Hadad and Shalim arrived next.

"He's a big one," said Hadad. He prodded the animal with his bow.

Shalim nodded. "Yes, and aggressive. It's mating season." He put a hand on Tobi's shoulder and looked at him up and down. "Any injuries?"

Tobi shook his head. His side still hurt, but his biggest injury was one of embarrassment and shame. *Now they know that I'm a coward.*

Hadad came over and handed Tobi's spear to him. "You dropped this."

"Keep it." Tobi turned and stormed off in anger toward the house.

"My lord!" Kenaz shouted.

Tobi ignored him. He needed to get out of there as fast as he could. As he reached the tree line, he heard footsteps come from behind him.

"Just leave me alone, Kenaz."

The footsteps continued.

He spun around. "Kenaz!" But it was not Kenaz.

Shalim stood there, his face full of sympathy and concern.

"What do you want?" Tobi asked.

Shalim spoke with gentleness. "To talk with you."

"I don't want to talk."

"But you need to," replied Shalim.

Tobi waved him away. "Don't you have a boar to gut?"

Shalim shook his head. "No. It's unclean, so it's not for eating."

Tobi threw up his hands in frustration. "The animal nearly kills me, but we can't even eat it because your God says so? Seems arbitrary."

"I know it seems that way," Shalim replied, "but it isn't. And this isn't about what to eat or not eat, is it?"

Tobi did not want to admit it, but Shalim was right. Brimming with anger and frustration, he pointed a finger at him. "Your God is just like any other god. He's as cruel as they are, maybe worse. Commanding the Israelites to kill men, women, and children!"

Shalim appeared unbothered by the outburst. "Tobi, my God judges evil because he is righteous and just. And even then he is long-suffering and patient with those who break his law."

"But what makes his laws any better than Moloch's?" Tobi snapped.

"For starters," answered Shalim, "my God gives value to all people because they are made in his image. Whether children or adults. Whether born or unborn. In fact, if a man hurts a pregnant woman and causes the unborn baby to die, God says that his life is forfeit."

Tobi stood silent, trying to figure out how to respond.

Shalim continued. "Moloch requires parents to murder their own children to get a blessing. But God says that the children themselves are the blessing. To sacrifice them for your own benefit is an abomination. That's why God has sent the Israelites to invade. And that's why they will win."

He held up a finger. "But still, the Lord will forgive all who genuinely repent and ask for forgiveness, without exception. For he is merciful."

Tobi crossed his arms in defiance. "My god is the same."

Shalim's voice turned firm. "No, he isn't, and you know it. Moloch demands and never forgives. His appetite is never satisfied. And even if you do everything right, there's no guarantee of his blessing. There is no peace." He pointed at Tobi. "You have no peace."

Tobi's face turned red with rage. "No, it's only because my people failed to serve Moloch that these things have happened. That's all!"

Shalim shook his head. "It's because you serve Moloch that the Lord is judging you. Moloch is no god. He is simply a piece of black stone that you carry in your pocket."

Tobi scoffed. "I saw the God of Israel. He's no different. I saw the golden box that the Israelites worship."

Shalim's eyes widened. "You saw the Ark of the Covenant?"

"The what?"

"The Ark," Shalim repeated. "It contains the stone tablets that bind Israel to God and God to them. Their covenant documents."

"But what about those winged creatures on top?" Tobi asked.

Shalim smiled. "Those are the angels who serve in the presence of God. I've never seen the Ark, but I've heard it described."

A look of confusion came over Tobi's face.

Shalim demonstrated with his hands. "The God of Israel sits between the angels."

Tobi paused in thought. "But—there's nothing there."

"Exactly," said Shalim. "The God of Israel is not made by human hands. He is not contained in an object, either natural or man-made."

Tobi laughed mockingly. "So, he is a god that can't even show himself?"

Shalim sighed. "He shows himself in his actions and in his words. His name is Yahweh, for he is the one who is. All other gods have ears but do not hear, eyes but do not see, and mouths but do not speak."

Tobi did not respond. The words caught him off guard.

"Your god is no god at all, Tobi." Shalim pointed at him. "Your name, Tobimelech, means 'Moloch is good.' You say that Moloch is your god and your king. Yet a good king does not sacrifice his people for himself. A good king sacrifices himself for his people."

How dare you! Tobi roared in anger and frustration as he charged at Shalim.

As if expecting it, Shalim dodged the attack and, with a few swift motions, sent Tobi crashing to the ground.

Both Kenaz and Hadad, who had kept their distance, ran up to them.

"My lord, stop this madness!" Kenaz shouted at Tobi.

Shalim held up his hand. "It's all right, Kenaz."

Tobi groaned as he got up. For a moment he considered rushing at Shalim again, but decided against it. Without another word, he stomped off, cursing repeatedly.

Shalim's words echoed in Tobi's mind as he went. He shook his head fervently. *He's wrong about Moloch. He's wrong about me. I have peace.* He let out a sigh. *No, I don't. But I don't care. I hate him and his God.*

Looking to the west, Tobi spotted the olive orchard. He decided to head there rather than return to the house. He could not face Nikkal. Not now. Not after what just happened. *I'm a failure. I failed to protect my son, I failed to protect my wife, and I can't even protect myself.*

After confirming that no one followed him into the orchard, he retrieved the wineskin from his pack. He took a quick drink, hoping that a little wine would make him feel better. It did not. He needed more.

He paced the orchard in frustration, muttering between drinks. "I'm not responsible. She's the one who ruined the ceremony. She cried out. Not me."

He drank again. "And it was her idea to go to the altar of Asherah, not mine. How was I supposed to know? It's not my fault."

War raged in his mind. *What about the Battle of Jahaz?* "Not my fault," he replied. "I did my part. Sihon had been stupid, arrogant, and hasty."

Another drink.

What about the farm? "Not my fault either," he answered. "I can't control the weather, or the insects. I did everything I was supposed to do." *Except protect your wife and son.*

After draining the wineskin, he threw it to the ground with a curse. *I need another drink, and then I'm going back to Rabbah.*

Glancing up at the sky, he realized that he did not have enough time to pack his things and leave the farm that day. He would just have to spend one more night here. After that, he would leave, with or without Nikkal.

Satisfied at his decision, Tobi stumbled his way back to the house.

When he arrived, he guessed that the other men must have not yet returned, for the women were surprised to see him enter the house alone.

Nikkal came up to him, her voice worried. "Is everything all right, Tobi?"

Ignoring her question, he grabbed a full wineskin hanging on the wall and climbed up the ladder to their room.

He heard Nikkal follow him but said nothing. When he reached their room, he sat himself on the mat and began to drink.

She came over and sat next to him. "What happened? Where are the others?"

Tobi drank deeply before answering. "Oh, they're fine. A wild boar came at us—er—came at me."

She began to look him over. "Were you hurt?"

He laughed and shook his head. "No, I ran like a coward while the others killed it. It worked out well." He turned to her, sarcasm in his voice. "You must be very proud, Nik."

"I—I love you, Tobi." She placed her hand on his arm. "It doesn't matter what happened."

"Would you still love me if I said I was leaving tomorrow?"

She nodded. "And I would go with you."

He paused, caught off guard by her response. *Is she trying to trick me into following the God of Israel?* Anger surged within him, and he shook off her hand. "Fine, but when we get back to Rabbah, we're serving my family's gods. No debate."

She placed her hands calmly in her lap. "I'll go with you, Tobi, as your wife, but I will not worship those gods." Her words were gentle, but firm.

He raised his voice, intending to break her defiance. "Yes, you will! You're my wife, and you'll do as I say!"

Her voice remained resolute. "Tobi, I can't stop you from serving your gods, but I cannot join you. I'll follow you in all my duties as your wife, but I will not follow you into sin."

"Then you are not my wife!"

Tears filled Nikkal's eyes. "If you wish to leave me, I won't stop you."

He lifted the wineskin to his lips, but she stopped his hand with hers. "I want to be your wife," she continued, "and I want you to be my husband. But I want you to lead me as a husband should—"

She paused and wiped her eyes. "And if you lead me down the right path, I'll follow you, always. I love you, Tobi."

Tobi tried to force back his own tears but could not. He began to sob.

Nikkal moved to put her arms around him, but he shrugged them off. "No, leave me alone."

"Okay," she replied. She got up and left.

Tobi did not look up, but heard her begin to cry as she departed.

He sat there alone with his thoughts. *Why was she so nice to him? What trick was she playing?*

He remembered the wineskin in his hand and put it to his lips. After draining it dry, he tossed it away and fell back upon the mat.

His mind raced with questions, questions that he did not have the answers to. Everything seemed to be spinning. The room, his mind, his life. He began to think of Ali.

As drunken sleep overtook him, Tobi slipped his hand into his tunic and touched his son's wooden horse.

CHAPTER SEVENTEEN

Betharan, Fall 1407 BC

NIKKAL FELT GROGGY WHEN she came down for breakfast. She had not slept well the previous night, having waited until Tobi had drunk himself to sleep before going to bed herself. Even then, the memory of his harsh words to her, coupled with her anxiety about returning to Rabbah, kept her awake.

When she entered the main room, she found Kenaz, Shalim, and Ishara already in casual conversation. Nikkal sighed in relief when she remembered that today was the Sabbath. She had no desire to work and wanted to enjoy what might be the last day she ever saw her grandparents.

Ishara smiled at Nikkal and gestured for her to join them. "Good morning, Nik."

"Good morning." Nikkal plopped herself down onto the empty cushion next to her.

Kenaz poured a cup of water and handed it to Nikkal.

"Thank you," she replied.

He nodded to her. "How is he, my lady?"

Nikkal took a sip before answering. "Drunk—and sleeping. He's leaving today I think."

Ishara gave her a concerned look. "And what about you, dear?"

Nikkal sighed. "It won't be easy, but I'm going to follow your advice. I'm going to submit to him in all things except sin."

"You'll leave us too, then?" asked Shalim. He did not conceal the sorrow in his voice.

Nikkal nodded.

Ishara placed a comforting hand on her shoulder. "I'm proud of you, Nik. You're doing the right thing. You won't win Tobi over by fighting him. All you can do is love him and leave the rest to God."

Nikkal gave her a weak smile. "I know, but it's easier said than done."

Ishara chuckled. "Absolutely. That's why we must rely on the Lord. And no matter what happens, know that God is watching over you."

"We will be praying for you both," added Shalim.

"Thank you," Nikkal replied. She looked over at Kenaz. "And what about you, Kenaz? What will you do?"

He seemed taken aback by her question. "My lady?"

She gestured to Shalim and Ishara. "Well, I imagine you could stay here with my grandparents, if you like. Or you could head back to Edom and rejoin your kinsmen."

He shook his head. "No, my lady. My place is with you and Master Tobi."

She respected his decision, considering all that he had done for them. But a question still lingered in her mind. "And what about the gods? Do you still serve them?"

Kenaz glanced over at Shalim and then back to Nikkal. "My lady, I've doubted the gods for many years. My people trace their line back to Esau, the brother of Jacob, who was called Israel. And ever since I learned of my people's history, I've believed in the God of Abraham, Isaac, and Jacob."

Nikkal let out a gasp of astonishment. "But you never said anything."

He shrugged. "I quickly learned that a slave is to openly follow his master's gods, and so I kept my own thoughts hidden."

He then gave a quick nod to Shalim. "But now I realize that I was living in fear, not in faith."

"So, what now?" Nikkal asked.

A determined look came upon his face. "Now, like you, I will follow Master Tobi, but I will not follow his gods."

"But what if you were free?" Nikkal replied. "Where would you go then?"

Kenaz paused in thought. "I would either stay with you and Master Tobi or stay here. But I wouldn't go back to Edom. Edom now hates Israel, although it was not always that way. Esau once embraced Jacob upon seeing him. I want to do the same with the Israelites."

Nikkal nodded. She did not expect to convince Tobi to set Kenaz free anyway. He had too much value as a slave.

As if anticipating her thought-process, Kenaz held up a finger. "But I do not want my freedom, my lady. I cannot abandon you and Master Tobi during such a time as this."

Nikkal considered dissuading him, but decided against it. *He can make his own decisions.* "Thank you, Kenaz. Your loyalty means a lot to me."

He bowed his head. "You're most welcome, my lady."

After Shalim led them in a time of prayer, they all ate breakfast together, and were soon joined by Hadad and his family.

After about an hour, Tobi came down. When he entered the room, both Kenaz and Nikkal stood.

Nikkal gestured for Kenaz to sit back down as she went over to Tobi. She pointed to her now empty cushion. "Why don't you sit and eat for a bit? I'm going to go up and start packing for us, okay?"

Tobi nodded but did not reply.

Nikkal left the room. She took a deep breath as she climbed the ladder to the second floor. "Lord, please change his heart," she whispered.

Tobi only half-listened to the conversation. His head hurt and he did not have much of an appetite. Still, he forced himself to drink some water.

No one, not even Kenaz, attempted to make conversation with him. And Tobi did not want conversation. He wanted to leave, and he hoped that Nikkal would not take too long to gather their belongings.

Hadad and his family finished breakfast and left the table shortly after Tobi arrived. Ishara soon followed. Only Shalim and Kenaz then remained with him. The three of them sat there as Tobi rubbed his head with his fingers.

Without warning, Shalim broke the silence. "Word is that Heshbon fell to the Israelites a few days ago. And now King Og has decided to avenge his brother and attack them."

Tobi looked up at him. "So?"

"So," continued Shalim, "with Heshbon destroyed and war between Og and Israel imminent, your journey back to Rabbah is going to be dangerous."

Tobi paused for a moment, considering the warning. He then shrugged. "I'll take my chances."

Shalim nodded. "Fair enough." He stood from the table. "But before you leave, Tobi, will you take a walk with me?"

Tobi felt confused. "Right now?"

"Why not?" said Shalim. "It's a nice morning, and it would be good to do something different today."

Tobi spoke with a mixture of curiosity and mockery. "Isn't this your day of rest?"

Shalim smiled. "Rest from work, but not from enjoying God's creation."

Tobi paused in thought. *The cool air would feel good, and Nikkal still needs time to pack.* He nodded. "Okay, but just for a little bit."

"Deal," Shalim replied. "I'll make sure that you, Nik, and Kenaz can depart by mid-morning." He turned and retrieved a walking stick that leaned against the wall.

Tobi drained his cup of water and moved to follow him outside.

The morning air felt refreshing to Tobi's lungs. He glanced up at the overcast skies. *Finally, rain. Maybe even today.*

As the two men walked side-by-side, they did not speak. Tobi took advantage of the quietness to reflect on Shalim's farm. It always seemed peaceful and well-ordered, a marked difference from his family's farm back in Rabbah. There, things were always in crisis, always intense.

They soon approached the olive orchard, which made Tobi feel awkward, given his previous day's bout of drunkenness. In an attempt to distract his own mind, he decided to talk business. "How have your harvests here been recently?" he asked.

Shalim glanced over at him and smiled. "Fairly good. I paid off the debt years ago and have been able to maintain a steady profit since."

Tobi's jaw dropped. "How is that possible?"

Shalim shrugged. "Well, the Lord has provided enough workers each year, especially during planting and harvesting. And Hadad has been very helpful, although the loss of Emet has hurt us."

Tobi stopped walking. "No, I mean, how have you avoided the droughts, floods, insects, and wild beasts? How have you avoided losing crops and livestock every year?"

Shalim turned to him. "I won't say that I haven't had my share of troubles. I'm familiar with what's been happening in your lands. Some of it has to do with your farming methods. But I think that the real reason is something deeper . . ."

"You mean judgment?"

Shalim nodded.

Tobi scanned the olive trees in front of him. They were healthy, unlike the fig trees back in Rabbah. Despair entered his heart, and, for whatever reason, he felt an urgent need to confide in Shalim.

Tobi looked down at the ground, his voice somber. "My father's farm is failing. The last few years we've seen crop failures, disease, and insects. And our livestock has been diminished, not only by beasts but also by thieves."

His hand moved to his recently healed wound. "I joined Sihon's army both to honor the gods and to save the farm. Sihon said that Israel had gold and silver that they had taken from Egypt. He promised us that, if we fought for him, we would be rich with plunder."

"He wasn't wrong," replied Shalim.

Tobi looked at him with surprise.

Shalim's face turned serious. "The Israelites did bring a lot of gold and silver with them from Egypt. It was payment that God required the Egyptians to make for the many years of Israel's slavery." He shook his head. "For Sihon to think that he could just take Israel's God-given inheritance from them was foolish."

"Yet you beat them," replied Tobi. "You even took one of them as a slave."

Shalim laughed. "Ha! And you see how that worked out for me and my family? Hated and rejected by my own kin—even my own son." He paused. "But in all seriousness, I would not change anything that happened. I did not capture an Israelite. The God of Israel captured me."

Shalim then walked up to Tobi and stared at him with piercing eyes. "And you did not lose to the Israelites. You lost to the God of Israel."

Tobi paused and reflected on the Battle of Jahaz. Somehow he knew that Shalim was right. He let out a resigned sigh. "Yes, I realize that now."

This time, Shalim seemed to be the one caught off guard. But he said nothing, and appeared to wait for Tobi to go on.

Tobi gazed off in the distance as he described the events leading up to the battle. He told Shalim about the stinging insects, the attacking lions, the cruel heat, and the intense dust storm.

"Everything was against us," said Tobi. "Even during the battle. The rocks, the wind, the earth. Nothing went right, no matter what we did."

He locked eyes with Shalim. "How is that possible? How could the gods of the Amorites be so weak in their own land?"

"Because," Shalim replied, "the God of Israel is not just the God of the hills. He is also the God of the valleys. There is not one plot of land that does not belong to the Lord. And he will have no rival."

Shalim placed a hand on Tobi's shoulder. "And now you must decide whether to surrender to him or to keep fighting against him. If you surrender to the Lord, he is merciful and will welcome you just as he did me. But if you fight him, you will lose. And you will die."

Tobi said nothing. *Surrender or fight?* He did not know.

After a moment, Shalim pointed to a small gap in the trees bordering the olive orchard. "Through there is a path, known only to me and Hadad, and now you, that will take you to the main road just east of Betharan, away from the town. From it you, Nikkal, and Kenaz can make your way to Rabbah."

He then turned and pointed to the way that they had come. "That direction leads you back to my farm, and to your new family, if you want them. But the choice is yours. It's a choice of either life or death."

Tobi's voice trembled. "But how can I trust in the Lord after all that's happened—after all I've been through? How can I abandon the gods?"

"How can you not?" Shalim replied. "Every man is responsible for himself and for those under his care. You abandoned your son when you let him be burned, and you abandoned your wife when you let her be ravaged."

Tobi winced at the words.

Shalim then pulled up the sleeve of his left arm, revealing several faded scars. "The servants of Baal say that victimhood is the key to power. That's why they cut themselves. They think that their blood, pain, and suffering will ultimately save them."

Images of the parade in Jericho flooded into Tobi's mind as he stared at Shalim's arm. He imagined him as a black-robed priest, spilling his own blood upon the ground. *He was once one of them!*

Shalim let his sleeve fall back down. "But it is not glorious to play the victim. Neither is it leadership to turn others into victims. So, you must ask yourself if you are being the leader that you are supposed to be."

Tobi bristled at Shalim's words. A concoction of anger, shame, and guilt bubbled up inside him. He wanted to lash out in defense of his honor.

As if anticipating hostility, Shalim raised his hands in a sign of peace. "You can't undo what's been done, Tobi. But you can decide what your next step is. The choice is yours. Your people have chosen to follow gods of wood and stone, gods in whom there is no life, only death; gods in whom there is no forgiveness, only guilt."

He then nodded to Tobi. "You have to decide whether to continue in the folly of your ancestors or to choose to follow Yahweh, the God of heaven and earth, who made all things and who can forgive all things."

A smile broke out on Shalim's face. "And if you choose Yahweh, you can be sure that you will have a new family. But you have to die first by giving up the old gods. Die now and live or live now and die."

Tobi did not answer. He could not answer. His mind swirled with conflict and doubt. *Life or death? Is it really that simple?*

Shalim turned and walked back to the house. Tobi watched him go, uncertain as to what to do next. He needed time. He needed to think.

Reaching into his tunic, he pulled out the onyx idol of Moloch. He had not looked at it since just before the Battle of Jahaz. As he turned the idol over in his hands, he considered the events of his life. Had his family been worshiping false gods? Had he been wrong to offer his son to Moloch?

He took out his son's toy horse and beheld it. If Moloch was a false god, then he had sacrificed his son for nothing. His son died a horrible death. And all of it was Tobi's fault. *What kind of a father does that? The wicked kind.*

Tobi's head swam. He found a nearby olive tree and sat down with his back against it. Holding Moloch's idol in one hand and Ali's horse in another, he began to weep. The tears came strong and sudden. He did not know how long he wept but soon the tears stopped, and he sat there in silence.

Fatigue hit him and he closed his eyes. He wanted to sleep. But more than that, he wanted to dream. His people had always valued dreams and visions. And though he had dreamed many times in his life, they had never been significant. They had been the typical ones: falling, appearing naked in public, or being unable to run while wild animals chased him.

As he drifted off, he whispered. "God of Israel, if you are real, show yourself to me . . ."

Tobi found himself back at the Battle of Jahaz, marching with Sihon's army toward the Israelite line. He could not remember how he had gotten there. *Didn't this already happen? And why am I in the front row?*

He heard a rumbling sound and looked up. Dark clouds hung above the battlefield, casting an eerie shadow over the landscape.

Gripping his shield and spear tightly, he moved forward. He glanced to his right to speak to Kenaz but stopped when he realized that he was not there. Another soldier, unknown to Tobi, stood in his place. *Where's Kenaz?*

Tobi turned and focused his attention on the Israelite warriors in front of him. They seemed larger, stronger, and more menacing than he remembered.

As if on cue, music and singing reached Tobi's ears and he shifted his eyes to the center of the Israelite army. There sat the golden box surrounded by priests, musicians, and singers. *The Ark of the Covenant.*

"Move forward!" shouted a man behind him. He recognized Commander Amurrum's voice.

Tobi turned in anger, spear raised, ready to run it through Amurrum's chest. But he stopped himself as soon as he saw his commander.

Amurrum did not appear to be human, or if he was, he looked like some grotesque version of a human. His body had become decayed, with bones and veins visible and bits of flesh hanging off him.

Frightened, Tobi glanced around him and saw that all the soldiers looked similar. Their ghoulish faces stared at him and grinned.

He looked down at his own hands and realized that they too were rotten. He screamed as he dropped his spear and shield.

"Coward!" The demon-like Amurrum moved toward him with his sword unsheathed.

Tobi ran away from Amurrum and toward the front line of Israel. The Israelites reacted by tightening their lines and lowering their spears. Tobi stopped himself an arm's length away from the deadly wall they formed.

He then heard Nikkal's voice. "Tobi!"

Scanning for the source of the sound, he found that it came from behind Israel's lines. Then he spotted her. She stood next to a figure clothed in white, but Tobi could not make out the figure's face. He gasped when he noticed that she held a baby in her arms. *Ali? How is that possible?*

He waved to her and shouted. "Nik!"

She waved back and beckoned him to come to her.

Determined to reach her position, Tobi began frantically searching for an opening in the wall of spears.

"Don't even try it!" barked Amurrum. "You think they'll welcome you? A man who kills his own son and gives his wife to another?"

Tobi froze as guilt and grief overwhelmed him. *Amurrum is right. How could they accept me? How could she accept me?*

Yet he still loved Nikkal. And he knew that she loved him too. *I want to be with her, to be the husband that she needs me to be.*

He continued probing for an opening in Israel's lines. In one instance, he came too close to a spearman and received a gash on his arm for it.

Tobi yelled in frustration at the Israelite who wounded him. "Please, let me pass!"

The warrior did not respond.

Thunder rumbled again. Louder this time. The area darkened to the point that Tobi could no longer see Nikkal's face.

Panicking, he glanced back over his shoulder. Amurrum was now just a few steps away.

He then heard Shalim's voice in his head. "You have to decide. Die now and live or live now and die."

"C'mon, Ammonite!" Amurrum shouted. "Pick up your weapon and fight!"

Tobi steeled himself and faced Amurrum. "No, I'm done fighting."

He then turned and ran full speed toward the Israelites. He felt their spear tips penetrate all throughout his body. Several spears entered his lungs, and he soon found himself unable to breathe.

The Israelite warriors lifted Tobi's skewered body so that his feet no longer touched the ground. The pain turned excruciating as their spear tips sank deeper into his flesh. He tried to cry out, but no sound came.

Fighting to stay awake, he searched for Nikkal. He soon found her among the crowd and realized with joy that he could see her face again. She smiled and then nodded to him as if she were proud of what he had just done.

With the last bit of his strength, he looked up at the dark sky. Rain drops hit his face and he closed his eyes.

Tobi gasped for air as he jolted awake. He still sat in Shalim's olive orchard, leaning against the same tree. His side felt sore, and he realized that he must have been sleeping in that position for a while.

A rain drop landed on him. And then another. They began to increase in intensity as thunder rumbled above him.

When he moved to get up, he noticed that he still held both the idol of Moloch in one hand and his son's toy horse in another. Seeing the black idol caused a wave of anger and disgust to wash over him.

He stood and turned toward where the orchard bordered the wilderness. Reaching back, he threw the idol of Moloch as hard as he could into the trees. The sound of stone on wood came back to him, and then there was silence. *What did I just do?*

Tobi waited for a feeling of guilt, but none came. Instead, he felt free.

He let out a sigh of relief and, satisfied that he had made the right decision, put his son's horse back into his tunic and turned toward the house. Even as the rain pummeled him, Tobi had never been more hopeful. He knew where he needed to go. *I'm going home.*

Nikkal fidgeted as she paced around the room.

"Don't worry," said Shalim. "He knows the way."

She nodded but remained unconvinced. "But why hasn't he come back yet?"

Shalim sighed. "He needed some time to think. He'll be all right."

She did not respond. Numerous thoughts flooded into her mind. *What if he was attacked by wild beasts? What if he needs help? What if he left me for good?*

She looked over at Kenaz, who sat near her grandfather. Kenaz appeared concerned as well, although he apparently hid it better than she did.

Nikkal considered asking Kenaz to go search for her husband when the front door opened. Tobi, drenched from head to toe, stepped inside.

"Tobi!" She ran over to greet him.

As soon as he saw her, he smiled. Not just a polite smile, but one of genuine love.

Not caring about getting her own clothes wet, Nikkal threw her arms around him.

He held her tight.

Both Kenaz and Shalim stood and approached him.

Shalim spoke first. "How was it out there? You were gone for quite some time."

"I fell asleep."

"I see," replied Shalim. He sounded disheartened.

Tobi sighed. "I also had some time to think about you said."

Nikkal turned and gave her grandfather a look of curiosity.

Shalim's eyebrows went up. "Oh? And what did you decide?"

Tobi shook his head. "I can't go back. The things that matter to me most are here. My family—is here."

"And what about the gods of your people?" Shalim asked.

Tobi glanced at Nikkal, then Kenaz, and then back at Shalim. "I want the truth, wherever that leads me. Moloch is a lie. But the God of Israel—I know he's real. He spared me at Jahaz, I know it. He's given me a chance to walk a different path. And I'm ready to do that."

Shalim smiled and placed his hand on Tobi's shoulder. "Then embrace me as a son would embrace his father."

The two men hugged. When they separated, both had tears in their eyes.

Shalim placed his right hand on Tobi's head. "You are no longer to be called Tobimelech but are now to be called Tobiah, for Yahweh alone is good."

Tobiah nodded. "Thank you—father."

Shalim then clapped his hands. "Well now, I think that a celebration is in order."

He turned toward the adjoining room. "Ishara! Our son lives! Come see!"

Nikkal felt tears of joy well up inside her. She had her husband back. No, she had a new husband. A husband who wanted to follow the God of Israel.

"What?" Ishara came in from the adjoining room, a look of confusion on her face. But after a few moments, she seemed to understand what had happened. She cried out in joy and threw her arms around Tobiah. "Welcome home, son."

She gestured towards Tobiah's clothes. "My goodness you're drenched! Hold on, let me get you some fresh clothes." She rushed out.

Tobiah turned to Kenaz and held out his hand.

Once Kenaz was within arm's length, Tobiah pulled him in and hugged him. "I never thanked you for saving my life." His voice quivered with emotion. "But thank you."

"I've only done my duty, my lord," Kenaz replied. "But you're welcome."

Both men laughed.

Tobiah cleared his throat. "Speaking of duty. I would like you to return to Edom, to your people."

"My lord?"

"You're free, Kenaz. You've earned it."

Kenaz at first seemed startled. But after a moment he spoke. "This morning. Lady Nikkal asked me what I would do with my freedom. I answered that question, not sure that the opportunity would ever come."

He looked at Nikkal and then back to Tobiah. "But my answer remains the same as before. I do not wish to have my freedom. I love you both as family and wish to remain with you. My people are here as well."

"Are you sure?" asked Tobiah.

"Yes."

Tobiah nodded. "Okay then."

Ishara returned carrying a stack of dry clothes. She handed them to Tobiah. "Here, now go change."

Shalim interjected. "And rest! For tonight we celebrate!"

Tobiah smiled, nodded, and left the room.

Nikkal walked up to Ishara. "How can I help prepare for dinner?"

Ishara chuckled. "You can help by bringing down your husband's wet clothes."

"All right." Nikkal turned to go.

"But take your time up there," Ishara continued. "I don't want to see you down here before dinner."

Nikkal nodded and smiled. She felt butterflies in her stomach as she approached the ladder that led up to her and Tobiah's bedroom. Her heartbeat grew faster with every step she took.

When she reached the top, Nikkal spotted Tobiah struggling to get his wet tunic off. Without a word, she went up to him. "Here, let me help you."

"Thank you," he replied.

As she worked to peel off his clothes, a wooden object fell out and hit the floor with a thump.

Startled, she bent down to see it. "What is—" Her eyes widened as she picked it up and examined it. "Is this—Ali's horse?"

Tobiah nodded. "Yes."

She turned it over in her hands. "Where did you find this?"

"At Tophet, after—after it was over." He seemed on the verge of tears.

A mixture of anger and confusion gripped Nikkal, but she fought to control herself. "Why didn't you tell me about this?"

Tobi wiped his eyes. "I was afraid, Nik. Afraid that if I showed it to you, you'd hate Moloch even more. That you'd hate me even more."

He laid his hands over hers as she gripped the horse. "For weeks I was afraid to even look at it myself. I was afraid that I'd grieve too much and anger Moloch."

Before she could respond, he covered his face with his hands and began to sob. "I'm sorry Nik. I'm sorry for everything. I—I'm sorry for not being a good husband and father. For not protecting you and Ali when I should have. Will you forgive me?"

Nikkal felt her own tears run down her cheeks. Without hesitation, she pulled his hands away from his face and looked at him. She nodded. "Yes, of course. And will you forgive me?"

Tobiah seemed confused. "For what?"

"For my bitterness and resentment toward you."

He smiled, nodded, and pulled her in close. "Of course, Nik."

They kissed. At first it felt gentle, formal. But soon it turned passionate. For the first time in a long time, Nikkal felt close to him. The tension, anxiety, and anger vanished. She now felt a deeper love for him than she had ever felt before. Time no longer mattered. All that mattered now was that they were together. They were one.

PART FOUR

The Family

CHAPTER EIGHTEEN

Betharan, Winter 1406 BC

TOBIAH DREW BACK HIS bowstring and focused his eyes on the man in front of him. Sighting his arrow onto the man's chest, Tobiah thanked the Lord that his target stood still.

Just before releasing, he held his breath as Shalim had taught him.

Twang. The arrow flew fast toward its target. Tobiah watched with anticipation as it impacted the man's left arm. The straw man did not flinch.

Shalim patted Tobiah's shoulder. "Not bad."

Tobiah shook his head. "I haven't hit the chest consistently yet."

"But you're getting better each time."

"I know, but still." Tobiah let out a sigh of frustration.

"Look." said Shalim. He stepped up next to Tobiah and pretended to draw his bow. "I've noticed that when you release, you are quick to see how your shot landed."

He lowered his bow as he continued. "Just try to consciously force yourself to follow through as we practiced, and not be too eager to see where it hits."

Tobiah nodded.

"All right," said Shalim, "let's retrieve the arrows and move on to something else."

They both walked in silence toward the straw man.

It had been about three months since Tobiah had chosen to stay with his new family, and since then he had felt a joy and a peace that he had not felt for a long time, if ever. He and Nikkal had begun being more honest and open with one another, although they still had some difficulty talking about Tophet and Jericho.

When Tobiah eventually recounted his own dream to Nikkal, she told him about hers. Both had marveled at how God had drawn them closer to him, and as a result, closer to each other. They then shared their dreams with the rest of the family, who also praised God for his grace and mercy.

Tobiah glanced over at Shalim as the approached the target. "Thank you, father."

Shalim shot him a curious glance. "For what? Teaching you how to shoot?"

Tobiah smiled. "That, and everything else."

"Well, all glory be to God. I'm thankful for you too." Shalim laughed. "Without you and Kenaz, the plowing and planting after the first rains would have been difficult, to say the least."

Tobiah nodded. Their extra hands had made things easier. And with olive oil production for the year complete, Tobiah had plenty of time now to learn, rest, and grow in his new faith.

The same was true for Nikkal. Over the winter, Ishara had begun teaching her how to manage a household and to read and write. Nikkal still had a ways to go, but she had shown herself to be fast learner.

As for Tobiah, besides learning about building repair and hunting, he also gained skills in self-defense. Hadad had given him some lessons, but most of them came from Shalim.

Shalim reached the target first and began to pluck out the arrows.

"I'll get the ones that flew far," said Tobiah.

"Thank you," Shalim replied.

Tobiah walked past the straw man to where some of his earlier arrows had landed. He had hit the target more times today than before, but still not as often as he wanted. Archery was not his favorite method of fighting, but he was glad to learn it.

Rapid footsteps approached him from behind. He turned and saw Shalim bearing down on him. Tobiah dropped his bow and arrows and dove out of the way. He felt Shalim's arms brush against his side but recovered his balance and turned to prepare for the next attack.

Shalim had also recovered and now stood facing Tobiah. His face broke out into a smile. "Well done. You were paying attention this time." He then rushed in, aiming for Tobiah's legs.

Tobiah jumped backward at an angle and then lunged in to attack Shalim from his now exposed left side.

Shalim tried to anticipate it, but to no effect. He let out a grunt as Tobiah's knee landed. Despite the hit, Shalim grabbed Tobiah's other leg and knocked him off balance.

Both men tumbled to the ground and began to wrestle for an advantage over the other.

Tobiah felt Shalim's arms wrap around his neck. Staying calm, he grasped Shalim's elbow and bent over while using his hips as leverage.

Shalim tumbled over Tobiah's shoulder and onto the ground. Holding onto Shalim's now captured arm, Tobiah twisted it and put pressure on the shoulder.

"I yield!" cried Shalim.

Tobiah let go of Shalim's arm and then helped him up.

"Very good—too good," said Shalim as he rubbed his shoulder.

"Thank you," Tobiah replied.

Shalim smiled. "You're definitely better at hand-to-hand fighting than archery."

Tobiah let out a chuckle. "Well, that doesn't help much in a real battle." He stooped down and retrieved his bow and arrows.

Shalim shrugged. "That depends. If you plan well, it can help." He retrieved his own bow and signaled for Tobiah to follow him. "Just be sure to close the distance between you and your opponent as quickly as possible. You have both strength and speed, so use them to your advantage."

Tobiah nodded and the two of them headed back to the house. Glancing up at the late afternoon sky, Tobiah felt glad to be done. Shalim had pushed him hard today and he looked forward to the evening meal and a time of rest.

When they arrived at the house, they entered the main room and found only Ishara, Ashima, Nikkal, and Liluri.

Shalim turned to Ishara. "Have Hadad and Kenaz not returned?"

"Not yet, dear," Ishara replied.

"Odd."

"Should we wait for them?" she asked.

"Perhaps just a bit longer," he replied.

She nodded.

Tobiah followed Shalim back to where they stored their weapons. He felt uneasy about Hadad and Kenaz. *Where are they? They're never late for evening meal.*

He glanced over at Shalim. "They only went to Betharan to sell olive oil and purchase some supplies, right?"

Shalim nodded as he unstrung his bow. "If they're still not back after the evening meal, we'll go search for them, all right?"

"All right." Tobiah unpacked and stored his own weapons before heading to the table.

As he approached, Nikkal came up and hugged him. "I missed you today."

"I missed you too." He kissed her.

They sat down, and Tobiah poured a cup of wine for them both.

Nikkal gave him a worried look. "What do you think is delaying Hadad and Kenaz?"

"I'm not sure."

"Could the Israelites have already captured Betharan?" she asked.

Tobiah shook his head. "I don't think so. Israel just killed King Og at Edrei and is now fighting the Midianites."

He took a sip of his wine. "Even if the Midianites were already defeated, I just don't see how Israel could have reorganized themselves quick enough to push west so soon."

She paused, lifting her own cup to her lips. "But don't they want to cross the Jordan before it floods?"

He nodded. "Yes, and there are several places where they still can. But when the spring rains come the river will be impassable, even for a few soldiers. So, unless they intend to get their entire army across in the next week or so, I don't think they'll rush to take Betharan."

She sighed. "I just—don't want anything to happen to Kenaz and Hadad."

"Neither do I, love."

Ashima and Liluri sat down next to Nikkal. Tobiah knew that it would only be a few more months until Ashima would deliver the baby. The thought of Hadad not being there for the birth of his child bothered him.

Ashima looked at Tobiah. He noticed the anxiety on her face and felt that he should say something. But nothing that sounded helpful came to his mind, so he just elected to pour a cup of wine for her.

"Thank you," she replied.

Once Shalim and Ishara were seated, Shalim cleared his throat. "Listen, I think we should pray for—"

The front door flew open, revealing both Hadad and Kenaz. They appeared tired but unharmed.

Shalim stood as if ready to come to their aid. "Are you both all right?"

"Yes, my lord." Hadad fought to catch his breath. After a few moments, he continued. "We're fine. I'm sorry we're late but—"

Kenaz interjected. "It's crazy out there, my lord! Lots of refugees and soldiers—"

Hadad jumped in. "And soothsayers, witches, and idol peddlers. People are desperate and anxious. It's because—"

Shalim held up his hand. "What matters is that you're both safe." He gestured for them to sit. "Please, let's eat first. Then we'll talk about what's going on out there."

"Yes, my lord," they both replied.

Hadad went and sat next to Ashima while Kenaz sat next to Tobiah.

Shalim bowed his head. "Let us pray and give thanks to the Lord, not only for this food, but for his protection . . ."

Once Shalim finished praying, an air of genuine peace and fellowship settled over the table. Tobiah knew that chaos ran rampant outside of their small farm, yet, on the inside, the joy of the Lord reigned. *This would never happen back at Rabbah.*

That evening's conversation focused upon life on the farm, as well as the excitement surrounding the pending arrival of Hadad and Ashima's baby. After that, Tobiah recounted his hours of training, particularly his ability to defeat Shalim in hand-to-hand combat.

As the meal came to an end, and everyone reclined, Shalim finally asked the question that had been on everyone's mind. He turned to Hadad. "So, what's the latest news?"

Hadad sat up in excitement. "My lord, it's confirmed that Og's kingdom has collapsed and that both Moab and the Midianites moved against Israel."

Shalim gave him a questioning look. "How many of the Midianite kings?"

"All five of them."

Shalim nodded as if unsurprised by the response. "And are you sure about Moab? I thought King Balak had decided to leave Israel alone."

Hadad shook his head. "Balak decided to take a more indirect approach. He's hired the prophet Balaam to curse Israel."

"Well, that must have been no small price. Balaam is the most feared prophet in the land!"

A grin appeared on Hadad's face. "Well, now he's dead."

Shalim's eyes widened. "What?!"

Hadad nodded to Kenaz. "You tell him."

Kenaz spoke up. "A few days ago, the Israelites killed not only all five kings of Midian, but the prophet Balaam as well."

The table fell silent. It was one thing for Israel to defeat Sihon and Og separately. But to then defeat the five kings of Midian and Balaam at the same time was unthinkable. Tobiah knew that this could have been nothing more than an act of God.

Shalim cleared his throat. "So, Israel is on the way?"

Kenaz's voice turned somber. "No, my lord. Their leader, Moses, has also died."

"In the battle?" asked Shalim.

Kenaz shook his head. "No. After Balaam and the kings of Midian were killed, Moses climbed Mount Nebo and never came down."

"Oh . . ." Shalim responded. He stroked his beard. "That's strange. I would not have expected that."

The table fell quiet again.

This time, Nikkal broke the silence. "Why would that be strange?"

"Well," began Shalim, "I just expected that such a righteous man would not die before entering the land promised to him and his people."

Nikkal pointed to where they sat. "But isn't the land east of the Jordan, where we are right now, part of the promised land?"

Shalim paused before answering. "Well, from what Emet told me years ago, the promised land starts at the Jordan and proceeds west to the great sea. But I imagine that they'll keep whatever territory they take in battle."

Tobiah spoke up. "But won't Israel want to cross the Jordan before it's fully flooded, if it isn't flooded already?"

Shalim shook his head. "No, they must wait until their formal period of mourning for Moses is over. It will last thirty days."

"What?" Tobiah replied in disbelief. "If they wait that long, they'll never be able to cross!"

"True," replied Shalim. "Either they'll consolidate their gains now and wait until the dry season or God will work a miracle." He looked at Kenaz. "Where is Israel's army now?"

"They seem to be staying at Mount Nebo."

Shalim nodded. "Then they're close. Once the thirty days is over, they'll come through Betharan on the way to the Jordan. Did you happen to find out who their new leader is?"

"I did," replied Kenaz. "It is Joshua the son of Nun."

"Hmm," replied Shalim. "Emet mentioned him to me a few times. He was one of the scouts who told Israel to invade forty years ago when God had commanded them to do so, but was ignored by the rest of people."

Hadad grew excited. "My lord, should we go to Mount Nebo and try to get a message to Israel? We could tell them that we're not their enemies and that we seek refuge."

Shalim held up a hand. "No, I think the best thing to do is to wait here. I don't want to violate their time of mourning. That gives us about four weeks to prepare. We'll need to gather extra supplies, since the roads will soon become even more dangerous than they already are."

He sighed. "We'll then wait here and, if the Israelites come to the farm, we'll ask for mercy."

"What about refugees?" Nikkal asked. "If the Jordan is already impassable, they'll have nowhere to go."

Shalim thought for a moment and then nodded. "Before the time of mourning ends, we'll make one more trip to Betharan. We'll pick up any final supplies we need and invite others to stay with us on condition that they'll surrender to Israel."

Everyone voiced their agreement with the plan.

Shalim took a sip of wine. When he spoke again, his words were solemn and serious. "The time of judgment has come. We must now trust in God's mercy."

CHAPTER NINETEEN

Betharan, Spring 1406 BC

THE NEXT FEW WEEKS flew by for Tobiah as he and the other men spent their days repairing walls and fences, securing the livestock, and gathering supplies. The women were equally busy making clothing and preparing food for potential refugees.

By the time that Israel's thirty days of mourning were over, Shalim's farm had the capacity to house several families for a few weeks. Tobiah did not expect that many would heed their offer of refuge, especially since any who stayed with them had to agree to surrender to Israel.

His prediction had come true. No one yet answered the call. Still, with the final day of mourning upon them, Tobiah, Kenaz, and Hadad decided to take one more trip to Betharan.

Hadad, who drove the oxen, glanced back at Tobiah and Kenaz. "We should be there shortly. You guys ready?"

Tobiah touched the sword that he had tucked into his tunic and nodded. He watched Kenaz do the same.

Hadad sighed. "I hate crowds. Let's not stay too long."

"I promise we won't," replied Tobiah.

They remained silent as the cart approached Betharan. It did not take long before they heart the expected chatter and shouting coming from the town, whose population had ballooned with refugees over the past several weeks.

When they emerged from the path, Hadad steered the oxen toward the road that ran through the middle of Betharan and west toward Jericho.

Tobiah saw an increase in traffic and felt the heightened tension. Those with children stayed close together and steered clear of any soldiers. As for the soldiers themselves, many appeared to be drunk and walked about as if in a stupefied, trance-like state.

Hadad stopped the oxen just short of the road's edge. "Okay, what's the plan, my lord?"

Tobiah jumped down and nodded to Hadad and Kenaz. "You two stay here with the cart. Offer sanctuary to those families and wounded soldiers who are willing to listen to you. But don't waste your time getting into an argument."

"And what will you do?" replied Hadad.

Tobiah pointed beyond the crowd. "I'll head to the market—if it's still functioning—to gather any new information and purchase the last items that Shalim asked me to get."

Hadad and Kenaz both bowed their heads in acknowledgment.

Tobiah left the cart and began to work his way through the crowd and into the town. As he walked, he scanned the alleys and the edges of the road for any signs of danger. All he saw were prostitutes, beggars, idol sellers, and fanatics.

"Doom! Doom!" one man shouted nearby.

Tobiah turned and saw an elderly man on the side of the road dressed in tattered clothing. The man's unkempt white hair hung over his face, partially obscuring it.

The man raised his hands to the sky and trembled. "The gods have abandoned us because we have abandoned them! Hurry, come back to the gods, and be rescued from the impending doom!"

Tobiah spotted a much younger man next to him, probably his acolyte, peddling wooden and metal idols. He recognized the images of Baal, Moloch, and Asherah. Shaking his head, Tobiah continued walking.

He soon found the market and strode toward one of the open stalls. He thanked the Lord that some merchants were still operating, although he soon realized that they had marked up their prices to ridiculous levels.

Realizing that he probably could not purchase all the items on Shalim's list, he decided to get the most important one, salt, if it were still available.

After trying several merchants, Tobiah found one that still sold salt. He stepped up the booth. "One mina of salt, please."

The merchant, of middle-age and dressed in a robe of fine linen, grinned. "Sure, if you have six shekels of silver."

Tobiah fought to contain his indignation. "Six shekels? That's almost a months' wages! I'll give you two shekels."

The merchant shrugged. "Tomorrow there won't be any salt. But just for you, I'll make it four shekels. Or else you can go do your shopping in Jericho."

"Fine." *This is robbery.* Tobiah drew out four silver shekels. He watched as the merchant weighed out the salt. Satisfied that he was not being cheated, Tobiah handed him the money and received the bag. He tucked the salt into his tunic. "So, what's the latest news?"

The merchant chuckled. "You're seeing it. Israel is headed this way. They'll be here tomorrow, but I won't be."

"Where are you going?"

"Leaving for Jericho in a few hours."

Tobiah nodded. "Sounds like a dangerous journey. Isn't the Jordan flooded?"

"Well, I'd rather take my chances with the river than stay here and die."

Tobiah's tone turned serious, and he leaned in close. "Listen, friend. You are welcome to stay at my family's farm nearby. We can provide food and shelter there."

The statement startled the merchant, who eyed him suspiciously. "And what? Wait for the Israelites to kill me there?"

"No," replied Tobiah. "If they come, we'll surrender to them and ask for mercy."

"Ha!" The merchant mocked. "Israel does not show mercy!"

Tobiah took a risk. "They will to those who repent and stop serving idols. And even if they don't, do you really think that the gods will save you?"

The merchant's face flushed red. "You're a member of Shalim's household, aren't you? Always talking bad about the gods." He pointed an accusing finger at Tobiah. "It's because of traitors like you that the gods have abandoned us!"

He sneered at Tobiah. "But don't worry, you'll get what's coming to you. I'll soon be safe behind the walls of Jericho with all the wine and women I could want, while you'll be here begging for your life."

The merchant dismissed Tobiah with a wave. "So, you go ahead and wait here to die. It's only a matter of time until Israel is gone. Then I'll be back, and life will continue."

Tobiah sighed and turned to leave. As he did, his eyes landed on a nearby soldier who had been staring at him. The man looked familiar, and Tobiah racked his brain to remember where he had seen him from.

Then it hit him. *He's one of Commander Amurrum's men! The one who brought in the deserters!*

Tobiah turned to hide his face, but he knew it was too late. The man had recognized him.

The soldier pointed at him. "Hey, you!"

Tobiah lowered his head and blended in with the crowd as he hurried his way back to Hadad and Kenaz. In the distance, he heard the soldier continue to shout, but the words were drowned out by the throng of refugees.

He breathed a sigh of relief as he approached the cart, but grew nervous when he noticed a family standing next to Hadad. It was a father, mother, and two small boys.

Tobiah addressed Hadad. "I got the salt. We need to go."

"Okay," replied Hadad. His face grew concerned. "Is everything all right?"

Tobiah glanced over his shoulder. "Yeah, I just don't want to stay here any longer than I have to." He gestured toward the family, hoping to change the subject. "Have they agreed to come with us?"

Kenaz nodded. "Yes, my lord, they were the only ones who would even listen."

Brief introductions were made, and Tobiah learned that the man's name was Rimmon.

As the others prepared to depart, Tobiah scanned the crowd for the soldier. *I think I lost him.* Still, he could not wait to leave, and he felt as if Hadad and Kenaz were moving purposefully slow.

Eventually, they were back on the path and on their way home. As soon as Tobiah felt confident that they were not being followed, he began to relax. For a moment he considered telling Kenaz and Hadad about the soldier, but then decided against it. *There's no point now. We're safe.*

He smiled at the two boys, who stared back at him. They appeared to be around nine or ten years of age. He then turned to their father. "So, where are you from, Rimmon?"

Rimmon, who wore close-cropped dark hair, seemed to have a warrior's look about him. "Originally, Heshbon," he replied. "But when Israel arrived, we went to Beth-Peor and stayed with some family for a time."

"Were you a soldier?"

Rimmon glanced down at his battle-scarred hands. "I was once. Years ago, I served in Sihon's army and helped him defeat King Zippor of Moab. In return for my service, Sihon granted me a plot of land in Heshbon."

Tobiah nodded. "If you don't mind me asking, why didn't you join Sihon this time?"

"A fair question," Rimmon replied. His face turned grave. "At first, I thought that Sihon would be a good king, like the great heroes of old. But in his war with Moab, he ordered us to do things that no soldier should do. So, after that, I refused to wield the sword for that man ever again."

Tobiah paused in thought. As a soldier, he had not been ordered to do anything wicked, although he supposed that waging war against the God of Israel was itself wicked enough.

Another question then entered Tobiah's mind. "What made you decide to flee west instead of staying at Beth-Peor?"

Rimmon sighed. "In the chaos that followed Heshbon's fall, the options were to be conquered by warlords or conquered by Israel. I did not think that either would show mercy, so I took my family and fled."

He then leaned forward and gestured to Hadad and Kenaz. "But thanks to your friends, I do believe that the God of Israel offers mercy, even to someone like me. I only wish that others would listen . . ."

Out of curiosity, Tobiah turned to Kenaz. "How many people did you talk to?"

"Probably a dozen, my lord," Kenaz replied. "But none of them would come. They all preferred trying to get to Jericho."

Tobiah nodded. "Somehow I don't think that the Jordan River, nor the walls of Jericho, will be able to stop the Israelites."

The others voiced their agreement.

The pounding on his door came a second time. "Sir!"

Annoyed, Commander Amurrum got up and stumbled to the door half-drunk. "I said I was not to be disturbed!"

He opened it to see one of his soldiers standing there.

The soldier opened his mouth to speak but noticed the scantily clad woman sitting on the mat behind Amurrum.

The woman took the opportunity to voice her own annoyance. "Are we doing this or what? Time is money."

Amurrum turned and barked at her. "Quiet!" He then addressed the soldier. "Speak, dog."

The soldier cleared his throat. "The Ammonite. The tall one. I saw him."

Amurrum raised his eyebrows. "Where?"

"He was talking to a local merchant. Just now."

"And did you see his Edomite slave with him?"

The soldier shook his head.

"Hmm." Amurrum's eyes narrowed. "Is he still in town?"

"I don't think so, sir."

Amurrum grabbed him by the tunic and spoke in a threatening tone. "Did you at least ask the merchant if he knew anything?"

The soldier stammered. "Y—yes, sir. He's nearby. Living on a farm owned by a man named Shalim."

Amurrum released the soldier's tunic.

As the man readjusted himself, he continued. "The merchant said that the Ammonite offered him food and shelter if he would abandon the gods and surrender to the Israelites."

Amurrum noticed the woman stand and put her cloak on. He spun around. "Who said you could go?"

She did not seem intimidated by him. "Time's up."

He yanked a small piece of silver from his tunic and tossed it to her. "How much will that get me?"

She picked it up and examined it. "Another half hour." She then dropped her cloak and sat back down on the mat.

Amurrum turned to the soldier. "Tell the men we're not going to Jericho."

"But sir, the Israelite army is on the way. Don't we need to keep moving?"

Amurrum grinned. "Well, if this place you describe is offering food and shelter, why not just take it for ourselves until Israel is gone?"

The soldier paused in thought, and then nodded.

"Besides," Amurrum continued, "I swore to the gods that I would have my revenge. That Ammonite, and everyone he cares about, will die." He lowered his voice. "Find out exactly where this farm is. We move out tomorrow morning."

The soldier bowed his head. "Yes, sir."

Amurrum slammed the door and leaned against it. After fleeing Heshbon, he and his men had stayed hidden, looking for opportunities to kill Nahash and take control of the city. But none came. Instead, the Israelites captured the city and burned it to the ground.

Unable to avenge Inanna and prevent the fall of Heshbon, Amurrum tried going to Rabbah. His plan had been to find the Ammonite and kill him and his entire family. But the Ammonites had locked down their border, refusing to let non-Ammonites into the city. And so, with no other options, Amurrum and his men fled to King Og's land.

Of course, they made sure to avoid getting drafted into Og's army, as Amurrum had no intention of fighting for that man. Instead, he and his six men spent their time among the chaos plundering unguarded houses and taking advantage of unprotected women. That was fun while it lasted, but when the Israelites defeated King Og, Amurrum knew he had to flee west.

The woman on the mat grabbed a nearby wineskin and took a drink. She then shot Amurrum a seductive look. "So, what would you like?"

"Right now, the wineskin," he replied coldly.

With an angry glare, she tossed it to him, laid down, and rolled over so that he saw only her bare back.

As he lifted the skin to his lips, he considered his change in fortune. He had been on his way to Jericho with no real desire to live. Nothing seemed interesting, not even the fun of pillaging and plundering. But now, after hearing about that Ammonite—Tobimelech—a fire sparked inside him. *I will have my revenge.*

Amurrum tossed the empty skin away and eyed the woman lying down in front of him. What if the Ammonite was married? And what if his wife were here too? That would make things even more interesting.

He smiled at his dark thoughts as he strode over to the mat.

CHAPTER TWENTY

Betharan, Spring 1406 BC

TOBIAH STIRRED WHEN HE felt movement next to him. Opening his eyes, he saw by the moonlight from the window that Nikkal sat awake. "Is everything all right, Nik?" he whispered.

"Yes, I'm just—not feeling well."

He sat up and turned to her. "Are you sick?"

She shook her head. "Not like that. It's a good thing."

He felt confused. "A good thing?"

She took a deep breath. "Tobiah. I'm pregnant."

A mixture of emotions struck him in that moment. At first, he felt elated. *I'm going to be a father again!* But then an image of Nikkal on the altar of Asherah entered his mind. *What if it's not my child?* He forced himself to dismiss that thought. *No, she would've known sooner.*

Tobiah cleared his throat. "How—how far along are you?"

"No more than two months." She paused, and he wondered if she had read his mind. Her voice turned defensive. "Trust me, it's definitely your—"

He reached out and took hold of her hand. "Nik, I believe you. And even if it weren't, it wouldn't matter. You're carrying *our* child, and I thank God for that."

Focusing his eyes on her face, he could tell by the dim light that she was smiling. He gave her hand a gentle squeeze. "I love you, Nik."

"I love you too," she replied.

He drew her in close and kissed her.

As they embraced, he noticed that her cheeks were wet with tears.

He pulled away and looked at her. "Does anyone else know?"

"Probably just Ashima and Ishara," she replied, wiping her eyes. "They didn't ask, but I think they're suspicious."

"All right, well, we should announce it today." He got up and began to dress.

"Wait, you're not going back to sleep?" she asked. "It's not yet dawn."

Tobiah laughed. "I can't sleep now, I'm too excited! And your grandfather will be too. He'll want to celebrate, for sure."

She laughed with him. "Yes, you're right about that."

True to his word, Tobiah shared the news with everyone at breakfast. The only exceptions were Hadad and Kenaz, who had left earlier that morning to go hunting.

As Tobiah had predicted, Shalim burst with joy and spent the entire breakfast planning the evening meal.

Over an hour later, after he had finished talking through the details, he gestured to Tobiah. "We're going to have to do our work fast today. It might be just the two of us for a while."

Ashima turned to Shalim. "May I ask Rimmon and his family if they want to join us tonight?"

"Of course!" Shalim replied. "They are most welcome. In fact, I might need his help with a few things around here if Hadad and Kenaz don't return soon."

Ashima stood and picked up a nearby basket. "I'm going to bring some supplies to them this morning for their breakfast. I'll ask Rimmon when I'm over there."

"Can I go with you?" Nikkal asked. "I was hoping to meet his wife."

Ashima nodded. "Sure."

Nikkal went to join her but stopped when the front door opened. Kenaz entered, empty handed except for his bow and quiver.

"I'm glad you're back!" said Shalim. "I was wonder—"

"My lord," Kenaz interrupted, "while Hadad and I were out, we spotted several armed men, perhaps half a dozen or so, headed this way."

Shalim gave him a confused look. "Were they Israelites?"

Kenaz shook his head. "I don't think so. They sounded Amorite, but I didn't get very close."

"Could they be fleeing the town?"

"No." Kenaz's voice turned ominous. "They moved purposefully, as if they knew exactly where they were headed. Here."

A sense of dread gripped Tobiah's heart. He cursed himself for not telling Hadad and Kenaz the truth when they were at Betharan.

Tobiah jumped up from his seat. "Where is Hadad?!"

Kenaz gestured toward the direction of the olive orchard. "I asked him to go find help. He said he knew a quick route to the main road and would look for aid there."

Shalim sighed. "I doubt anyone will come." He turned to Kenaz. "Go tell Rimmon to gather his family and bring them here."

"Yes, my lord." Kenaz hurried off.

Shalim then addressed Ishara. "We need to collect what food and supplies we can and be ready to leave right away."

"Okay," she replied. She then gave instructions to Nikkal and Ashima.

Shalim walked up to Tobiah and lowered his voice. "Grab our swords, bows, and arrows and come back here."

Tobiah did not respond but stared off in the distance. *It's my fault.*

Shalim raised his voice. "Tobiah? Did you hear me?"

"I'm sorry," Tobiah whispered.

"Sorry for what?"

Tobiah looked straight into Shalim's eyes. "It's my fault."

Shalim began to reply, but the door opened, and Kenaz rushed in. "Rimmon and his family are coming," he said. "They're just gathering their things."

Shalim nodded and turned back to Tobiah, his voice firm. "Son, if you know anything at all, tell me now."

Tobiah glanced at Kenaz and then back at Shalim. Despite the shame he felt, he knew he needed to tell the truth. "They're soldiers from Sihon's army, serving under a man named Amurrum. When I was wounded at Jahaz, I fled, and he swore that he would find me and kill me."

Kenaz's eyes went wide. "Amurrum? How . . ."

Tobiah turned to Nikkal. She must have been listening as she worked, for she now stared at him with a look of fear and confusion. "Nik," he began, "I'm sorry I never told you. I thought it was over, that I had escaped. But yesterday in town, one of Amurrum's soldiers recognized me—"

Kenaz interrupted him. "Why didn't you tell me?" He sounded hurt.

Tobiah lowered his eyes. "I'm sorry Kenaz. I thought that Amurrum was gone. I thought that he wouldn't find us here, that he would just flee across the Jordan like everyone else."

Kenaz looked as if to respond, but Shalim held up his hand. The room fell silent. "You made a mistake, son. One that I've made before."

He then placed his hand on Tobiah's shoulder. "All is forgiven. We cannot change the past. We can only give it over to God and seek to make the next right choice."

Tobiah looked at him and nodded.

Shalim smiled. "Now go."

Tobiah rushed to the storage room at the back of the house. On his way there, he passed Rimmon and his family, who had just walked in. Rimmon gave Tobiah a nod of understanding. Tobiah returned it. *He knows what's about to happen.*

A few moments later, Tobiah returned with both his and Shalim's weapons. He found Kenaz positioned at the front window with his bow at the ready. Shalim stood next to him, scanning the tree line.

Tobiah handed Shalim his sword, bow, and arrows.

"Thank you," Shalim replied as he armed himself.

Glancing outside, Tobiah saw no one. Just the line of trees off in the distance. "What's the plan?" he asked.

Shalim kept his eyes moving. "We hold them off until the women and children can get clear. Then we'll slip out, gather everyone together, and work our way east toward the Israelite camp."

"Will the Israelites welcome us?"

Shalim sighed. "I pray that they do. But if Hadad does not come back with help soon, we might have no choice but to abandon the farm. A half-dozen trained soldiers is no easy fight."

Tobiah nodded as he watched the tree line in silence. *Lord, protect us, and give me courage.*

Then he saw them. Several figures emerging from the wilderness. He counted seven men, with four of them holding bows.

Shalim moved away from the window. "They're here, time to go." He went up to Rimmon and held out his hand. "I'm sorry that things have not been as hospitable as I'd hoped, but we'll do our best to keep you and your family safe."

Rimmon gripped it. "Thank you, sir." He then drew out a sword that had been tucked into his tunic. "I'm willing to fight for you here if needed."

"No," replied Shalim, shaking his head. "Your job is to protect your family. It may come down to you."

Rimmon nodded.

Shalim gestured to Tobiah. "Take everyone out the back and head to the olive orchard. If I'm not there by midday, or if you see them coming, take the path through the wilderness to the main road. Then find the Israelite camp."

Tobiah held up his hands. "Wait. You're staying here by yourself?"

"Yes."

"No," Tobiah replied. "I should be the one to stay. You should lead everyone else to safety."

"Tobiah, no," Nikkal replied.

He turned to her. "It's my responsibility. They're here because of me."

"That might be true," Shalim replied, "but this is my house and my land."

Tobiah said nothing, and for a moment he just stared at Shalim. He had made his choice and would not budge.

Eventually, Shalim gave way. "Fine, then you and I will stay together." He turned to Kenaz. "Take them to the orchard. We'll meet you there soon."

"Yes, my lord." Kenaz gestured for everyone else to follow him.

Tobiah walked up to Nikkal. Sensing her anxiety, he hugged her. "I don't plan on dying."

"But what if—" she began.

He stopped her. "Last time I fought for the wrong reasons." He placed his hand on her belly. "I fight for different reasons now. This isn't about pride or money. I believe that God is with us, not against us."

She nodded and whispered. "I love you."

"I love you too." He kissed her.

A man shouted from outside. "Ammonite!" Tobiah recognized the voice as Commander Amurrum's.

"Go with Kenaz," he said to Nikkal.

She turned and followed the rest out through the back of the house.

As Tobiah approached the front door, Shalim notched an arrow and gestured for Tobiah to open it for him.

Tobiah unlatched the door and pulled.

"Stay hidden," Shalim whispered. He then stepped outside.

Tobiah listened as Shalim addressed the soldiers. "Greetings. My name is Shalim of Betharan. Do you come to my home in peace?"

"That depends," Amurrum replied. "I'm Commander Amurrum, servant of King Sihon. You have an Ammonite soldier with you, named

Tobimelech. He's wanted for desertion. If you hand him over, I'll spare you and your household."

"There's no one of that name here," replied Shalim. "Just my family and a few others seeking to survive the coming judgment. And if I'm not mistaken, Sihon is no longer king over anything these days."

Peeking through the window, Tobiah watched as Amurrum's face turned red.

Shalim continued. "And if you wish to avoid judgment yourself, lay down your weapons and we can arrange for you to stay with us in peace."

Amurrum laughed mockingly. "You're the one who should be worried about judgment, old man. I know that the Ammonite is here with you. This is your last chance to turn him over."

Tobiah felt torn. *Shalim wants to keep me safe. But dealing with Amurrum is my responsibility, not his. How can I just stand here?*

After sending one more prayer to God, he made his decision. "Amurrum!" he shouted. "I'm here!" He exited the front door and stood next to Shalim.

Shalim whispered to him. "I thought I told you to stay hidden."

"I'm sorry," replied Tobiah. "But I need to face him."

Shalim nodded in understanding.

Commander Amurrum grinned. "Well, well, the deserter has come out to fight, and with an old man as his protector. What happened to that Edomite slave of yours? Did he realize how much of a coward you are and decide to leave?"

Tobiah felt anger rising inside him but forced himself to remain calm. "You need to go, Amurrum. Nothing good can come of this."

Amurrum paused as if deep in thought. "I suppose you're right. No point in making a big deal of it now. We'll go." He turned to leave.

Tobiah felt shocked. *Is he really going to go? That's strange.*

He then noticed Amurrum make a slight gesture with his hand. The four men with bows aimed and drew.

But before they could release, an arrow flew out from Shalim's bow and struck one of the archers in the chest. The man fell.

Shalim grabbed Tobiah's tunic. "Inside, now!" He pulled him through the doorway and dove to the ground. Three arrows followed them in but just missed their bodies.

Once they got up and closed the door, they stood with their backs against it. Shalim glanced over at Tobiah. "It was a feint. A very good one."

Tobiah nodded. "For a moment I thought he'd actually leave."

"I have to give it to you," said Shalim. "You sure picked a good soldier to piss off." He chuckled.

Three more arrows flew through the open windows on either side of the door.

"So, now what's the plan?" asked Tobiah.

Shalim spoke calmly. "Give everyone else time to get to the orchard, and then join them. And if these guys keep coming, we try and stop them."

Shalim notched an arrow. As soon as another volley of three arrows flew through the window, he turned, drew, aimed, and released. A man screamed.

"Wounded him," said Shalim. "I expect now that they'll have one archer shoot at us while the other tries to protect him from any return shots."

"Get up!" they heard Amurrum shout to the injured man.

Shalim gestured toward his window. "I'll feint an attack and draw their fire. Then you take aim and hit one of their archers."

"Okay." Tobiah stood, notched an arrow, and nodded to Shalim.

When an arrow flew through the window, Shalim turned and made the appearance of taking a shot before ducking back behind the door. A second arrow passed the space where he had just stood. "Now!" he shouted.

Tobiah turned to his window, drew, and aimed for the closest archer. The man was in the process of notching an arrow. Tobiah heard Amurrum shout just as he released. The archer jumped out of the way and Tobiah's arrow flew past him.

Tobiah turned back to Shalim. "Missed."

"It's all right," replied Shalim. "It won't be easy now. We also need to worry about them closing the distance and climbing onto the roof. They might try that soon."

"And what happens then?" Tobiah asked.

Shalim smiled. "We run."

Another arrow flew through Tobiah's window. After it passed, Tobiah glanced outside. The first man who Shalim hit remained unmoving. Tobiah presumed him dead. Another man stood holding his shoulder, grimacing in pain. Two others had bows, while Amurrum and two soldiers held swords.

He then saw Amurrum point, and his two swordsmen sprinted toward the wall of the property.

Tobiah turned back to Shalim. "Amurrum's sending two men over the wall. They'll be able to see everyone heading to the olive orchard."

Without hesitation, Shalim turned, drew, aimed, and fired. The shot caught Amurrum's archers off guard.

Tobiah heard another scream and looked to see the same wounded archer now on his knees clutching his stomach.

Shalim pointed toward the rear of the house. "Go to the others and protect them. I'll stay here and keep the rest occupied."

"All right," Tobiah replied. "I'll come back as soon as I can." He sprinted out the back of the house and toward the olive orchard.

CHAPTER TWENTY-ONE

Betharan, Spring 1406 BC

TOBIAH PUMPED HIS LEGS as hard as he could. In front of him, he saw the two swordsmen enter the orchard. A few moments later, the sound of shouting men and screaming women reached his ears.

As soon as he entered, Tobiah spotted the two men. One stood over Kenaz, who had fallen to the ground. The other still fought against Rimmon, who remained standing but clutched a wound in his side. Beyond them, Nikkal and the others were running toward the wilderness.

Nikkal spotted Tobiah and stopped. "Tobiah!" she shouted.

The soldier near Kenaz turned in response. Upon seeing Tobiah, the man charged full speed at him.

Tobiah notched an arrow. He felt panic threaten to take hold off him, and debated whether to drop the bow and run or try to take the shot.

The soldier began to shout as the distance between them shrunk.

Time slowed down for Tobiah. Forcing himself to stay calm, he drew his bow and held his breadth just before he released. He remembered what Shalim had taught him and made sure to follow through all the way with his shot.

The arrow hit the man in the chest at nearly point-blank range. The force of it caused him to spin and fall. He landed near Tobiah's feet and did not move.

Tobiah dropped his bow and drew his sword. Out of the corner of his eye, he caught sight of the other soldier running toward him with his sword brandished.

Tobiah turned to block the blade. And though he deflected the attack, the men collided, knocking them both to the ground. The hard landing stunned Tobiah and he felt his sword slip from his grasp. He turned his head and saw that it was just out of arm's reach.

The soldier, who had dropped his own blade, quickly regained his feet. He drew a dagger and lunged at Tobiah. The blade would have hit home but Tobiah rolled away just in time.

Tobiah reached for his own sword but changed his mind as the soldier launched another ferocious attack.

When the soldier came down upon him, Tobiah grabbed the man's arms and, with all his strength, fought to keep the dagger from going into his heart.

The soldier shifted his weight and pressed down with a grunt.

Despite Tobiah's strength and size advantage, the blade drew closer and closer to his chest. His arms quivered with fatigue, and he knew that he would soon be a dead man. *Lord, help me!*

He then heard Nikkal yell and saw the soldier's eyes grow wide with pain. The man instinctively turned and swung his fist backward, catching Nikkal in the mouth and knocking her to the ground. Tobiah noticed her own dagger sticking out of the man's back.

The distraction gave Tobiah just enough time. He reached out, snatched up his sword, and swung as the soldier turned back to face him. The blade caught the man in the neck.

Blood poured out of the wound as the soldier fell, clutching his throat and gurgling for air. The man soon went limp and stopped breathing.

"Nik!" Tobiah shouted as he rushed over to his wife. He let out a sigh of relief. Aside from her bloody lip, she appeared to be unharmed.

He helped her up and she put her arms around him.

"It's all right, I've got you," he said. "It's over." Once he felt certain she could stand on her own, he searched for Rimmon and found him sitting up against a tree, wounded, but alive.

"Are you all right, Rimmon?"

The man nodded. "I've had worse. Go, I'll be fine."

"Okay. I'll come back to help you." Tobiah then turned and sprinted to where Kenaz lay.

When he arrived, he knew right away that it was bad. He noticed dark red blood pouring out of Kenaz's right side.

Tobiah dropped his sword and knelt next to his friend. "Kenaz!"

Kenaz looked at him with glazed eyes, but did not speak.

Tobiah gripped his hand. "I'm so sorry."

Kenaz shook his head. "Don't—be—my lord . . ." He gave a weak smile before his hand went limp and his breathing stopped.

Tobiah began to sob. "Lord, no . . ."

Nikkal ran up to them and stood there in silence.

Continuing to hold Kenaz's hand, Tobiah stared down at his lifeless friend's face, unsure of what to do or even what to say.

Amurrum's shouts soon interrupted his thoughts. "Ammonite! Where are you! Come and face me!"

"Oh no! Shalim!" Tobiah gasped. He turned to Nikkal, who appeared to be in shock. "I need to go, Nik. I left Shalim back there."

She looked at him but did not respond.

"Nik," he repeated.

She snapped out of her daze and seemed about to protest but then nodded. "Go, help him."

Tobiah picked up his sword and placed his hand on Nikkal's shoulder. "Stay with them, and if anything happens to me, take everyone and go."

He did not wait for her to respond but sprinted back to the house.

As he drew closer, he heard Amurrum's voice. "Over here, Ammonite."

Tobiah stopped and saw Amurrum standing over Shalim's body. Next to Shalim were the last of Amurrum's soldiers.

Amurrum sneered. "He fought well for an old man. Got one of us with an arrow when we charged through the front door, and then he took out another in close combat. He was good. But not good enough."

Tobiah held up his sword. "I won't be running from you this time."

Amurrum laughed. "We'll see."

They circled each other. When Tobiah reached Shalim's bloody body he knelt, keeping his eyes on Amurrum. He then checked Shalim's pulse. It felt weak. *He's still alive!*

Amurrum charged, but Tobiah expected it and jumped out of the way. Yet he had misjudged Amurrum's speed and received a slice in his left arm as a consequence.

Tobiah cried out in pain but forced himself to stay calm. Amurrum lunged to press his attack, but Tobiah blocked it. He then focused on maintaining his balance and his breathing, waiting for Amurrum to make a mistake.

Amurrum launched several attacks, which Tobiah either blocked or dodged. But then, out of frustration, Amurrum overextended himself. Tobiah noticed the opening and counterattacked, slicing Amurrum's side.

Amurrum grunted in pain as he clutched his wound. For the first time, Tobiah caught a glimpse of fear in his former commander's eyes.

Taking advantage of the change in momentum, Tobiah moved in to continue the attack, but Amurrum kicked dust up into his face.

Tobiah failed to shield his eyes in time. They closed instinctively and burned with every attempt he made to open them.

Sensing an attack but unable to see where exactly it came from, Tobiah chose to dodge to the right. He realized he had made the right choice when he felt Amurrum's blade graze his tunic.

Still blind, Tobiah knew he had to do something. He lunged toward Amurrum's last known location with all his strength and felt his left shoulder hit Amurrum's ribs.

Both men tumbled to the ground. Tobiah landed on top and heard Amurrum groan in pain.

Tobiah stood and blinked his watery eyes repeatedly to clear them. Just as he regained his vision, he felt Amurrum's fist slam into his cheek.

Fighting through the pain in his face, Tobiah prepared for another punch. When it came, he took hold of Amurrum's arm in an attempt to subdue him. He knew he had an advantage in grappling and did not want to lose it by allowing Amurrum to retrieve his sword.

Amurrum seemed to realized Tobiah's strategy and twisted his body to try to free his arm. He then used his other hand to strike at Tobiah, but Tobiah lowered his head to avoid getting hit in the face again.

Still, the hits caused Tobiah's grip to loosen just enough that Amurrum broke free. He then spun around to the rear and wrapped his arms around Tobiah's neck.

Tobiah began to panic as the pressure increased. He clawed ferociously at Amurrum's forearms, but to no avail.

"The gods are with me, Ammonite," Amurrum sneered.

Tobiah prayed. *God, give me strength.* A sense of calm suddenly came over him. Ignoring the taunt, he gripped Amurrum's elbow as

Shalim had taught him, gathered all his strength, and pulled. Using his hips as leverage, he lifted Amurrum into the air and over his shoulder.

Amurrum released his grip on Tobiah's neck as he smashed into the ground. The impact knocked the wind out of him, and he began gasping for air.

Their roles reversed, Tobiah reached down and wrapped his arms around Amurrum's neck. His former commander struggled to break free, but Tobiah held on. He clenched his teeth and began to squeeze.

"Tobiah . . ." he heard a voice say. It sounded like Shalim.

"Tobiah . . ." the voice repeated. "No . . ."

Keeping hold of Amurrum, Tobiah glanced over at Shalim.

"No . . ." Shalim whispered again.

Tobiah felt Amurrum's body begin to weaken, and he realized that the man was losing consciousness. *I can end this, once and for all! I can get him back for what he's done!*

"M—mercy . . ." Shalim whispered.

"Why?" Tobiah asked. His eyes teared up.

Shalim raised one finger and pointed it toward heaven. "God—had mercy—" He then pointed it at Tobiah. "On you . . ."

"But he doesn't deserve it!" Tobiah yelled.

Shalim looked at Tobiah, his eyes piercing, and gave a weak smile. Tobiah knew what it meant. He had not deserved mercy either.

"And what about justice?" Tobiah asked. "Justice for Kenaz!"

"God—will—judge . . ."

Tobiah realized that Shalim was right. He sighed and, choosing to let go of his rage, he let go of Amurrum's neck.

Amurrum began to cough and sputter.

Tobiah stood and walked over to Amurrum's sword. He kicked it away before retrieving his own.

He returned to Amurrum and used his foot to force the man onto his back. "It's over, Amurrum." He pointed the sword at him. "You trusted in the wrong gods. Do you yield?"

Amurrum hesitated at first, and then nodded.

"Then, in the name of the God of Israel, I offer you mercy." Tobiah held out his free hand.

Amurrum looked at the hand with suspicion but then accepted it. He groaned in pain as Tobiah pulled him to his feet.

Once standing, Amurrum gave him a confused look. "Why do you invoke the God of Israel? Isn't Moloch the chief god of the Ammonites?"

"Yes, but he is no longer my god," replied Tobiah.

Amurrum shook his head and chuckled. "So, you've really deserted your people, haven't you?"

"No," Tobiah replied, "they deserted the truth a long time ago. But God showed mercy upon me and has granted me peace. True peace."

Amurrum did not respond.

Tobiah took a step backward and lowered his sword. "This conflict between us is over, Amurrum. I desire peace, and I pray that God will grant you the same peace that he has given to me. You are free to go."

"Tobiah!" he heard Nikkal shout.

He turned and saw her running toward him.

"Peace?" Amurrum mumbled. "There is no peace!" He pulled a dagger out from inside his tunic and drew back his hand to throw.

"Tobiah! Watch out!" Nikkal screamed.

Thud.

Tobiah spun around and saw Amurrum's dagger fall just short of where he stood. Glancing up, he noticed an arrow protruding from Amurrum's back. The man's face contorted in pain, and his mouth opened as if to scream, but nothing came out.

After a moment, Amurrum's eyes rolled back in his head, and he fell to the ground.

Tobiah looked up to see several archers within bowshot. They appeared to be Israelites. Hadad stood next to them pointing at Tobiah and talking to another Israelite who carried a spear.

As the group began moving toward his position, Tobiah dropped his sword and rushed over to Shalim. "Shalim!" he shouted as he arrived at his side.

"You—don't have to yell," Shalim whispered.

Tobiah laughed as tears began to fill his eyes.

Shalim smiled. "You—fought well."

"I have you to thank for that."

Shalim shook his head. "No, thank—the Lord." He then extended his arm to Tobiah. "Take—" His breathing began to sound more labored.

Tobiah looked down at Shalim's hand and noticed that it held a crumpled-up animal skin. "Shalim?" he asked.

Shalim closed his eyes as he continued. "Take—care of them—Tobiah—my son . . ."

He let out his final breath.

Tobiah felt his pulse. Nothing. A wave of sadness and grief over-came him, and he began to weep. "Oh Lord—Not him—Not Kenaz—Not both of them!"

As he held Shalim's hand, he remembered the animal skin in its grip. Tobiah took it out and unfolded it. Though now stained with Shalim's blood, the words of the Ten Commandments were still legible.

Tobiah heard Nikkal's footsteps. She then knelt next to him, weep-ing. Tobiah wrapped his arms around her and held her tight.

For several moments the two of them mourned together, unable to speak between sobs.

A shadow soon obscured Shalim's body and Tobiah remembered that they were not alone. He and Nikkal stood and turned. His heart pounded as he realized that he was about to meet the Israelites for the first time.

Three men stood in front of him. The man in the middle, clearly the leader, wore a helmet and armor and carried a spear. An Israelite archer stood on the man's right side while Hadad stood on the man's left.

The man in the middle spoke first, his voice commanding, but gentle. "I am Joshua the son of Nun, commander of the armies of Israel. Are you for us or for our enemies?"

Tobiah knelt and lowered his eyes. Nikkal mimicked his action. "We are for you, my lord," replied Tobiah.

"Then have no fear. You may rise."

Tobiah and Nikkal stood and waited.

Joshua stuck his spear into the ground as the archer next to him relaxed his posture. "Who is the master of this house, that I may speak with him?" Joshua asked.

Tobiah gestured toward Shalim's body. "My lord, this farm belongs to your servant Shalim of Betharan. Yet he is fallen in battle."

Joshua nodded and, seeing Shalim's body, his face grew sorrowful. "And who speaks for him now?"

Tobiah took a deep breath. "I do, my lord."

"And your name?" asked Joshua.

"Tobiah."

Joshua voiced his surprise. "Tobiah?"

"Yes, my lord."

Joshua smiled and nodded. "A good name, for Yahweh is indeed good." He then gestured toward Hadad. "Your man here found us and said that you were under attack by Amorites. Is this true?"

Tobiah nodded. "Yes, my lord." He pointed to Amurrum's body. "That was Commander Amurrum of King Sihon's army. He meant to harm us."

"And are there any more of his men on the property?"

Tobiah shook his head. "No, my lord. Commander Amurrum was the last to be slain."

Joshua nodded. "Are you aware that both Sihon and Og have also been killed and that this land now belongs to Yahweh, to be given to whom he wills?"

"Yes, my lord."

Joshua moved his hand in a sweeping gesture. "The land has been polluted by idols and by blood. Those who serve false gods will be devoted to destruction, while those who serve the God of Israel will be spared."

He locked eyes with Tobiah. "Whom does your household serve?"

Tobiah held out the animal skin. "We serve the God of Israel, maker of heaven and earth and all that is in it. Your God is our God."

Joshua took the skin from him and examined it. A broad smile came across his face. "Praise the Lord. The Ten Words." He looked up at Tobiah. "How did you come to possess this?"

"Forty years ago," Tobiah began, "the master of this house, Shalim, fought against Israel. He captured an Israelite named Emet, from the tribe of Simeon, who taught him the ways of the Lord."

Tobiah gestured to the animal skin. "Emet died before Israel came out of the wilderness. But before he passed, he gave those Ten Words to your servant Shalim. And now, they have been passed on to me."

Joshua nodded and handed the skin back to Tobiah. "Then you are most welcome, Tobiah, son of Shalim of Betharan, to dwell among the people of Israel. This part of the land has been allotted to the tribe of Gad. You shall keep your property and dwell with them in peace."

Joshua then reached into his tunic, withdrew a red cord, and held it out to Tobiah. "Fasten this to the doorpost of your house. It will be a sign to the rest of the armies of Israel as they march through. So long as they see it, no harm shall come upon you and your household."

Tobiah took hold of the cord and bowed his head. "Thank you, my lord."

Joshua gestured to the archer next to him. "Phinehas here will stay and help you bury the dead and tend to the wounded. If there is anything you need, don't hesitate to ask him." He retrieved his spear. "Peace be upon you and your house, Tobiah, son of Shalim." He then turned to go.

Nikkal stepped forward. "My lord?"

Joshua stopped and looked at her.

Nikkal bowed her head. "My lord, I am Tobiah's wife, Nikkal."

He nodded. "A pleasure to meet you, Nikkal. How may I be of service?"

She hesitated a moment before speaking. "My lord, will you be marching on Jericho soon?"

Joshua paused, considering her question, and then nodded. "Yes, God has deemed that the city be devoted to destruction."

"My lord," Nikkal replied, "there is a woman who lives there, my cousin. Her name is Rahab. She—she is a prostitute."

To Tobiah's surprise, Joshua did not react with anger, but displayed an expression of curiosity.

She continued. "I believe that she fears the Lord. I think that she would be a friend to Israel and would be of great help to you in taking the city."

Joshua nodded. "Thank you, Nikkal. I appreciate the information. The Lord is always willing to show mercy on all who fear him and turn from their wicked ways. So, if what you say about her faith is true, she and her household will be offered mercy."

"Thank you, my lord." Nikkal bowed her head again.

"Farewell now," said Joshua. "And may the Lord be with you." He turned and strode back to the rest of his men.

Tobiah reached over and took Nikkal's hand. He held it tight as they watched Joshua depart.

Betharan, Fall 1406 BC

NIKKAL STOOD AND BREATHED in the autumn air. She closed her eyes. "Thank you, Lord, for this day that you have given us."

She looked down at the baby boy in her arms. It had been almost a year since she had first come to her grandfather's farm. A lot of things had happened since then, some bad, but many of them good. The most recent blessing was the son born to her and Tobiah just a couple of months ago. Tobiah had named him Shalim, in honor of her grandfather.

Nikkal turned and looked at the doorpost behind her. The red cord still hung there. Although Israel's armies had long since passed through the area, she and Tobiah kept it visible as a reminder both to them and to others that they were followers of the God of Israel and were under his protection.

And God had protected them. Ashima had given birth to a healthy girl several months before baby Shalim had been born. Ishara still lived and seemed filled with increased energy now that two new babies had arrived. And although Tobiah still missed Kenaz, a strong friendship had developed between him and Hadad.

As for Rimmon and his family, they had decided to stay and work as hired servants for Tobiah and Nikkal in honor of her grandfather's hospitality.

Nikkal heard a cart off in the distance and soon saw Tobiah and Hadad emerge from the tree line.

She smiled and spoke to baby Shalim. "Daddy's back from town."

Tobiah waved at her.

She waved in reply and watched as the cart drew near.

Once it had reached the house, Tobiah got down and retrieved his pack.

As he walked toward Nikkal, Hadad spoke from the cart. "I'll take care of the oxen, my lord."

Tobiah glanced at him and nodded. "Thank you, Hadad. We'll see you back at the house soon."

The cart moved off as Hadad drove the oxen forward.

Tobiah's face alighted with joy when he came up to Nikkal. He leaned over and kissed baby Shalim on the forehead and then kissed her. "I'm home."

"Welcome home," she replied.

He reached into his pack, drew out the small wooden horse that had belonged to Ali, and held it in front of baby Shalim's eyes.

The boy just smacked at it with his hands.

Tobiah laughed as he spoke to his son. "I guess you're a little young yet." He put the horse back into his pack. "But that's yours when you're ready for it."

"How was the trip to Betharan?" Nikkal asked. "Was it successful?"

"Very," replied Tobiah. "I enjoy dealing with the Gadites. A lot less likely to get cheated, and a lot higher quality merchandise. They've rebuilt most of the town and are even planning to add fortifications."

"Really?" Nikkal asked. She felt relieved. "That'll help me sleep better."

He nodded. "And if the area becomes safe enough, we might even be able to start raising larger herds and flocks again."

"Do you think we should?" she asked.

Tobiah shrugged. "I'm not sure. It'd be a lot more work." He let out a chuckle. "And I'm still trying to get used to the whole clean and unclean animal concept."

Nikkal laughed. "Ha! Well, I wouldn't want to raise pigs anyways."

"Agreed," replied Tobiah.

Her voice turned serious. "Any news from Rabbah?" She and Tobiah had tried to send messages back to his family, but had not yet heard anything.

He shook his head. "Sadly, no."

Nikkal sighed. "I've been praying for them."

"That's all we can do at this point," he replied.

"Do you think they're all right?"

He shrugged. "The Israelites never attacked Rabbah, so I imagine everyone is fine. But the peace is tenuous, and it's not yet safe enough to travel there."

She nodded. *I wish I could talk to Arsay again, to tell her the truth about God.*

Tobiah's eyes lit up. "On a happier note, I did receive something else." He reached into his tunic, pulled out a small clay tablet, and handed it to her. "I was given this by a messenger in town."

Nikkal shifted baby Shalim in her arms and, with her free hand, took the tablet and examined it. Although she still had difficulty with some words, she was able to read it. "A wedding invitation?"

Tobiah nodded. "Apparently, your cousin Rahab is marrying an Israelite named Salmon from the tribe of Judah."

"Wow!" Nikkal replied. "That's unexpected. But I'm really happy for her. God is good."

Tobiah grinned as he pointed to the tablet. "And we're all invited to attend the celebration at their new home in Bethlehem."

"Where's that?" she asked.

"It's a small town outside of Jebus. The Jebusites still control the city, but the surrounding area is in the hands of Judah."

He paused as his face turned serious. "Nik, word is that the Israelites just discovered Tophet."

Her eyes shot up from the tablet and locked onto his. "And what will they do to it?"

He placed his hands on hers. "They'll destroy it, I'm sure."

She breathed a sigh of relief. "I pray that they do . . ."

"Amen." He put his arms around her and held her in silence.

After a few moments, he let out a chuckle. "By the way, how is Rahab going to manage going from city life to life on a farm?"

Nikkal laughed. "I have no idea. She must really love that man."

Tobiah grinned. "As much as you love me?"

She gave him a playful look "Maybe."

They kissed.

Hazael pulled his spear from the priest's chest. A gurgling sound came forth as he did. After confirming that the man had died, Hazael looked around for his commanding officer, Jamin, and found him not far away.

Jamin stood in front of a large bronze statue. It had the body of a man and the head of a bull. Jamin's second-in-command, Ethan, stood next to him beholding the statue with a contemptuous look on his face.

Other Israelite soldiers continued to search the area, to ensure that all enemy soldiers and priests had been devoted to destruction. Commander Jamin's unit had been assigned to that area, known as Tophet, by Joshua himself. When they had arrived earlier that morning, they had found the place only lightly defended. After gaining entry, they had spent the rest of the day hunting down all the priests and priestesses of Moloch.

Hazael scanned the area around him and, despite still hearing a few moans from those who had not yet died, he perceived that there were no immediate threats. Shouldering his spear, he walked over to Jamin and Ethan, who both continued to stare at the statue in silence.

Hazael cleared his throat. "So, this is Moloch, sir?"

Ethan spat upon the statue. "Abomination! How many thousands of babies were murdered here?"

No one responded.

"Commander Jamin!" shouted a nearby soldier.

Jamin turned as a soldier approached him, accompanied by a woman whose hands were bound behind her back. The soldier held her arm and shoved her forward until she stood before Jamin.

"Commander Jamin," the soldier repeated. "This is one of their high-ranking priestesses, named Anat."

"Thank you, soldier," Jamin replied.

He turned toward Anat and spoke with firmness. "Where is your high priest?"

She did not answer.

He grabbed her by the arm and dragged her to the area behind the statue of Moloch. There, near the base of it sat a large pit containing the bones and ashes of thousands of children. Portions of the pit still smoldered with hot cinders, while the cooler parts teemed with worms.

Jamin pointed to the mass grave. "Look at what you've done! Have you nothing to say to me?"

Anat looked at the pit and then back at him. "The high priest is already dead." She nodded toward the man that Hazael had just speared. "That was him. He had disguised himself as a regular priest."

Jamin looked at Hazael for confirmation.

Hazael just shrugged.

Turning back to Anat, Jamin drew a dagger and held it up to her throat. "In the name of Yahweh, the one true God, I hereby devote you to destruction. Do you have any last words?"

She trembled as she spoke. "I was only trying to help people."

He pointed to the bones in the pit. "You failed to help them! And just as you helped to pass others through the fire, so I will now pass you on to the fiery judgment that awaits you." He slit her throat.

Her eyes went wide as blood flowed from her neck. She tried to cry out, but no sound came.

Jamin tossed her bleeding body into the smoldering pit and then turned to address his men. "Soldiers!"

Everyone stopped and looked at him.

He pointed to the grave behind him with his dagger. "I want everything thrown into here. They called this place Tophet, the place of burning. Well, let it all burn, then. Everything and everyone will be devoted to destruction. Do not take anything for yourselves. You know what happened to Achan and his family, so be sure to guard your hearts. Any questions?"

No one responded.

"All right, move!"

The soldiers began to work, gathering treasures, bodies, and any objects that could be burned.

Jamin walked up to his second-in-command. "Ethan, get the pit as hot as you can. Once it's ready, pull down that statue of Moloch and destroy it. I want all memory of him blotted out from the land. Nothing is to remain."

Ethan bowed his head. "Yes, sir."

Jamin then turned to Hazael. "Hazael, check the priest's body and see if there is any way to prove that he was the high priest. I don't want him escaping if he's still alive."

Hazael nodded. "Yes, sir." He turned and strode back to the body of the man he had speared.

When he reached it, he knelt and began to search the priest's robes. He soon found a small clay tablet that every priest and priestess of Moloch seemed to carry. It bore an image of Moloch on the front, with a set of titles on the back. Hazael had seen many such tablets before, but the words on this one indicated that the man had been no ordinary priest.

He hurried over to Jamin and handed him the tablet. "Sir, I think she was telling the truth."

Jamin examined the tablet and, after a few moments, nodded. "Well done, soldier." He tossed the tablet into the pit before turning back to Hazael. "Burn the body."

Hazael bowed his head. "Yes, sir."

He ran back and grabbed the high priest's body from beneath its arms. When he did, he felt another hard object inside the black robes. He had missed something.

Curious, he reached inside and removed what he believed to be the most ornate idol of Moloch that he had ever seen. Made of solid gold, it contained detailed etching and had been embedded with numerous jewels.

"Wow," Hazael whispered to himself.

As he gazed at the idol, he heard his own voice whisper in his mind. *Don't destroy it.*

Then a second thought came to him. *Why not keep it?* He paused, considering the idea. It's not like he wanted to follow Moloch. And he had no desire to sell the idol or make a profit from it either. That was how Achan had gotten into trouble. Achan had wanted wealth. Hazael just wanted a souvenir.

Besides, he had been the one who killed the high priest, hadn't he? God would surely honor that. The souvenir would only serve as a reminder of what he had done for the Lord. Nothing more. *God will understand.*

Glancing around to ensure that no one was looking, Hazael shoved the idol into his tunic. He then grabbed the high priest's body and dragged it to the pit.